THE HELIX BLINK

By

Jeanette Appel Cave

THE HELIX BLINK

By

Jeanette Appel Cave

Copyright 2015

Outside Parameters Press

Sacramento, CA

ISBN-13: 978-1516894604

ISBN-10: 151689460X

Editor: Elizabeth T. Greer, www.moonshinewidow.com

Cover designs: Matt Musselman, www.invokedesign.us

Disclaimer: Actual places have been used in this novel. Everything written about them in the novel is meant to be considered as fiction, not a reflection of them in real time, 2015.

No part of this book may be used, except for excerpts for reviews, or copied in print or digital formats, without the permission of the author.

Dedication

I want to dedicate this book to all adult children of the world, especially those who think and dream outside the parameters of conventional thought. You will give us a future worth living.

The Helix Blink

Desolation was the first word that filled her mind. Heat was the unbearable feeling that drained her body of the will to put one foot in front of another and continue. She could see it as well as feel it, the heat rising in waves from the cracked and broken tarmac miles ahead in the flat terrain. She knew that effect was what caused the parched to see an oasis and believe they were approaching water. Her clothing was drenched with sweat and uncomfortable, her hair wet and sticking to her face; she wiped the back of her arm across her forehead, a brief respite from having the sweat stinging her eyes. She felt gratitude that, starving and thirst aside, her body was still very strong. Her leg muscles had developed dramatically from the hundreds of miles of ceaseless walking.

She looked down at the sturdy hiking boots she had been lucky to find at an REI Sporting Goods store still intact in what was once Santa Rosa, California. Most of the merchandise had been taken. The store was nearly stripped bare, but she found a pair of boots in her size high on a shelf in the stockroom. She also was able to find some camping equipment and rope. When she had almost given up finding anything else, she discovered a box of energy bars beneath the broken and empty cash register.

This find had been one of the most valuable and she had managed to stretch the precious sixteen bars over the weeks of walking. And with the cans she had found in a house that she had risked sleeping in, she was able to stay reasonably nourished. During her stay in the deserted house she found a full-length mirror on a closet door of a bedroom that had looked like it once housed a teenager. She sighed at the posters on the wall, the messages taped around the mirror, the hope for a bright future reflected in the postcards and college applications she had found. She stared long and hard at her reflection to see what the face and body she was occupying looked like. The face looking back at her was sunburned, young, and pretty; the body was strong and healthy and it had been well cared for. Her own green eyes stared back at her but her hair was black, unusual considering she was usually a ginger.

She searched her body's memory to find that her name was Gayle Cooper-Lesko. "Oh, great," she thought, "I'm finally hyphenated...whatever THAT means!" The two names, combined, were strangely familiar to her. Her host self was a scientist, specializing in auto-immune diseases and their cures. A long-distance runner before the apocalypse, Gayle was both intelligent and strong. "Thank you, Gayle, for taking such good care of yourself!" she said into the mirror.

She knew that she was burning far more calories than she was taking in, but this body was alive. That alone was miraculous. Her hipbones were visible, as were her ribs. But she remained well-muscled.

Her most precious finds before the food and boots had been the knife and the gun with ammunition she had found three days ago on the body of an emaciated, heat-swollen body of a man. He had chosen weaponry to carry, rather than food, perhaps relying on the weapons to steal from other scavengers. He had died from exertion, perhaps a weak heart, and starvation.

Everyone alive was following a road, or hiding in what remained of dead forests, trying to decide whether they wanted to live another day. Afraid of one another, afraid of the hunger, the heat. Afraid to be alone, afraid not to. Many had chosen to end their own lives. She had seen bodies of every description, enough bad memories to last several lifetimes. Navigating around fissures in the earth had become a full-time occupation.

She stared into the distance: how many times had the heat looked like water on the tarmac ahead? She knew that it didn't matter either way. Surface water was dangerous now. Water was poisoned in the ground and on the ground. Only finding caches of food squirreled away in deserted cellars or in grocery stores that had not been stripped to the bone allowed one to survive. The proof of human habitation had already begun to crumble into ruin: no villages, no towns, certainly no cities. Just a few buildings left standing here and there. Ash buried them. Lava buried them. It had been days since she had seen or heard a sign of human life and then it had been gunfire in the distance. She knew better than to walk in the open toward such activity, so she had circled around to observe and to examine the possibility of encounter.

Her caution had been wise. The gunfire came from marauders who attacked a helpless group of people walking the road. They were in the process of stripping the bodies, doing unspeakable things to the bodies, to the women and children. She could do nothing to help the dead and wanted nothing more than to put distance between herself and the armed and dangerous thieves. She quietly slipped deeper into her cover to await the night. She was sick to the soul and hoping to leave this nightmare behind.

Weeks ago, the road had taken her to the edge of the world. She had stood on a cliff on what was formerly Highway One in what was formerly California, possibly close to Bodega Bay. It was hard to be sure, so much of the highway had given way to the ocean as the water level continued to rise. She had felt exposed and vulnerable looking down at a deserted beach. The ocean still had a tide and there were still waves but this was nothing like the ocean she had known and loved in all of her previous lives.

She knew that nothing lived on the other side of the Pacific. Those people had died long before this continent began to fall apart. The news had been filled with the war, the attacks, the bombs dropped. Much of Asia was gone. Life in Australia had ceased to exist. The news had been filled with stories of the eruptions, the tsunamis, the famine, and death. And on the heels of this news the apocalypse had begun on this side of the sea. The ocean tore at the coast, waves washing away entire villages. She remembered reading about Fort Bragg and Mendocino being lost to the tsunamis overnight. Little by little, the entire continent experienced natural phenomena--floods, earthquakes, eruptions-- as never before.

She brought her thoughts back to her observations and she held on desperately to her sanity as she looked out over the coast.

Bodies had washed ashore: dolphin, seal, whale, fish, crustaceans, no doubt human, as well. Bones everywhere, the overpowering stench of rotting corpses and rancid saltwater. If there were carrion birds now, they were elsewhere. No gulls, no crows, no buzzards, except those twisted, feathered bodies of gulls and cormorants that lay among the bones; the sky was empty of life, nothing cleaned the corpses, no benefit here for the carrion eaters. The ocean was a muddied brackish red, dead water, poisoned water. Never had she known herself to feel a more helpless sense of grief and loss. Why struggle to survive? Why were any one of those walking the roads struggling to survive? And yet, she did.

Each day brought new horrors. The smell of sulfur hung in the air; ash covered the ground; volcanoes everywhere had been rumbling; the earth was splitting open, breaking the road, swallowing whatever might be left of trees and roots, poisoning the air. Entire forests had ceased to exist. Cities had ceased to exist, many swallowed by the earth.

She followed the coast up from San Francisco, her former home, for no reason but that there seemed fewer people here than there had been inland. But near Jenner she decided to turn inland. Something told her to put distance between herself and the fault and volcanic activity. She had seen so many bodies along the road. She hid from the living. The living were far more frightening than the dead. She rejected the adage that there was safety in numbers. She had seen the strength of those who armed themselves, but could find no comfort in joining them, those who were hungry for human blood, those who took what they wanted by force. Each day she talked to herself, reminding herself, "I am Gwen. I am strong. He thought me prepared for this, he thought me ready...he was so wrong...he promised he'd be with me."

Two days ago, just west of Sacramento, she had opened the last can of food in her knapsack. A dented can of peaches, nothing left of the label but part of the word, "ea..e," on a torn little piece of paper, but somehow she had known they would be peaches. They had been ambrosia. Every drop of juice, although it made her thirsty, was felt in every pore of her parched body. She felt she could taste the TREE they had grown on.

Now there was just the road and the need to be aware of every single noise around her. Would she be able to hide if someone was watching her? What if someone followed?

What was she walking toward? What was her journey? Why, when it seemed like everyone else was walking the other direction, was she being drawn eastward?

Suddenly the air around her changed and, not for the first time, the coming sensation known to her as the "Blink" filled her with hope and the thought of salvation, wherever it might leave her. She hoped that it would lead her to wherever he might be. The smell of ozone overpowered the smell of organic rot and decomposition. She felt the shimmer and pull of the Blink and leaned back into it, willingly, not for the first time in all of her lives, a smile breaking through the grime as she invited it to take her...but she knew that this was a nightmare she would return to time and again. This was not her first trip to 2062 and it would not be her last. The Blink. It was as if she closed her eyelids and then a tornado took her. This was her personal destiny, her holy grail. Her last thought was, "Good-bye, Gayle Cooper-Lesko, and good luck."

BLINK

There had been other times when they had felt the approach of what they had come to call the Blink. They had come to call that foreknowledge, the "Fade." There had been times that they had felt the Fade long before the Blink took them, often when the person they were occupying was going to die. It was like the calm before a storm, like electric charges gathering around, like the drop in atmospheric pressure. Air and time stood still but they could feel turmoil just beyond the veil, turmoil pulling them.

"Kiss me!" he said, urgently. "I can feel it, I'm beginning to fade into it."

"No, nooo...." she cried. She shook her head in frustration and reached for him. Her lips found his and moved against them but it was like moving through water, nothing solid, but the shimmer. The Blink included her as the kiss gained intensity and she, too, was pulled into the tumultuous void. A tear traced a path down her cheek. Her fingers had no choice but to release the warmth of his skin.

The Blink was not quick. There was always the sensation of falling, dropping from high above, falling for hours, falling down into her new host. Strange that, once lodged, the host never felt that sensation and did not feel anything but a strong sense of dislocation and disorientation. Spinning, not falling....

BLINK

When the dizziness wore off, she looked down to see she was now in the form of a very small child of three, perhaps four years old. Quickly she searched her mind for a new name to which she would have to become rapidly accustomed to answering and found that she was now Harmony. It was very difficult when the new host was a child. The disorientation was often mistaken for an illness or serious malady so she had learned to search the brain and orient herself very rapidly. Harmony. She pushed aside the ironic thought that her new parents might either be musicians or hippies and drew out every bit of self-awareness she could find. She was four-and-a-half but was very small for her age.

Her mommy had brought her to the playground because this was one of the nicest spring days in weeks. "No rain!" her mommy had pronounced happily, as she had dressed her this morning. She had let her wear her favorite outfit, a creation that her mother, Sydney, had sewn for her. Tinkerbell in all green leotards and green tulle, complete with the wings! She was sitting beside her "mommy" on a blanket in what was obviously a park. Her mother was engrossed in a book whose title was "Time and Time Again," by James Hilton. Gwen smiled at the irony.

The costume was a guide: Harmony was obviously a fan of Disney's latest release, the classic, animated version of "Peter Pan." This, and her mother's apparel, the cars in the parking lot, the memories in the toddler mind, helped Gwen set the year as somewhere around the early fifties. She searched her mind for the release date of "Peter Pan" but could not determine why she would know that. Ah, what a wonderful time to be alive. This lifetime would see so much growth and change, it was a welcome respite. She could only hope and dream to spend some time here, to grow with Harmony through the coming, exciting decades.

Her daddy was at work and this was mommy's day off so this was why she was not at a sitter's. Grass, thick grass lay beneath her as she edged off the blanket. Trees and cool, organic air surrounded her. She buried her hands in the grass and sighed in relief. People alive in this era had no idea how lucky they were: trees and grass and little to fear but the development of weapons that would make the future into a terror.

It always surprised Gwen that there was residual memory of things that happened to her host before the Blink took place. She had stopped wondering what might have become of the child she replaced. Sometimes she felt that she was still "in there" but had relinquished control, or was sharing control. She had reasoned some of their predecessors either Blinked somewhere themselves or they might simply share space waiting for their chance to return. Path contended there was always a reason for the Blink, but it wasn't always apparent. After struggling, however, with guilt over the fact that she might be kidnapping someone else's body, she resigned to realizing that there was absolutely nothing she could do about it. She didn't ask for the Blink and she certainly didn't control it. She had learned to adapt, only hoping that she didn't feel like a repulsive parasite to her host.

It was difficult to imagine that there might be other simultaneous dimensions or answers beyond her ability to research but, after all the hundreds of years of struggling with her dilemma, she had come to accept that, whether going backward or forward in time or dimension, there was absolutely nothing she would ever be able to do to stop this from happening. Their physiques and genders might change and be affected by exercise, disease, musculature, but she was nearly always relatively familiar to herself in the mirror.

"In the middle of a kiss this time," Gwen, rather HARMONY, moaned to herself. Would this be one of those lives where they would cross paths early and then spend the rest of the life waiting, alone, until the next Blink? In several of the lives she had mourned Path's early death, remarried, raised a family, and lived a long, long life waiting and hoping for the Blink to happen. Although she had certainly loved those children and grandchildren, she was lonely and full of awareness that this was temporary, and a life without Path was a life lived too long. She had come to realize why some people, if they, too, were "travelers," as Path called them, chose to end their own lives, because of that horrible feeling of yearning.

"Oh, Pathogent, where are you?" she sighed, under her breath.

"What did you say, honey?" Her mother looked up from her book, giving her full attention to the tiny, beautiful, red-haired child seated in the grass beside her.

"Mallysent!" Gwen declared in her new voice, in Harmony's voice, (what the hell is a mallysent...a...oh, a black cat?) "Where is she?"

"Oh, honey, you know we can't bring Malificent to the playground with us. Malificent is home playing with her toy mouse...the one daddy bought her at the pet shop. Aren't you having fun here? Want to go home? I thought we could nap in the shade."

Another reference to Disney, and Mallysent was "childspeak" for Malificent. Harmony must be a child raised on a diet of the fantasy world of cinema. Sleeping Beauty's nemesis prompted the name of her black cat. That made perfect sense. She would have to remember to continue to be charmed by the magic Walt Disney was creating for the world's children, even with the future knowledge that she would not approve of the molding of the helpless princess image so dominate in the themes. This would have to be incorporated into her play, names like Flora, Fauna, Merryweather, Wendy and the lost boys...she would be aware of Snow White, but not Pocahontas or Belle or Ariel. But HER heroines would save the day! HER princesses would not be so needy and weak!

"No, I want to play." Harmony scrambled to her feet. "Can I swing without you, mommy? Can I swing myself?"

Her mother looked over her glasses at the swings and saw that they were close enough for her to keep a close eye on the child. "Can your feet touch the ground on that swing, the one closest to me?"

"Yes, I can push on that one. Daddy let me swing myself when he was working on his dipusiton!" She remembered to mispronounce an adult word that might actually be familiar to a child of an attorney. Asserting her independence, Gwen walked to the swing, her eyes searching the faces of the other children on nearby swings, the slide, the teeter-totter. She smiled at her mother and pushed off with her feet, swinging happily. When she saw her mother relax and return to her book, Gwen allowed her mind to wander. This one could be another very long life, indeed.

*

Swings. That wonderful feeling of flying high. In one of her lives, she had built a tree swing for the village children in Sauri, Kenya. The African heat was sweltering and swinging on a rope from a tree made just enough wind to cool their little bodies.

One of the village teens had been able to climb skillfully up the tree to loop the rope over a strong limb. He felt so helpful and important, helping the teacher work on their growing play area. "Asante, Jabari, thanks so much," she called up to him. "Kazi nzuri, good job!" her Swahili stumbling and imperfect. His wide grin beamed down at her as he tied off the rope just as he had been taught. Once it was securely anchored and tested, the children would jostle in line to be the next ones to enjoy the knotted rope.

Watching Pathogent working nearby and taking breaks to play with the children was the most wonderful part of the memory. She was sure that during the parts of his lives when he was a father he was a good one. He was a natural with kids. She often filled with regret that she would never know the feeling of having children with him. Little dark-haired, gray-eyed boys, green-eyed, ginger girls. A stab of jealousy went through her mind, jealous of the women who bore his babies.

Pathogent had helped her with the wooden teeter-totter, built from leftover lumber from the makeshift hospital, and together they also built a climbing platform that was quickly taken over by the village mothers who used it for drying clothing. All the children were given sandpaper to smooth the wood so that fewer splinters invaded little feet and hands. There was no arguing with the fact that the mothers had found a better use for the structure, so they added more width to it and the mothers allowed the children to play close by when there was no clothing to dry. It was a rudimentary playground, but it caused many years of joy for those children and children after them.

Thinking of Kenya made her smile as the memories moved soothingly and slowly through her mind, the golden grasses, the heat, the celebrations, the dancing and singing, the chirring sound of the cicadas, the feeling of being "family" with all the village, and the smiles, there had been so many smiles. She had been a teacher, sent by a government program to the village, working closely with the missionaries and doctors, and he had been a surgeon, born in the village, educated in France. He had returned home to help his people. So like him to do such a thing.

That romance had been closely watched by the children and the young mothers. They loved that their new teacher and the young doctor, their native son, were so happy together. All the smiles...all the supportive happiness. Primitive and poor but without guile and greed, the village was a precious memory. It had been a wonderful life until her body had become so very ill, too ill to be saved by medicine...or smiles. Path did not do well when she preceded him in death. It made her feel guilty to leave him, as if she had a choice to fight the Fade.

*

"Now, I just have to get my bearings," she thought. Grateful to be anywhere but the future again, Gwen relaxed and enjoyed the fresh air, the lush trees, the thick grass. Even the dust beneath the swings seemed fresh and soft and pleasant on her bare feet. The 1950s. What a great time to be a child. Soon the turbulent but wonderful 1960s would push more social change than any other decade. Many important and fascinating brave young people would die; assassination would become almost commonplace, unfortunately. But change would be wrought and it was change for the better. Things would begin to swing toward a more just world, a more accepting world. She smiled and hoped that she would be given yet another chance to enjoy that decade.

She watched a crow land on the grass nearby and, like any child her age, she allowed the swing to slowly come to a stop as she sat and studied the beautiful, shimmering bird. He strutted through the grass and looked at her, tilting his head from side to side as if to check her from different angles. She smiled. She had always been drawn to crows, their intelligence and their beauty. Crows and Ravens, her corvid companions. She held her breath to keep from alarming him and he strutted closer.

*

Once a crow had been identified as her "familiar," back when she was accused of witchcraft because of her talent as a healer. She fed the crows and they just loved to hide out in the open rafters of her hovel when they came to visit. Why superstitions had to make evil of something as beautiful as a crow, or a raven, or a black cat had always been far beyond her realm of understanding.

The fact that she shared knowledge so very far beyond this dark age of existence worked against her at the tribunal of priests. There were times when living in the future and the past could be hazardous and this had been one of the most dangerous of times. She had not been careful. She was too full of herself and her knowledge to pretend to be ignorant of the things she knew, the things that time had taught her.

The Inquisition, started in the 15th century, had, in her opinion, been one of the most hideous times to have been alive and joyous. The Church had declared her a heretic *for expressing her "beliefs" when she made the mistake of stating something that her fifty to sixty accumulated years of college courses had taught her.*

She was guilty of realizing too late that there was no way someone in her time would have known anything about the science she was putting to use in her attempt to heal. Dangerous times. It was especially dangerous to truly be "magic" or have some of the powers she and Pathogent possessed. He was wise enough to suppress his powers but when she pulled some of her powers and knowledge to play in healing a very sick mother of ten she exposed herself irrevocably.

The village priest was a hideous, sniveling hypocrite and peeping tom, hiding in his robes the attraction he felt for her and blaming her sins for that attraction and his "sinful" lust. He had always been suspicious of her healing powers and had deemed her a "witch" when he heard that she had snatched the dying woman from the jaws of certain death by actually performing an impeccable and impossible surgery. The woman was a neighbor with ten children to feed. They would have been orphaned without her. Gwen had been foolish enough to scoff at him when he accused her outright of being a witch. When he called in the tribunal, she was made to pay dearly for her contempt of the disgusting "holy" man.

That was one time when the Blink happened at the most fortuitous moment, for when Pathogent released his powers to try to save her from beheading, which would have resulted in his own torture, they both Blinked into the next incarnation. It was one of the few times when she had not had to suffer her own painful death or someone else's, for that matter.

*

She had died brutally so many times, too many times to number. Car accidents, cancer, old age, drowning, shot, stabbed and beaten to death. Perhaps because of the Blink and her full acceptance of it, she was fearless and sometimes tempted death. She had walked on the edges of cliffs and tall buildings, saved others from fatal attacks, run through fire to help her fellow, wounded highlanders, ridden horses at breakneck speed chasing buffalo across the plains, faced down a predatory polar bear to save an Inuit child, saved a woman from the bite of a king cobra, only to be bitten herself. She considered herself fortunate to have been able to live life to the extreme in so many ways. She smiled at the many memories surging through her mind, none of them distressing in their portrayal of danger to her body. Being immortal allowed for the acceptance that death was not an end. The Blink taught her to be prepared for any climate, any situation. She had learned many times that the sacrifices were often well worth the risks. Her courage, sometimes foolish and reckless, made Path crazy. She smiled at the memory of his face draining of blood as he witnessed her extraordinary bravado. There were times when she knew that she teased him this way just to see that very reaction.

She had tried to explain the Blink to one of her children in the past. It had been so difficult to find the words to explain such a strange phenomenon. "It is like when you close your eyes very, very slowly, very similar to the last moments before you drift off to sleep. Then you feel yourself pulled into the eye of a hurricane. It isn't so much painful as it is disorienting. I can only tell you that it is like waking from a dream that you desperately do NOT want to awaken from and the dream pulls you back again, only to scramble the images that you sought not to vacate. Then you feel everything stop, just before the fall. It's like falling from a great height. You spiral down and down and down, but there is never impact; you simply awaken in a new body and the dizziness is evident to both you and the person occupying that body. I don't know where they go from there; perhaps they wait, perhaps they Blink. I have no way of controlling or knowing that." Her daughter had thought that the description she had just heard was caused by delirium and medication, but soothed her mother and nodded.

This particular and new Blink was a treat. Nothing was better than being allowed the joy of a childhood with loving parents. All too often she had been the victim of heinous abuse, enduring a life in which each day seemed unending, the pain a constant reminder of what was to come. Determined to enjoy being a treasured child, at long last having no responsibilities beyond just enjoying life and the moment, she pushed off and started the swing again, enjoying the cool air on her face. Like any child of four, she quickly grew bored and stopped. When she looked up from her dusty Kelly green ballet slippers, she noticed a little boy standing just a few feet away, staring at her and smiling.

She would have known those pale gray eyes in any face. She smiled slowly. He walked over to the swing, his hands on the chains above her, a dark-haired boy not too much older than she, but tall and slim for his age, and he smiled. "No, they can't do this to us." He arched a brow and touched the wired contraption attached to the back of her leotard, "Fairy wings? How appropriate!"

She grinned, "This will be interesting...and, yes, a faerie. Apparently I wear this almost every day, when I'm not wearing tap-dancing shoes and black leotards. What can I say? I'm a weird kid, but I'm cute!"

He smiled, bemused. "Just moments ago we were...and now I can't kiss you, can't touch you," he complained. "It's a cosmic game. The gods or game-players or whatever they are, are laughing at us. Oh, this is so unfair..." he paused and grinned, "you are so little. I feel like a giant even in this small body. I want to pick you up and put you in my pocket."

"No, you should want to shove me down or pull my hair or something," she teased. "Isn't that what little boys do to little girls? That's what I've been told."

He looked over to where her mother sat engrossed in her book and dropped his voice even lower, a scant whisper,

"Do you know where you live?" he asked, desperate not to lose the quick connection they had been fortunate enough to have this time. They had learned, from experience, how fleeting these moments of connection could be. "My mother will be looking for me any second, I have been running all over, looking at every little girl, hoping, getting tongues stuck out at me. Little girls make the strangest faces for absolutely no reason. It's been interesting..."

"We walked here, we live over there." She pointed. "You?"

"My mother drove us here. It took about fifteen, maybe twenty minutes, you know how time measures differently when you're a child, so it's not that close," he whispered, "what's your name?"

"Harmony Tipton," she answered, ready to memorize anything he could tell her. They needed to find one another again. It would be difficult to accomplish given the limitations of their ages. Who knew if they would see each other again? It could be years! People could live in the same city and rarely, if ever, cross paths. "We don't go to church. My parents are proud to be secular. I think, yes, they are musicians. She is in a symphony orchestra, haha, I almost said, 'simpfee orgster'...first violin, but she also works at a bank. My father, hmmm, yes, has his own band. They play. HE plays drums, blues...he's in a blues band but he works at an office during the day...depositions...he's a lawyer! I am so glad this little brain I'm in has been so curious!"

It always seemed to them like they were reading something similar to the binary code in the brain of their new body and they, skilled technicians, had become adept at pulling up useful information.

"My name is Jacob, Jacob Coen. My parents are both professionals. He's a doctor...good, that will help you to find me. She is a professor at the college just outside this city...I can't see the name at all...but she's on a 'hiatus.' Yes, don't look at me that way; she used the term 'hiatus' with a child. I guess they don't talk 'down' to him. She plans to break away until I am in school." He paused, trying to read the inside of his new collective mind to remember experiences he had not really been part of. "I think this is Cleveland, Ohio. I can see myself writing or trying to write that in school. The climate seems about right, huh? Good, we've been here before. I am familiar with the neighborhoods." He used memory to try to get the lay of the land, to figure out where he might be but it was difficult with no landmarks.

Harmony kept an eye on her mother. Of course, they would just look like two children jabbering at one another if the woman looked up, but she had to be careful that none of this was overheard. Just for good measure, she added, almost too loudly: "I have a CAT. Do you have a CAT?"

"Did I mention that I can't kiss you...can't touch you?" He sighed quietly, then answered, louder, "Cats are DUMB, we have a dog, he's SMART, his name is Mohawk, he's a GOLDEN RETRIEVER! He is smarter than your cat!"

"Can't kiss me? Why not? Children kiss all the time!" She giggled, teasing. "Nothing like the kiss we were sharing just moments ago, but..."

"And then you have to cry and pretend you hated it."

"I would hate it, it would be too weird." Then, aloud, "Mommy!" Harmony called out, "I have a new friend, his name is Jacob. He has a dog! Can he come meet Mallysent, he said that she's DUMB, that's not nice!"

"That would be up to his parents, honey. And maybe he means that she can't talk, that is what dumb really means," her mother answered, smiling up from her book. She marked the page and lay the book down beside her. "Nice to meet you, Jacob! My name is Mrs. Tipton."

Their attention was drawn in another direction when they heard an imploring shout, "Jacob! Why did you wander away without telling me? You know better, you gave me such a fright!" A lovely, well-dressed young woman who was obviously either Jacob's mother or caretaker approached, scolding, concern written in the furrows of her brow. Gwen realized that the woman could easily have been Pathogent's mother, not just Jacob's. She had the black hair, the thin face, the soft gray eyes. Jacob's mother smiled at Harmony's mother and rolled her eyes, "Please don't judge me for this. I'm really not world's worst mom. Honest, I only took my eyes off him for a second..."

"No judging. I have a toddler and I know what you mean. I get engrossed in my reading and look up and my daughter is establishing a lifelong relationship without my even noticing, I'm ashamed to admit..." Harmony's mother laughed. "I'm Sydney Tipton, nice to meet you. It seems my daughter and your son are now 'friends'. So cute."

"Oh, hi! Catherine Coen," Jacob's mother offered. The two women chatted, allowing Jacob time to squeeze Harmony's hand, surreptitiously.

"It's going to be a trial growing up now that I know you're close," he whispered and smiled. They realized that two children would not just be standing around as their parents visited, so they chased one another, enjoying their young bodies and endless energy. The play of children was a welcome release after the years of growing older in their last life. A chance meeting in a chance place yet a connection broken by time.

BLINK

"Shawnee, do you think we might need to take more penicillin?" a male voice asked. She could hear shuffling off to her left where the voice had originated but the

dizziness was making her hesitate to move. She put her hands out to both sides to steady herself, wondering if they were experiencing another quake.

Gwen shook off the dizziness that filled the mind she had entered and closed her eyes. Gwen searched the memory and realized that her name was Shawnee and that she was once again in the future where the smells of fires and destruction and rot filled the air. "No…no...no," she thought, "take me back to Harmony, I want to be there."

She found herself standing in a huge building that had collapsed. There were parts of the store that were still intact and she recognized the familiar red logo in the shape of a giant target. Part of the big red circle had broken off but it was still identifiable. The man's voice had come from behind a counter she recognized as a pharmacy. She looked down to see that she was holding a bottle of acetaminophen. She tucked it into one of the pockets of her vest and walked to the counter. She looked down at her arms, dark brownish-red skin, strong hands.

She moved toward the counter and looked over it to the man on the other side. He was young and tall, dark-haired and thin. He had labored to turn over a collapsed shelf and was weeding through baskets and bottles that had been hidden beneath it. He was searching through the rubble and was talking to her as he held up large bottles containing pills. "There isn't much here, most of everything is nearly empty. The penicillin is a good find. What is the shelf life? I know that a lot of stores were running out toward the collapse. They couldn't get supplies anymore, this is evident here. I did find some pain killers. Would that be too much temptation?" He grimaced at the reality of the fact that someone in their group might choose the option of oblivion.

"Pain killers are essential;" she voiced her opinion, "what are they?"

"Percocet. Some, no, just a few Tylenol with codeine." He read the label. "We can break them down...offer it in grams of powder if necessary."

She nodded and watched as he carefully put the pills into smaller containers he had found. All that he gathered then went into a large backpack, the kind used for long-distance hikes. "The kids found shoes," she told him. "Good thing they did. The shoes that Yellow Feather was wearing were getting too tight; I swear that his feet grow every day! Barefoot is okay but shoes are essential if we hit some areas of lava rock. Little Sandy found a rope, those bright eyes don't miss a thing. There are some clothes I've got them gathering and I gave Jill permission to carry a doll she found in her backpack. I hope no one objects. I know we said essentials only but I think she needs it...a link to sanity, perhaps." She took some of the containers he handed her and put them in her pocket after reading the labels. "Layla went into the stockroom and found some cans squirreled away in the back. We'll eat tonight! I don't trust that part of the structure over where the freezers and food stuff used to be and had to stop Clint and Mary from going in there. I think they are tired of my bossiness, but it doesn't look safe."

For the first time since Felix hosted her [another Blink, from a California life], Gwen felt like she was merely a passenger in the body she had Blinked into. She was watching through Shawnee's eyes but the woman controlled her actions, not the other way around. Gwen decided to relax and just observe. Perhaps this was a quick visit. Obviously she would not be guiding this young woman through much that she couldn't have handled on her own. This young woman was so strong-spirited, she was able to keep Gwen's thoughts and desires at bay. Gwen was hoping to get a chance to see her host when she caught a reflection in a part of the counter that had broken away from the rest and lay at an angle, the sheet of metal reflective and caught in sunlight coming down through the broken roof. She stared, fixedly, at the dark-haired Shawnee. She was the image of herself in that long ago life when her "tribe" had carried the same name as this woman. The girl looked so wild and strong that her appearance was incongruous in this modern building with twenty-first century baubles and colors. Beautiful, strong, her hair as black as raven wings, high cheekbones in a noble face, untouched by make-up or glamour. She looked to be in her late teens, perhaps early twenties. It was hard to tell. She was dressed in a flannel shirt and jeans, hiking boots on her feet. Much too thin. Her face was gaunt but this girl was a survivor in a world where few were able to survive.

A little girl approached and said, in a voice almost too soft and shy to be heard, "Mary says that I may keep this, may I? Keep it, that is?" She seemed to need Shawnee's approval, seemed to want it. The girl was blonde and small, perhaps nine, very thin, very troubled. She held out a pocket knife and allowed Shawnee to pick it up, open it and look it over.

"It's a fine knife, Haylie," Shawnee told her, smiling. "Don't let the younger children touch it. And be very, very careful with it, okay?"

Haylie smiled up at Shawnee, standing within the protective reach of her hero. "I will be very careful. I told Jill that I will help her care for her new baby. Shawnee, she doesn't really think it's real, does she?"

"I think she may need to just now," Shawnee told her.

Gwen grimaced at a world where it would seem wise to allow a small child to carry a knife for protection. But her own experience with the future told her what Shawnee was feeling. The children faced more intimate peril than even the adults in this ugly, post-apocalyptic world. Having a knife of her own, learning how to use it safely, gaining confidence in her own ability to protect herself might indeed be a lesson that even so small a child should learn. Shawnee squeezed Haylie's shoulder and smiled. "Tonight I will show you how to keep it sharp and how to oil it. Remember, don't let any of the younger children know you have it."

"It's smaller than Yellow Feather's and Coyote's but they said it's a good knife for a little sister to carry. I like that they call me little sister even though I'm not really their sister," Haylie said, smiling. The most talkative of the children, she had seen her own share of tragedy but seemed to process it better than some of the others. Shawnee admired the little girl's strength and resilience. From what Conner had told her, this kid had suffered. Shawnee frowned at those thoughts, swearing to herself that Haylie would suffer no more, not while Shawnee lived and breathed. "I found some bands for our hair, and a brush...tonight Jill and Mary and I will wear braids!" With that, she ran off to join the other children in their scavenging.

Shawnee smiled and watched her cross to talk to Coyote, a patient and kind little boy. Then her attention was drawn down to something caught beneath a collapsed shelf. She brushed aside the layer of insects covering the magazine and read the words, "Vacation in the Rockies." A beautiful image, a mountain trail with a blue sky above and a mountain stream running down beside the trail captivated her and she smiled...wondering if the Rockies were still there, if there were still mountain streams.

"I will never get used to the sound of crushing insect bodies as I walk," Conner declared, approaching, his backpack firmly seated on his back. He caught her eyes and grimaced. "They are thick beneath our feet here; I wonder if this whole state is going to be nothing but dry air and dead insects...why did they survive? How are they surviving?"

"They eat each other," Shawnee told him, rising to her feet.

He looked down at the magazine she had been examining. "Is that where you want to go?" he asked.

"Why not? What if there are still forests there? What if the mountains remained above the ash and poisonous gases? What if the canopy held and protected the flora and fauna there? Got any better ideas?"

"I was just thinking we should head south before winter...but there's still plenty of time. Let's talk to the others and see what they think."

BLINK

It had been a relief to Blink back into the life she had just left. She had been right. The trip to the future was simply momentary, almost like a flash of memory, but too real to have been anything else but a Blink. She found herself sitting in her familiar room. Harmony made faces at herself in the mirror, testing her new lipstick and eyebrow pencil. She could not do a perfect, skilled job with her make-up, she reminded herself. She had to pretend that she was just getting the hang of it, to be in the learning stage of adult activity.

As frustrating as it was not seeing "Jacob" since that day on the playground, her life was nonetheless fun and fullfilling this time around. She felt she would willingly stay here forever, this age, in this time. Her young parents doted on their only child and she had grown in the warmth of their combined love and attention. She had gone to blues clubs with her mother to watch her father play for as long as she could remember; she also enjoyed the prestige of being the child of the first chair violinist and allowed to stand behind the curtains during symphony performances. Music surrounded her. It was a strong influence in her family life and her own lessons were progressing beautifully. She could play both harp and violin and was learning guitar so that she could express herself in the music of her own era.

Years before, a band from Liverpool had stolen the hearts of many of her friends as well as her own and her dose of Beatle mania was actually shared by both parents who made sure that her record collection always contained the latest release. Piles of albums and forty-fives were evident in her spacious room. Having lived in the future and full of the knowledge of what would happen in the lives of the "Fab Four" made her case of Beatle mania all the more bittersweet. She couldn't tell her father that many of his favorites would die so young. She would tease her drummer father and call him "Ringo" and he would respond by calling her "Little Miss Hendrix" (to show how "hip"' he was and to refer to what he considered to be one of the most talented guitarists to hit the music scene). San Francisco had already peaked as the Mecca for all good hippies and marijuana was the drug of choice while many across the nation were dropping LSD and barbiturates at an alarming rate, something Harmony avoided like the plague. Knowing the future and the effect that some chemicals could have on genetics, neither she nor Path had ever indulged in chemical highs, although "grass", wine, and an occasional beer were enjoyed.

Harmony's long hair hung in a curtain of straight shining auburn past her shoulders in the current popular style. She was wearing madras (it's not true madras if it does not "BLEED", she remembered being told by the owner of a "head shop" where she found the shirt) and bell-bottoms, and her room was a flower child's dream come true. She found that she had truly enjoyed being a child again, especially a child of such amazingly bright and progressive thinkers.

Of course, her maturity and obvious thirst for knowledge thrilled them and they were convinced that they had given birth to a prodigy. Her education (possibly the twentieth time she had been through school) was enhanced by their interests, and they made it a point to travel all over the country on every vacation, introducing her to history and culture everywhere they went. The current plan was to go to Europe next year for her birthday and celebrate that special day in Paris. It would be so good to experience Paris again, not the Paris of the Revolution (those were hard memories), nor the early twentieth-century renaissance Paris of writers and other artists, which she had enjoyed witnessing firsthand, but a new vision of Paris, a relaxing vacation, strolling along the Seine or visiting the Louvre. She thought of the years in France when she and Path had been participants in the bloody Revolution, justified, noble their cause…until it had gotten out of control and the guillotines and the nouveau riche of the Reign of Terror turned life into another witch hunt, disillusionment growing among those who had fought for the greater good.

She thought of him often, wondering why their paths had never crossed again in this life, not in school, not socially. She would look for him in department stores, at concerts, in every public place. But those arresting gray eyes of his, his raven's wing black hair, and his slim, straight posture were nowhere to be found. Her biggest fear because it would take him so much longer to reunite them was that his family had moved away. There were many Doctor Coens in the city and she didn't know anyone who went to that university so there was no way to encounter Catherine, Jacob's mother. However, he was old enough to be mobile now and should have found her. She and Path had made a pact a long time ago to enjoy each life and just "let it happen," so, while frustrated that this city was larger than it seemed sometimes and conspired to hide her lover from her, she was determined to enjoy this wonderful decade of discovery and freedom.

Her parents pleased her. She could not have been more fortunate. Both of them were highly intelligent and extremely moral and far-sighted. Her father's friends had been to marches in the South. He had gone, himself, to Selma. And although his wife, Sydney, had been proud, she had feared for his safety. Change was steamrolling: the world was starting to demand equality, racial and gender; and she couldn't dream of a more exciting time to be alive. The era of change and growth. Discovery was happening in all aspects of society. The medical world was taking leaps and bounds. There were musical awakenings and happenings, social unrest and resolution; campuses had come alive with energy and activism. It was almost as exciting as it had been living during the Renaissance in Italy.

Her parents had weathered her tantrums when she was younger, the little green-clad fairy demanding to go to the park daily, insisting on waiting and waiting...she was embarrassed to think how she must have made their lives stressful by insisting that they somehow produce her "new friend," Jacob. And it wasn't that they didn't try, but her mother had forgotten Catherine's last name and Harmony didn't dare prompt her because there would have been no reason for a four year old child to have remembered it. After all, why would a child remember such a thing? Poor Sydney Tipton wracked her brain trying to remember but it eluded her. Even when Harmony would leave hints, magazines left open to articles written by a writer named Coen, the phone book opened to the pages of physicians with one of the many Dr. Coens at the top of the page, Sydney had completely forgotten the details of the encounter. There had been so many playmates, so many children, daily encounters that drowned that one incident in the sea of life.

Harmony had even played the childish game of dialing, with operator assistance, random people with the last name Coen, hoping that Jacob would answer. Her ears would strain listening for his voice in the background when a woman would respond. Not able to think of anything to say other than, "Sorry, I must have the wrong number," when the operator connected the call, Harmony felt embarrassed and intrusive in her desperation.

She put the needle down on a forty-five RPM record and *"The Sounds of Silence"* by Simon and Garfunkel filled her room. She found herself singing Art Garfunkel's harmony much more easily than Paul Simon's lead. Art's voice was sweet and pure and easy to follow; it tested vocal acumen more efficiently.

It wasn't that her life wasn't full. She had great friends, went to a fabulous school, really loved this life. It was the knowing that he was there, somewhere close, probably searching for her just as desperately. In all of their Blinks, they had not accumulated much time together. It was one of the reasons that they both felt this thing they called the Blink a curse. They had watched each other die young, remarry, and have families. They were never able to produce a child of their own union, which was probably just another aspect of this curse. Perhaps immortals, or "travelers" as Path sometimes called them, could not create other immortals. Their children with other spouses had always been perfectly normal and very human. In only one incarnation, in one glorious Blink, they had met and married and spent nearly three years in marital bliss. But there was never a child. It had been the part of history that historians referred to as the Dark Ages and he had been a fisherman, somewhat of a hermit.

Feeling this memory overtake her and wanting this vision to last, because it was especially dear to her and pleasant, Harmony fell back to lie down on her bed and let her mind remember. The details were so rich in her memory she could almost smell the ocean.

*

With her father and a group of fishermen from their village, she had crossed the Straits of Moyle from Scotland, shortly after the death of her mother. Their plan was to return to her father's own people in a small Irish village on the north coast. Though his Scottish friends were sad to see him go, they arranged the passage on their boat for him, knowing that his grief had become a great burden and that he needed to share it with family. It had been like "coming home" to her as well, as she roamed the land of her original people, the Tuatha de Danaan, sometimes referred to as the fey folk, or the fairy, the red-headed original people of Ireland who, legend had it, went beyond the veil to leave the ugliness of the violent, less evolved, warlike human world behind.

The Samhna, or Samhain, festival prompted a huge celebration in her father's village, her new home, and it took place just a few months after their arrival. The celebration had been known to be deeply rooted in mystery and legend, pagan, exciting, pulsing with life. The air was crisp yet filled with wood smoke from the fire, winter was yet a few weeks off and the harvest had been good. Larders and root cellars were stocked and the hard work of the fields was turned and plowed under to await spring. Now was the time to celebrate, to rest a little before the coming of the cold.

Villagers danced drunkenly around the great fire built to keep the spirits at bay, for the space between the living and the dead is believed to be very thin on All Souls Night of the Samhna. Couples, tempting the fate of meeting banshee and kelpie, disappeared together into the darkness and those left behind mingled and teased and danced and flirted. Laughter, wit, music and camaraderie made her heart feel light as she lifted her skirts to skip around the fire with newfound neighbors, friends and family. Bawdy comments and drunken boldness made the men seem rough and the women loose but she knew these were good people who meant no harm. Not less than a few of the young men tried to gain her attention but she frolicked and played with abandon and joy simply to be alive.

He stood on the other side of the fire watching her and when she saw him, her heart skipped a beat. Rugged, rough and mysterious, he seemed a dream. His look drank her in. She stopped, afraid to lose sight of him, afraid to drop the connection. She smiled and struggled through the crowd to find him but, when she reached the spot where he had been standing, he was no longer there.

She had felt her heart racing in her chest and wondered if she had simply imagined him. Turning slowly in circles, she must have looked bewildered, maybe a little too intoxicated. Then her father's youngest sister, a woman her own age, came dragging Path toward her to introduce them.

"Happy All Souls, Sabd, my lass, and I want you to meet the very best friend of my very own dear husband." She then turned to Pathogent, "Nuadu, you must be on your best behavior. This comely lass is my dear brother's only bairn!" She chattered on, telling Sabd that it must have been a long stretch of lonely to bring Nuadu down to the village from his fishing hut high in the hills. She told Path, who wore a bemused look of feigned interest and patience, that Sabd had crossed the waters to sweeten Ireland's gene pool, making Sabd blush.

The crass but honest people of the village were often capable of making her blush with their blunt and easy style of teasing. Sabd and Nuadu allowed her aunt to dominate the conversation as they both waited patiently to be alone. They spent the evening talking, and he did the expected, and asked her father's permission to walk with her and they walked in the moonlight, along the craggy coast, high above the waves below. Stopping her, he drew her into his cloak to keep her warm...bending his head down toward hers...

"In all of our lives, in all the many incarnations, you have never looked more beautiful than you looked in the firelight tonight. Your wild, uncontrolled red curls, that dress, your white teeth gleaming in your smile, those green, green eyes...I wish I could paint the spell you cast, the vision I saw. I didn't want you to notice me. I watched a long while...and it wasn't just me watching you...I'm just the lucky one who won a walk in the wild with you, bonny lass. I will carry this memory in my heart until our lives are no more..."

*

"Harmony! Are you ready to go?" Her mother burst into her reverie.

"Omigosh, Mom, I forgot!" Harmony apologized, jumping up from her bed. "I'm so sorry! It will only take me a few minutes to change." She sighed as the memory faded...at the romance of it, at the fact that it had actually happened; it wasn't just the plot of a book or a movie script. Her young hormones were stirred greatly.

"Daydreaming again, kiddo? You don't have to change your clothes, you look great! It's just the Blue Note. You don't have to worry, it's so dark in there no one can see you anyway!" Sydney teased, but relented. "Okay, I'll go get the car out of the garage...you have TEN minutes! Seriously, honey, that would be pushing it."

She combed her straight hair and shed her "hippie' garb," struggled into her most "bohemian" look, black from head to toe, (kids in the future would call this Goth), trying to decide whether to wear a beret on her head or not, decided not to...drew a darker eyeliner under her bottom lashes for "drama." Ah, now she looked less a flower child and more like the daughter of a "blues man." When she got in the car, her mother examined her. "Change costumes?" she smiled after the light tease. "Honey, I'm going to drop you off. I don't even have time to go in and wave. I can't be late for rehearsal. Since you don't have school tomorrow, you can stay with your dad until he's finished, or, you could give me a call."

"It's okay, Mom, I'll stay with dad and 'close the joint down'," Gwen said, with a smile. "After all, I'm almost old enough to drink."

"Not quite, Stinkerpoo! Dad and the Azure Mojos will be finishing up early tonight since they are opening for another act. You'll be home by eleven, little 'Outré' BOHO!" Her mother teased, then winked. "That is, if your father doesn't get into a four-hour conversation with one of the other musicians!"

"We can hope," Gwen grinned.

"He has a deposition tomorrow. Remind him! Especially if he starts reliving the history of the blues."

Her father's first set was well underway when they arrived at the Blue Note Club and Harmony went directly to a table reserved for her near the stage. Harmony smiled and waved, at first, to her father then the other members of the band. She threw her sweater over the back of her seat and went to the bar for an ice water, then she folded her long legs under her on the chair and made herself comfortable to enjoy the familiar songs.

The bar was crowded as usual with old blues followers and young students drawn to get a taste of the blues experience, awakened in many of them by singers Janis Joplin and British groups like The Stones and The Animals. She knew each song of the set by heart and listened intently as the band honored many bluesmen throughout history with their covers of the old songs. They alternated with originals that one member of the band, or another, had composed.

She wasn't seated long before a soft whisper, close to her ear, "Hey there, beautiful, it's about damned time!" She turned slowly and met Path's eyes. She tried to hide her excitement from her father, who she KNEW was watching this encounter but would not miss a beat on his drums. Jacob pulled out a chair and sat down across the table from her. "Is this okay? Will he be okay with me joining you? When I saw you come in, I had to wrestle with myself not to jump up, immediately, and approach you right then and there!" He put a bottle of beer to his lips and took a drink to try to slow himself down. "Gwennie, damn it, you were so hard to find! Where have you been hiding?"

"ME! I have been looking for the Coens for years. This is a big city but I didn't think it was going to be THAT hard!

You didn't go to any of the places we shopped, never returned to the playground. I thought we'd at least meet in high school!"

"Ha! There was one thing I didn't know to tell you: I'm Jewish! We moved in completely different circles, went to different schools...I knew it was going to be a needle in a haystack, so I went the music angle and learned everything I could about the blues scene in this city. You know I've loved the blues since my other life in Louisiana. It was easy to become the resident 'expert', with my father's financial help. He considered it a wasteful way to spend my time but, fortunately for me, he is loose with his money. My record collection would probably blow your dad's mind! I know every axeman, blues harp blower, sideman, roadie, groupie and lightman in this town and can name off all their idols. Problem is, your father doesn't allow his name to be used on the promo posters. He goes by that crazy pseudonym...what, Slim Maxie Brown? How am I going to find a Tipton when the poster says BROWN? I've already been here before, watching this band, but I never made the connection, I never knew that he was Max Tipton. Okay, I know, I'm talking a mile a minute. I'll slow it down. Couldn't get into the clubs until I turned eighteen...so there was that. And my parents would never think to go 'diving'. They consider clubs like this 'frighteningly risky'," he said this with air-quotation marks, then he winked.

Gwen smiled slowly, drinking in the vision in front of her

of Path at eighteen, young, handsome, enthusiastic, energized, wild, carefree, and hyperactive.

"Gwennie, look, I am leaving for college next week."

"Next WEEK!" she breathed, unable to believe that she finally had him within reach only to lose him again so soon. TWELVE YEARS! She closed her eyes and collected herself, "And, you have to remember, you've got to stop calling me Gwen. I'm Harmony in this life." She struggled past the lump in her throat.

"No, honey, don't cry...I...I refuse to lose touch this time. I'm going to make your father WANT me for his little girl...I'm going to be both of your parents' favorite suitor, that is, if you have other suitors...you don't, do you?" Erratically, he changed the subject, so upbeat, so joyful, "This has got to go down as one of the best lives I've had a chance to enjoy!"

"Your...your friends are trying to get your attention," she whispered. She was trying hard to digest the news that he would be gone again within a week, trying to control anger that she could not let him sense. How could she be angry with him for having such a good life without her when she had just been thinking the same thing only an hour or so ago?

"Um, okay, I told them that I was going to finally get to meet this very important drummer...it's not their gig, so it won't matter to them. I thought they would let it drop at that. Give me a minute to shake them free...don't leave. I'll be right back."

Gwen couldn't believe how very young Path actually seemed. He was playing the part of an active, crazy teen so very well. He would make a great frat boy. She closed her eyes and moaned...college...leaving. She looked up at her father who gave her a questioning look. She knew that he was wondering if he should stop playing to come to her rescue. She smiled to reassure him. "He's okay!" she mouthed and assured him with a thumbs up. People often came to talk to her at the club, this was nothing unusual, but she knew that her father was a little disturbed at this young, handsome "lad" being so "familiar" with his "little girl," even though she was sixteen.

Path returned to sit beside her and smiled. "I know I'm being frenetic, I'll reel it in a little. It was the surprise and excitement of finally seeing you. And the beer. I've had a lot of beer," he admitted, shaking his head. "Please don't be mad at me, Gwennie, um, Harmony, I didn't plan for it to be this way." He changed the subject. "I don't want your father to think I'm making passes at you but, damn, how I'd love to BE making passes at you!"

Gwen laughed, then looked serious. "Tell me more about this 'going to college' thing...where? How far? Why?"

"I'm going back to New York, can you believe it? Remember New York? I have always had such a great time there."

*

Did she remember New York? She had worked her way through college which, of course, came so very easy since she had been through college so many times. Scholarships practically fell in her lap. She continued through the school of "hard knocks" in the literary world to finally land a job as the assistant advertising editor of a new innovative and progressive magazine for women. She had worked there many months, getting caught up in the insanity of working in Central Manhattan. For nearly twenty-six years she had been Megan Cassidy, hungry for success and quickly climbing that ladder, earning an italicized listing under the heading of "Staff" in the table of contents.

Her job was her breakfast, lunch, and dinner and her only respite was to struggle through the teeming throngs to the apartment she shared with two roommates to sleep at night and begin again the next day. She had actually gotten so drawn into it that she thought of nothing else, forgetting about the Blink or anything of former lives. When she did muse about the past, it was like something that had happened to another person, like a dream life. Her life had consisted of looking through stills, arranging shoots, editing copy, and working with the proofreaders to make each article perfection. She would not even dream of anything less than perfection, holding herself personally responsible for each word that made it into print. She was driven and she was happy, caught up in the excitement of being skilled and appreciated, knowing that she was on the fast-track to having her own byline.

Forty minutes to get home and change, thirty more to get to the dinner being held for one of the investors. The publisher had demanded her presence at this one, much to her unbridled joy; this meant she was doing exactly the right things to gain notice. She moved through the crowd, weaving through skillfully, not allowing anything or anyone to slow her down. She looked at her watch and cursed the bustling streets: so crowded, so many people. When rush hour hit, the sidewalks were a tide going in either direction; to swim against that tide took skill and the ability to shut it all out. She passed businessmen, brokers, models, shop clerks, factory workers, shoppers, all blending together like sardines.

Suddenly the hair stood up on her arms and she turned a half circle looking back at the person she had bumped past in her hurry. He, too, turned slowly, and, just as slowly his lips curved into a half-smile. She felt weak. How could she have forgotten, how could she have given up the search? She pushed through to him and he enfolded her...what was this, a cape? "Oh, Gwennie, this time I'm letting the magic just happen...I feel like I'm caught between Blinks. I don't think we have much time. We are now invisible. Don't worry, they can't see or feel us." How was it that she understood what he meant, that it made sense to her that he called her by another name? How could any of this have seemed normal?

In the middle of the madness of rush hour pedestrians, they kissed, oblivious to all but that hungry need. In the hundreds of years they had been jumping from era to era, proportionately they had only a handful of days together. She had only ten minutes with him before the Blink took him elsewhere. It left her feeling desolate, abandoned, adrift. She was left turning in circles on the sidewalk, looking like a lost tourist. She shook herself and finally went on her way and actually arrived for the fund-raiser just a few moments late. But her mind had shifted and she felt disoriented and dazed for several hours. Had it all been a dream, an illusion?

Desperate to have an identity of their own they could recognize in one another and hold onto when alone, and after spending many lives in other identities, yet having no real "birth," no real beginning or end, they had decided to choose their own "real" names. These would be their names of choice, the names they would carry in one another's heart throughout each ordeal, throughout all times. They were, after all, obviously not human and would always carry too many names, too many identities. Though they might present themselves as beings in each life, they knew themselves to be immortal energy, nothing more.

Although completely and totally non-gendered and ambivalent when it came to preferences with others, they also embraced an identity that would make them a "couple" to validate the very human feelings they evoked in one another when they were in the bodies of humans.

He had chosen to be Pathogent Lachesis, both virus and remedy, but also from the Latin for passion and change and even chaos, a play on words he found amusing as someone who was often a physician holding true to his attempt to improve the lives they touched.

She chose Gwen, because she loved the Celtic meaning of the word Guineviere: "white wave," reflecting her love of the coast, the draw of the ocean in her heart. She was also a hopeless romantic and embraced the story of the star-crossed lovers, Lancelot and Guineviere. The name meant more to her than most. It suggested strength and independence to her, someone who would risk a crown for true love. She took no last name as her personal identity, but identified strongly as one of the Tuatha de Danaan of Ireland. The feelings those tales evoked resonated in her mind, which would have made her one of Ireland's fey folk. It fit because he often called her his fairy, his muse. So, in his mind, she was Gwen de Danaan, his eternal lover.

*

"Gwen? Um, Harmony?" he asked, as the sax player finished his solo and the singer stepped to the microphone.

"I was remembering New York..." she admitted, smiling slowly and looking directly into his eyes.

His smile was blazing. "Yeah, remember New York," he paused, letting his own mind enjoy the memory, then continued, blushing, "Back to this thing about college.

I'm going to Yeshiva in NYC. It's a great school, a good start...Kosher, haha. Then, hopefully to Ivy League, it's my...um, my father's dream. I owe him this, really. He has dedicated his life to this...Leo wants another doctor in the family. I mean, we have to LIVE these lives; we have to have believable careers...this one will be easy."

She grinned, "You've already gone through college seven times to become a doctor. This should be a breeze for you."

"Yeah, and another residency. I am NOT looking forward to my interning days," he groaned, "but I won't be struggling like the first time. The second best thing about this Blink thing. You're the first best thing, you know that, don't you?"

She laughed at his blatant enthusiasm, his energy, the fact that he really actually talked and seemed like a very young man, but then, Path had always shown the energy of someone meant to be young. He continued, "I am hoping that will help me accelerate my courses. I am planning to fast track it, if possible. I want to finish with it all as quickly as I can, particularly NOW. Maybe you've got something there. Maybe there are no geniuses. They're just immortals who've Blinked enough to appear that it all just comes so easy to them. And, you're one to talk, my world-famous micro-neurosurgeon! 2028 was a good year for you! Your picture was everywhere I looked! Scrubbing in with your team that day was the highlight of all my careers as a physician."

"Scrubbing onto a TEAM. Doctor, there were nurses and technicians on that team that made that surgery possible; it could not have been done without you, without them. No one person should ever get the credit for such success when all those skills and talents come to play. Do you KNOW how frustrating it would be to do that kind of surgery with the limitations of this decade?" she moaned. "I don't know how you're going to stand it, knowing the procedures you've already performed and the advanced instruments you've had at your disposal. Do you realize that Dr. Barnard just did the first transplant not too long ago?"

"Um...yeah, I kinda follow things like that!" He grinned at her blush, took another drink from his beer and looked up at the band. "So here's the plan tonight. I am going to pretty much ignore you and engage your father in a walk through blues history. It's all going to be about him and the blues. You tell him that I asked to sit here to have you introduce me to Slim Maxie Brown. I hope to be your dad's new protegé by the end of the night. You're going to see a lot of me in the week before I leave...and hopefully on every vacation."

"No, seriously, you're leaving in a week?"

"Shhhh, Gwennie, dammit, Harmony. The set is almost over. Dayum, this axeman has lips." He moved his foot under the table to touch hers. Connection. "Oh," he teased, "and stop being so damned pretty and looking at me with those eyes...I'm having a hard enough struggle trying to ignore that face!"

And that is how the evening went, just as he had planned. Harmony's father approached the table, a little wary at first, but then flattered and amazed by the knowledge that was coming out of this young guy's mouth. And Max's initial fears were unfounded. The kid completely ignored Harmony to talk Muddy Waters, Bessie Smith, Lightnin' Hopkins, genuine enthusiasm for the genre rolling from him, and yet was polite and inclusive when Harmony or a member of the band joined the conversation.

They talked non-stop during the break and Max Tipton shook Jacob's hand and said, "At first, I thought you were making moves on my daughter, Jake. Glad to find out I was wrong. Hang out. I've got one more set, then we can get down to some serious conversation." Turning to Harmony he said, "Hey, this kid's the 'real deal'." He jumped onto the stage to join his bandmates, then turned back to address his daughter. "Harmony, give him our phone and address, there are labels I want to share."

Path leaned back in his chair and sighed...but under the table, his hand found Gwen's. The night was endless as she watched her eternal lover charm her "father" to integrate himself into their lives.

As planned, he and Max formed an instant bond. He told Max that he had thought of forming a band of his own after college and, at Max's urging, played his own wailing sax for them the following night in their living room. He added riffs taught to him by a future sax-player and idol, Clarence Clemons, who would be a very important name in future rock and roll circles but would not be known in this time and place. Her father was impressed with Jacob's talent and innovation and wondered why he was not already playing on stage. He turned to his wife and said, "Does this kid have any idea how good he is?" Harmony smiled at this. If only her father knew how many of those famous blues musicians they were listing and talking about had been joined at jam sessions by the young, skinny, black saxophonist Path had been in several other lives. This music drew him like a moth to flame.

True to his word, he was at their home every night before leaving for college, encouraged by Max, who was thrilled at his endless research into the music. Max was excited at having found such a talented protégé. He had other band members over to witness the savant. Never once did Jacob appear anything more than polite to Harmony. He would listen intently to her opinions, but as any friend of her father's would, respectfully and engaged. She had to admit to herself that it was driving her crazy to be this close, at this age, with all the raging hormones rushing through her young body. So this was what "puppy love" felt like? Each night she went to bed with him in her thoughts, yearning. Was she showing the part of "starry-eyed smitten teen" to her parents? Was she hiding this very real attraction?

It was the last night before he left for school and he dropped in to bring over a few forty-fives he had talked to

Max about. "No, really, I bought three copies of each of these when I found them. You're not taking my only record. I want you to have these, a gift," he assured her father. "I know it's not blues, but you've got to listen to this bootleg of Sandy Nelson." Filtered into the later conversation, she and Max let Jacob know that she would be studying music at the Cleveland Institute next year.

"Why not Juilliard?" Jake asked, reaching for the very best to suggest to them, led by the bonus of the fact that it would bring her to New York. He smiled up at Sydney in thanks for the coffee she put in front of him.

"Because she's not going that far away from us her first year, is why!" Max teased. "And I'm definitely not going to allow her to be alone with you in New York City! I like you, Jacob, but there's a limit! We both find NYC to be too worldly at this point in her studies...maybe in another year or so."

Jake slowly smiled, "Why not? I'd be a great guardian. I'd keep the crowd from crushing her...protect her for all I'm worth! [The irony of the allusion was not lost on Harmony and she smiled.] You wouldn't have to worry...I know New York, I have a lot of family there, Coens everywhere! She'd have a lot of people looking out for her."

"Oh, Jacob, get real!" Sydney interjected, "As if you and Harmony don't realize how good looking the other is! We'll chaperone this friendship for a while, thank you very much! Besides, New York City is just too...um, stressful. I don't know what I'm trying to say, too worldly."

"What my mother is trying to say," Harmony teased, pulling a lock of 'Jacob's' hair, "is that she may trust ME, but the jury's still out on YOU, bluesman! We've only known you a couple weeks!"

Jacob nudged Max, "She called me bluesman. I will take that as a high compliment coming from THIS family. And that jury...counselor, will you represent me? I'm sure you can convince the jury of my innocence."

Sydney seemed relieved to hear Harmony's words. It was a very mature tease and yet she realized that Harmony was visibly attracted to Jacob. Perhaps Harmony, in her youthful crush, was almost afraid of what this attraction was doing to her. Sydney could certainly identify with that uncertainty, the coming-of-age-without-knowing-where-to-put-the-feelings dilemma so many young people went through.

Max took a long look at his wife and raised an eyebrow. It had just occurred to him that something might develop between his new protegé and his daughter. Sydney stifled a laugh at his naïveté. Her radar had detected the chemistry between the two young people from the day she met Jacob. She had no memory of their encounter when Harmony and Jacob were children so they had never mentioned it. However, they knew that she was watching them closely whenever they were together.

When it was time to leave, Sydney even suggested that Harmony could walk him to his car to say goodbye. Max gave her a puzzled look, but she just took his arm and yawned. "We need our beauty rest, tomorrow's going to be a busy day; you have court and I have an audit at the bank in the morning. Good night, Jacob, and enjoy your time at Yeshiva. I've heard it's a great school! And, you'd BETTER write and tell us all about it! Harmony, no more than a few minutes. You have flute class in the morning."

As they walked the half-block to his car, he said, petulantly, like a REAL teen, "I wish I'd parked a couple miles away." He turned to her. "Gwen...miss me...miss me half as much as I'm going to miss you."

He stepped closer to her. "Do you suppose they're watching?"

"I'm certain that Dad wanted to, but I'm just as certain that Mom won't allow it. After all, she suggested this...I think Mom's an empath..." She moved into his warmth and took hold of his lapels. "Damn it, Pathogent Lachesis," she asserted, calling him his chosen name, "this is horrible." His kiss was warm, soft, gentle. One hand moved through her hair to her neck to pull her closer. "We've been through worse, you know. I can't risk making your parents regret meeting me so you'd better get back. We will make it through this. Come visit me in the city!" He wiped her tear with his thumb, gently, as he held her face in his hands to stare into her green eyes. "I love you, faerie girl. You make me want to always be the man you deserve, the man you seem to see in me."

She broke away while she knew she still could and turned away to walk home. He watched her, tears shimmering in his own eyes. Star-crossed and doomed to be torn asunder time and again.

True to his word, he wrote letters to her father and mother and notes with hidden meaning to her. Every holiday he spent more time with her family than he spent with his own, and he and Harmony were having trouble hiding their attraction from her parents, to the point that Sydney seemed to be warming up to the idea of them as a couple. His plan to accelerate his courses came true as he was proving to be the "genius" that his father hoped for.

She went to the Cleveland Institute and made her parents proud when she received commendations from her professors and, of course, there were recommendations that she consider Juilliard. Even her parents thought this might be a good direction for her next year, so she was given permission to apply for scholarships and auditions. Her talent was getting noticed, both in voice and in her skill with many instruments. She was chosen to perform at governor's galas, community fundraisers. She moved through crowds of the gifted and wealthy patrons of the arts. Any style of music seemed to come so easily to her, but she had already decided what she wanted to be; while she loved classical music and high arts, her heart, like her father's was in the blues.

She found a pianist and started listening to and learning torch songs from the past like, *"Cry Me a River"* and *"My Funny Valentine."*

When her parents visited the nightclub, she seated them at the front table, right in front of the stage where she was being featured and she sang her heart out for them. It was their anniversary and she determined to make it very special, having invited several of their closest friends. She sang Billie Holiday's version of *"I'll Be Seeing You."* It nearly broke her when she saw the tear tumble down Max's cheek...and she blew him a kiss.

They turned the table of surprise on her and she was shocked to see Jacob approach their table with red roses for Sydney and pure white roses for her. He brought them to her at the piano and kissed her cheek and the audience applauded their approval. He took a seat with her parents. She leaned over to whisper to her accompanist and looked straight into Jacob's eyes and told the microphone, "This song will have to go out to Jacob Coen." She buried her nose in the roses, then set them aside and threw herself into Ella Fitzgerald's version of, *"Can't Help Lovin' That Man." "Oh, listen sister, I love my mister man...and I can't tell you why..."* When she came to the lyrics, *"it must be somethin' that the angels done planned,"* she winked at Sydney.

When she finished her set, she joined their table, kissing her parents and then pausing to kiss Jacob. The evening was beyond anything she could have planned for them.

Her parents were the celebrities of the night and everyone in the club came to congratulate them and tell them what a wonderful young woman they had raised. She had invited all their friends and the club was filled to capacity with their friends, band members, and musicians.

Then Jacob proposed to her with her parents as witness. And Max and Sydney declared it to be one of the best gifts they could have received.

During a moment when her parents' attention was drawn by a chatty couple nearly their same age, Jacob took advantage of the distraction and turned to her and whispered, "What are you doing this weekend?"

"I had nothing planned, spring break...Mom and Dad are going on to Niagara Falls tonight...tonight is my last show until..."

"Neither have I," he broke in, "no plans at all...all day...and all night Saturday and Sunday...and Monday," he whispered, his lips close to her ear, his breath warm on her neck. "I need a place to stay...would you be interested in putting me up for the weekend?"

"I can't wait," she whispered back softly.

It was like another honeymoon for them. Reveling in the strength and stamina of their young bodies, they spent one another to exhaustion. Between kisses, he declared, "If either one of us Blinks right now...I...swear...I..." Hours later they were both exhausted but happy.

He watched her as she moved through her rooms, economy in motion. She came back to bed with cups of coffee and a bowl of strawberries. "I love watching you move around your little place. I can almost picture wings on your back, fey filly."

"I thought this day would never happen," she admitted. She sat cross-legged on the bed and handed him a berry. "I was a bundle of frustration - a horny co-ed is a dangerous thing indeed. AND, I can stop calling you Jacob for a while!"

He lifted her hand and kissed the ring he had placed on her finger at the end of her performance the previous night, much to Max and Sydney's surprise and delight. "How am I going to break it to my folks that they're going to have a 'Shiksa' for a daughter?" he teased. "Can you imagine, after all the lives we've been through, we end up being a...oh, the horror...another 'mixed marriage'?"

"So when you gonna break it to them that I'm also an atheist?" she snorted, laughing. "It will be enough to make their eyes bleed, no?"

"No, really, they're great. Very modern. My mom isn't one of those, 'Eat...and give me grandchildren' kinds of Jewish moms," he laughed.

She rose to her knees in front of him and brushed her hands through his dark hair. "God, you're so fucking gorgeous!" Gwen told him, "When you walked into the club in that tux...with those roses...my knees got weak...you could have had me then and there...well, if my parents hadn't been sitting beside you and...you know, all those other people hadn't been watching!" They both laughed. "And," she moved her hands down over his arms, "you've been working out, my love!"

"Something has to vent MY sexual frustrations, my fey. I spend myself in the gym on weights, then drop into bed still thinking pornographic thoughts about you. Speaking of gorgeous, you and that slinky black-beaded number sizzled on stage. Do you know how many men you were turning on?"

"I only cared about one!" She took a bite of the berry he was holding and let the juice drip from the corner of her mouth. He licked it, and worked his mouth over hers, kissing her deeply. "I want to throw back my head and howl to the moon right now," he smiled, his lips still against hers. "FINALLY, god damned FINALLY!"

*

She should have taken it as a premonition. That weekend had been too perfect. She got called out of class three weeks later, her father standing in the hall, hesitant, white as a sheet and obviously grieving, unable to know how to begin to tell her. "It's Jacob," he began. She fell to her knees, unable to breathe, unable to think. "Harmony, honey...accident...instant...honey, he felt no pain." She screamed, "No, so unfair...so....god....damned...unfair." She was with Harmony for only another month before her own Blink, drowning in her music, the sad love songs, her torch burning through the nights. She had been in this situation too many times. It had seemed like a rehearsal for grief. The thought always haunted her: with no control over their Blinks, might this have been their last together?

BLINK

Louisiana, 1992, in a different life:

Sirens, flashing lights like a strobe somewhere to her left. The most unbelievable, unbearable pain wracked her body. She was lying on the tarmac and could not move even her head to look around. The emergency lights intermittently lit the world above her, flashing on a dark night sky. It was summer. She could feel the warmth of a summer night, hear the tree frogs singing at a nearby pond. The tarmac was still warm from the day's sunlight. She could feel rocks digging into the back of her left arm, that arm obviously in the berm of the road, on gravel. She heard the sounds of cars moving around her.

Someone was crying, radios were making a noise that sounded like endless static, occasional distorted voices barking through the annoying din, there was broken glass everywhere, she could hear shoes crunching as they walked on it. She felt like she could sense it, not see it. All that she could see was what was directly above her, constellations, stars twinkling above...darkness broken by the rhythmic strobe of the light. She could not move her head, could not move her body at all.

A voice, possibly that of a policeman, talked into the radio, breaking into the static, "We got an 11-44, the driver of the truck." Unintelligible noise followed; she heard broken phrases, from other positions around her, "Passing a semi on a curve," and, a choking sob from someone, a woman, "hit head on, I think her neck is broken, they practically had to cut her from the vehicle." A gravelly voice, coughing, then, "Yeah, three dead, one injured, no, probably won't." Another official report into the radio, "Squad is on the scene, coroner is just arriving."

A face came into view, white coat. She saw a medical insignia patch above the breast pocket as he leaned over her to adjust something. She thought the word, paramedic. He leaned close to her ear and whispered, incredulous, "You transitioned! I saw it. I saw her leave and you come into this body. You're one of us. I'm one of us, there are...others. It's not just me...I'll be damned, I'm not alone." He put his mouth closer to her ear to whisper, "I am so sorry, this just always means so much to me, to know I'm not alone."

Gwen moaned, blood in her mouth, blood in her nose, not able to breathe in, swallow. She knew this feeling, the feeling of dying. She had done this so many times, endured so many different deaths.

His face moved close again, in and out of focus now, his voice soothing, "I'm a transitional, too. Thank you for letting me witness this. Now I know I'm not a freak. Good god, I'm not alone," he repeated over and over in wonder in a voice only she would be able to hear. He put his mouth closer to her ear, "I'm a traveler, too...time traveler. Look for me. I go by the name Dave Carson, when given a choice." Then he brought himself back to the task at hand. Aloud he asked his partner, "Are they on the radio? Ask if we can administer something more to ease the pain. IV drip administered...blood pressure dropping to...."

She moved her left hand to his sleeve, weakly trying to grasp. "Path?" she asked.

There was no recognition in his eyes. This was "another," not Pathogent. A voice, perhaps his partner said, "Were you praying with her? Not that she's not going to need it...but...."

She could hear someone out of sight above her head, say softly, "She's not going to make it, no one can survive this." The strangest thought went through her mind. Just like Bessie Smith, it's a blueswoman's death. It's a righteous death.

They were right. She did not "make it."

BLINK

One night, as they shared memories and talked about the Blinks, Pathogent contended, "Tesla Blinked, you just know he did; there was nothing of the capitalist in him, he was working toward the betterment of mankind; I'm sure that Alan Turing certainly was a 'traveler', too...he was a loner, did not know how to relate to so-called 'normal' people. He didn't understand nor embrace his own genius and how it was so blazingly advanced that it set him apart. He might have been one of those 'travelers' who have no memory of the past times." He shifted his weight and stretched his feet toward the fire. She was comfortable, her head on his stomach, the warmth of the fire chasing the winter cold outside the cabin away.

"Einstein, Marie Curie, Edna St. Vincent Millay, Harriet Tubman, Van Gogh, Rachel Carson, Alice Paul," she added. The wind rattled the makeshift shutters on the windows. She hoped they would hear the howls of the wolves again. Last night their music had been incredible to witness, rich with overlapping tones as the pack took to song. What kind of world would wish to be without the existence of wolves? Why were they hunted down to the point of extinction in the future? Why were humans often so ignorant of the balance wolves brought to the world around them? The presence of wolves filled her heart, the presence of beings with such a strong sense of their own society. "I've met many who don't call it the Blink; several called it 'transitioning'. Others, as you've said...travelers..."

"Oh, no doubt. And I'm sure there are so many others. Some may not ever realize WHY they were gifted with so much knowledge, why things came so easily to them and not others. There may be people who Blink and remember nothing at all of the former lives, unaware that they've taken classes in those subjects time and again through time."

"Former and forward," she reminded him. "We have seen the future, and we know it's grim. For all the accumulated knowledge, for all the 'genius', ignorance is winning...ignorance will win. The troglodytes or morlocks, or whatever word humans contrive to explain those who battle against empathy and knowledge, are continuously trying to make species extinct. And I can't believe that we are the only ones with full imprint from our former existences. I just wish we could control it! I would NEVER Blink forward. One day we may Blink into a horrible oblivion."

"We don't know that for sure. We only know what happens within the realm of our own experiences. Somewhere, some way forward, there may be one Tesla, one Einstein who will have the answers and enough charisma to make the changes necessary. It's logical, you know. We are very fortunate to have one another. It's almost impossible to find others except by accident and I've never met another 'traveler' more than once, no repeat connections, except with you."

"I always listen to your logic. It is, after all, PATH-a-logical." He groaned at her insane pun, then she laughed but continued with a more serious observation, "That horrible future, Path. It will be impossible to remove the poisons from the water, from the earth. No one can reverse the damage."

"My pessimistic, misty-eyed wanderer, never say never. Time and nature can reverse the damage. I believe that hundreds of years after humans cease to exist, the earth will be lush and fertile and ready to begin again."

"In all the lives we've lived, you can honestly think that something can be done to reverse the damage to the atmosphere?" she argued, incredulously. "You are aware that there are planets that once sustained life but are now dead. You have been a scientist, you know about the gravitational pull of the sun, about solar flares."

"In all of the lives we've lived, we know that you can never say never. When we give up on seeing one another, something throws us another bone and we get to share moments like this." He paused and ran his fingers through her hair, "Maybe it will be you. You have the knowledge that it takes and you have more than a boatload of charisma and empathy. I can see you fostering change, inspiring people with your endless passion. And then, there is the possibility that our mission isn't on this planet. Maybe we will be somewhere, sometime else."

She closed her eyes, enjoying the feeling of him stroking her scalp, and sighed, "Empathy can be painful. I think of all the extinct species, the way the ocean looked in 2062, barren, poisoned, the earthquakes, the volcanic eruptions. The lives I visited were living in terror. You know yours were, too. Being a minority in the times leading up to those horrors was almost a death sentence in itself...as if the struggles of the nineteen-sixties...and the twenty-teens hadn't even happened. I never want to go back there. I never want a life without wild wolves, whales, teeming nature..."

"Teeming nature...remember the insects? As all other species died, the bats, the birds, and the insects increased...they were everywhere. I'll never get over the sound of walking on insects with each step we took outside."

"Remember them? In one of my families, they were our protein! Oh, I was never so glad to Blink away from a time; even the most violent times in our histories could not have prepared me for that post-apocalyptic nightmare." She shuddered and stretched in the luxury of being safe with him in their primitive cabin. Outside, the year was 1814, somewhere nearby in this "new" nation (oh, the arrogance of the whites, people had lived here for centuries. Yet they deemed it "new" on their arrival). The Treaty of Ghent had been signed. She and Path/Siginak (or "raven") lived at peace with their Shawnee neighbors and the Ohio River flowed somewhere to the south. She sighed, "I love being Shawnee. I love these people. I wish we could just Blink back to these two bodies after every single trip to the future. This heals me, living in tune with the heartbeat of the earth, living in awareness of the value of all manner of life. That would be a reward I could strive toward. I'd be happier suffering the deaths, the loss, the frustration, if this were at the end waiting for me."

"You love living in a matriarchal society where women are not only listened to, but obeyed," he teased.

"Your point? It's as it should be!" she retorted, smiling, then changed the subject again to a more serious thought. "I'm glad Tecumseh revealed himself to you as a fellow 'traveler'. It made mourning his loss so much easier. I wanted to ease his sister's pain, to tell her that he was just somewhere else in time. I wish I could have but I knew she would not believe me. It just is not part of their belief system. They prefer to believe that he will rise again... Shawnee," she sighed. "That day was so very hard to face, even though you and I knew it was coming, that it was inevitable. He was such a great man, a great leader."

"He's another with enough charisma and knowledge to enact change in the future. It may be the reincarnation of Tecumseh's energy who leads us back to sanity," Path mused. "Have you ever noticed that, whatever the belief system in place, there is always a shade of the myth that the hero will rise again to ease change and retribution for his people? King Arthur, Genghis Khan, Jesus, Buddha. But neither of us can say that he may never rise again Shawnee. They just won't be aware that it is him next time."

"Maybe that's how they see us, those of us who are travelers. Maybe they know there is something at work here outside of what their religions and traditions tell them. Fairy tales, legends, sagas, oral histories are filled with larger than life heroes and heroines who will return again to make righteous those who follow and believe." She turned and faced him. "Maybe in some era somewhere there are people who talk of our return." She smiled and reached up to lace a finger through his long, raven-black hair, "And maybe we have to struggle to contain our egos."

"I don't want to be anyone's legend," he declared. "I just want to spend one long, whole life with you...just ONCE!"

"Who sets out to be a legend?" she whispered. "Do you think that Tecumseh did what he did to form legend around himself? He was visionary; he saw that history might be changed, if only...if only his brother had not invited the attack by Harrison, despite Tecumseh's exact warning of the outcome; if only the tribes had all sent emissaries to Tippecanoe earlier and there had been a stronger force to defeat Harrison; if only the British had not withheld their support at the Thames leaving the Shawnee so vulnerable. You know he knew that things would and could go wrong. He was aware of the future and that his mission would be foiled. History is filled with all the possibilities of a different outcome."

"Or, perhaps, with all that we know from the future, there is nothing we can change about the past because of the effect that it would have had on that self-same future," he drawled, sleepily. He was drifting off. It had been a long day. She watched him as he fell into sleep and smiled. Contentment was hers, if only for a little while.

"Can't Help Lovin' That Man."

BLINK

San Francisco, CA, 2014

She stood in front of her closet and sighed. Turning toward the full-length mirror on the adjoining wall, she touched a hand to her silvering hair. Her reflection showed her to be drawn and pale, losing weight, her clothing hanging on her, her cheeks sunken. She certainly wasn't doing her vessel any good.

2014 and they had found themselves living in San Francisco. They had Blinked simultaneously and linked, unheard of in their past, and found themselves to be, conveniently, already married. Offered this unique opportunity, they were overjoyed. Their lesbian marriage was legal and recognized by this wonderful, vibrant and fascinating city on the bay. Path was now a beautiful, sultry, sophisticated, slender Sophie, Jewish again, which suited and complimented the usual dark, handsome looks Gwen had grown accustomed to. And Gwen's new host identity was Marisha, caramel-skinned and of Jamaican descent. She had found herself often looking into the mirror in wonder at the beauty of her smooth brown skin, her green eyes, almond shaped and long-lashed, her full, well-defined lips. Sophie teased and wondered at this newly-awakened vanity but delighted in complementing her unusual and strikingly attractive spouse.

The year that they had together was filled to the brim with happiness, outings with friends in their circle, visits to the coast, boating on the ocean, exploring, hiking, filling every single day with new discovery and joy. The cultural overload of the city offered them concerts, extraordinary spontaneous events around every corner, open-aired markets, North Beach, Fisherman's Wharf, Chinatown, Mt. Tamalpais. They lived in the Castro district but harbored a boat in Sausalito that they took out to sea often.

Retired from an extremely lucrative corporate law firm, the previous occupier of Sophie's existence had been able to set them both up with a substantial savings, and a beautifully decorated townhouse just north of Market Street, allowing Marisha to continue her own exploding career, painting incredibly beautiful fantasy landscapes. She had been asked to illustrate several book covers as her fame as an artist grew. It was a delight for Gwen to recognize a style she could warm into and share. They owned a small cabin on the Russian River to escape to when they needed to get away. She insisted that they spend every single day finding something new and exciting to do and each day brought adventure and laughter. They saw it as a dream come true for them both, a gift, repayment for all the grief and hard lessons of the past. Their time would be short. They were both retired and considered elders.

Days were often spent just walking together, hand in hand. Sometimes they would find themselves walking east beyond the Castro and the Mission District. But exploring

Golden Gate Park to the west of them was one of their favorite day hikes. The Japanese Tea Garden, the de Young, so many favorite haunts as well as new discoveries. When they found themselves in the Haight, at the southeast corner of the park, they strolled along through the tourist attraction it had become. They often thought about the Tipton family, particularly Harmony, back in Ohio and how they would have loved the shops. Marisha felt that visiting the Haight was almost like reliving part of Harmony's history for herself.

Laughing and teasing as they walked past the strip joints and sex clubs in North Beach, Sophie once pressed her to share which of their incarnations had been the most memorable, sexually. Since there were so few times they were actually able to enjoy such closeness, such a luxury, she confessed curiosity over which might have been the best for Gwen. "Come on, baby, there were so many different bodies, so many different physiques. We do not even know what gender we are or if we have one, essentially, deeply, truly. We know what gender we often find ourselves occupying, but we've been both, and every race, creed, color. Was I better as a Roman soldier or when we were both male pagan warriors? Was it best when we were teens or when we were older? If you could relive just one or two moments...you know there are moments like that..." She stopped and turned her head to the side, reflecting. Marisha took in the beloved profile. "I know that there have to be one or two outstanding memories."

"Which would YOU pick?" Marisha retorted. "I have never really given this thought. You seem to have given this a lot of consideration. You first!" She was blushing and a little uncomfortable about where this conversation might be leading. Was the Path inside of Sophie going to reveal that there had been a better lover? Was he fishing to find out if she had had someone in her past that surpassed his prowess or her attentions? Or was this Sophie talking in an effort to find if Marisha had been changed by Gwen's presence.

"Well, it's pretty damned good right now. You are smoking hot, woman! But, if I really had to pick a singular experience, I relive one most often in my mind and it feeds my fantasy when I need it to be stoked...and you have to be well aware of the fact that I seldom need to stoke that fire when you are near."

"Go on..." Marisha said, smiling.

"You were an extremely passionate freedom fighter in Ireland. One of my favorite moments to relive was that time when you thought I'd been shot, when someone had given you the wrong information about no one making it through the barrage of gunfire. You were already grieving, torn to pieces by the fact that we had argued just before I went out as a sentry. You looked exactly like the Gwen I've always held in my mind, your wild and tawny mane, the intensity in your green eyes, your heritage embraced and practiced. You were an Irish warrior, a blazing Celt. So like that Celtic goddess I saw across from me at the Samhain fire centuries ago."

Sophie continued, "The British troops had killed another guy who fit my description and your intelligence was that I was lying dead in an alleyway. You had already begun to mourn. In truth no one could touch you as you raged. I walked in the door and you looked as though you thought you were seeing a ghost. Then, talk about aggressive! I could have been paralyzed for all I was needed."

She blushed and laughed. "Oh, when you were Brendan Donnelly. Talk about a passionate person! Believe me, your part in that was appreciated. You have to admit, Brendan was more than just a comely lad. But it was you inside of him that made him equally irresistible. Yes...that was good..." She smiled at the memory and touched Sophie's arm...running her fingers down to trace the delicate wrist.

"Okay, your turn..." Sophie reminded her, arching a brow.

She stopped walking and stood deep in thought. How on earth could she put this? "It's pretty damned good right now, you know. Yeah, I'd have to say it's more than just a little good. I think about it all the time and your libido seems to be on fire. Don't you REALIZE that you're supposed to be slowing down? I am madly in love with you, Sophie, both of you. Marisha is here in this conversation, too, and there is that love to consider, not just what you and I feel, Path."

"Ouch, you just emasculated me, my love! This conversation will have to go down in our personal history as the neutering or castration of the Pathogent I've built in my mind for the 'between Blinks'. I guess there's a part of me you won't be needing again anytime soon."

Marisha laughed, "No...no, that's good, too. Ha, ha, no, seriously, I don't think I can separate each time into something I could rate as good, better, best. My heart is always so filled with love, every brush of skin is memorable, every touch takes my breath away. If we're talking about fantasy fodder, sometimes I see you as the Shawnee warrior...pensive, intense, your long dark hair lifted in the wind. Sometimes I remember you in that tuxedo at Harmony's concert, holding those roses and looking like a model for a magazine. When I think about you in armor with leather armbands, or in that long, black magician's cape or in your kilt, or out on your currach, nearly naked, fishing. But this feeling, when we are intimate, this is so beautiful, this feeling of growing old together with nothing dimming the intensity of our love. Those moments I mentioned do feed Gwen's fantasies, believe me, but Marisha certainly does NOT share them. But I am equally as capable of loving you, Sophie, immensely attractive, kind, smooth, brilliant. That love is genuine, that love is there, Marisha's love is there. I don't think that it's ever been about the skin we find ourselves in. We both adapt. Yes, I love you and am aware of your presence, but I also feel the love that was there before we Blinked. It is not only residual, it's ingrained. Do you not know that when I was Felix, I genuinely loved Tommy, not just the Pathogent inside him. I loved Tommy."

"Good save, you little diplomat!" Sophie smiled and mused, "I was pretty muscular and hot in that armor, eh?" she said, breaking into an exaggerated strut. "No, I brought this up, not so much for the ego or the sexual validation, which, by the way, you neutralized effectively." They both laughed at this, although Gwen knew that it pressed Path to admit it. "But to talk about how much I've learned from the times that I've reincarnated as a woman, or when I've Blinked into a gay man's life...into Tommy's life, in particular. I've been a gay man in so many lives now, but Tommy was the only one I shared with you. I've learned a lot about the psychology of human sexuality and attraction. It's an enlightening thing to learn about the pleasure zones and how it helps to 'hone that skill', that's a given. But it's also extremely enlightening to feel the feelings, know what happens in the brain, understand the endorphins. But I'm glad you brought up the inherent connection between the two people we occupy; that strong relationship remains and something of that has taught me that love is a-gender; it really is just love, want, need for another person, the right person."

"I agree. My lives as a man have made me wonder about so many things in life. You know that I hate to generalize but it's almost impossible not to when one has lived as many lives through the ages as we have. Even surveys and data are influenced by the times in which they were conducted. What was true about men and women a hundred years ago certainly is not applicable today, which makes it difficult to actually justify such generalizations. Time and social constraints, culture and interactions play such a big part in the molding of a psyche. Why it is that men have such a need to be surrounded by their peers, almost tribally, definitely athletically? And this is a carry-over since primitive times, yet seldom seems to cement those relationships with a truly deep and revealing bond. And why women will have so few friends that they truly trust or even wish to spend time with, but, when they find that confidante, lay bare their souls and open up their vulnerabilities so willingly? And you and I? We are a contradiction."

"Darwinians address that part about why men and women view friendship so differently in their analysis of human sexuality as being a throwback from our ape-like ancestors. But that theory has always bothered me because it really often has the two-gender foundation stone, or paradigm, and we know that's all wrong," she continued. "But then, the gay life breaks all those generalities into pieces so I know that there's something more, something much harder to put into words. It's not just about the sexuality between genders or lovers or friends, it's about the trust process, the formation of miniature 'tribes'. When people of this age get a new job, they often look about for a clique they can become part of. Will this person have my back if something happens to me? Can this person mentor me to help my advancement? Is this one just waiting to find fault and bring it to everyone's attention? Worse yet, why don't they like me? Why don't I fit in? How will I fit in, it's always about, how I fit in? Often, people find a mate who doesn't fit the mold of their work experience to be able to break away from the psychological strictures placed on them in all their other walks of life."

"I think this is why we sometimes experience a lot of lives without one another. It almost takes away our own 'crutch', or as you just said, the break from the norm," Sophie said, smiling. "No, don't look at me like that. You really do know what I mean. Yes, it hurts to find that we can love others, but it's there and we face it. There is nothing to learn if we aren't forced from our comfort zones to meet others, observe them, get close enough to learn from them, genuinely love them."

"As a man, you are much, much more aggressive than I. But, as a woman, you are also commanding and strong. There is nothing demure or reticent in any of your genders. Look how effectively you rallied your people without me when you were a tribal queen and they fought because you loved them and you understood the love they had for their spouses and families. We didn't reconnect until you were already a formidable leader. You were able to do this because you understand the psychology of patriotism, loyalism, sectarianism, the need to love and protect, defensive postures humans have performed since cave times when threatened by an opposing force, whether that force be other humans, nature, or other species. I think I came into the picture to validate what you had already started, to be your helper, to help protect you, because Lord knows, you risk yourself far too bravely. I think sometimes that I play the part of anchor, to keep your feet planted on the ground. There's something very important at play here. You've so seldom had an 'ordinary' life."

"You seem to think that our lives are leading toward something, like they aren't just a cosmic accident of some sort. You honestly see patterns, like we are being formed into something for a purpose, like all of the grief, pain, torture, and hurt we have been through has purpose. You have a belief. That is too hard for me to relate to. I can't see this as lessons we are learning toward a higher purpose. I don't see these people we've inhabited as lab experiments to form us into something," Marisha admitted. "What did you mean about me being more aggressive as a man?"

"Nothing important, just a thought," Sophie said, shrugging, then added, quickly, "I know you don't want to think about the higher purpose in all of this. And yet, how many times have you felt that some force is playing with us, cursing us, purposely causing us pain, whether emotional or physical? You know we've both cursed the 'gameplayer' in all of this." Sophie took Marisha's hand and brought it to her lips. "Whatever the end, if there IS an end, if this is truly immortality, then so be it, but, whatever the outcome, you live in here," she put Marisha's hand over her own heart. "Every rebirth, every incarnation, you're as much a part of me as my own brain, my own limbs. And I know that you feel the same. If there ever is an 'end', we will be there together, I know that without any trace of doubt."

The summer night in the city was warm, full of noise, excitement and adventure. They walked often, through the night, talking about psychology, the future of the earth, whether they would someday walk in the stars above, and love.

Life was so good, so there was no warning, no feeling of impending disappointment and grief. No indication of the weak heart in Sophie's chest. Considering their conversations, this was another cosmic irony. It had come so suddenly and was over so quickly that Marisha had no thoughts of preparation, no way of coping with the unfairness of it except for the experience of their previous lives and deaths. While fully aware that death was not an end, this was the end of a beautiful relationship, the end of something she cherished.

Stepping into the closet, she ran her fingers down the sleeve of one of Sophie's shirts, a custom-made Souster and Hicks, Sophie's very favorite. There were many times that she had to stop Sophie from wearing it to every occasion that demanded something formal and stylish. She brought the sleeve to her face and inhaled the scent of her beloved's cologne. Through her tears she worked the buttons and took it from the hanger, slipping her arms into the sleeves. She disappeared into the soft cloth. Sophie had been slim, but taller and stronger, so it fit Marisha as though she were a child wearing her father's clothing. She closed her eyes and remembered a night just a few weeks past.

*

"Here, let me," she had said and reached to tie a Windsor knot at Sophie's neck. Fussing with it until it was perfect, she looked up to find Sophie smiling and staring into her eyes. "Oh, no you don't!" she said, patting Sophie's chest, "You've got to stop doing this. We are meeting Jill and Marnie in an hour and I'm not even nearly ready...we don't have time...."

The kiss was intense, demanding. "We need to make time then," Sophie whispered against her lips. "They love us. They'll both understand and forgive."

*

The thrill of the memory made her warm with a flush through her body. Then sorrow burrowed so deeply into her soul that she wrapped her arms around herself and sobbed. "Why do I have to experience so much grief, so often?" she thought. "What terrible wrong have I done? What possible lesson could I be learning from this?"

She curled up on their bed and, as was habit, her arm reached out for Sophie's side of the bed. Knowing full well it was empty, she gave in to her feelings and allowed herself to weep. What started as silent tears escalated into wracking and painful sobs and her sides ached with the force of her despair.

How was she going to put one foot in front of the other and go on? Why would that even be expected of her? "Okay," she cried aloud, "God damn it, BLINK ME! I'm ready! Take me anywhere you want, you damned curse! I'm tired of it, so tired, destroy me...let me out of this eternal hell. You let us get so close, so close only to jerk my loves away from me every time, like a monster torturing a pet."

*

Suddenly she could so clearly see one of their conversations. It had been following a battle in ancient Britannia. Her men had fought under her banner. The battlefield was red with enemy blood and her kingdom safe from yet another invader. She and Path had fought back to back, their swords slick with blood. They were both clad in leather and armor, leaning against one another, exhausted.

The village women were out walking among the dead and injured, knives in hand, finding survivors to finish off, identifying their own villagers so that they could be either buried or carried back to the village to be healed. The crows and other carrion birds circled above. The strong iron scent of blood hung in the air, overpowering in intensity. Death everywhere, death and mourning and wailing. After the din of a battle, death was a heavy silence even with all the sound.

He saw that she was weary and sorrowful at all the death and destruction on the field and how that it affected her. He had taken her hand and kissed it, saying, "You have to keep this moment in your heart, Gwennie, don't allow yourself to be discouraged by things that are always so temporary. You saved your people. Evil men were trying to kill them and you saved lives, the lives of their children. These men and women died because they, too, needed to protect their way of life. I know you're destined to be the salvation of this planet, or you're going to somehow be involved in educating, maybe raising, maybe giving birth to the person who will." He wiped his sword clean with the tail of his shirt, then continued.

"I just know that this is all somehow connected to you and that's why I've always felt this aura of magic and power around you. It's like we're doing this to gather all the knowledge and preparation you ...WE... will need to have when the time comes. It's the activist in you; it's the fighter, the one who sees injustice and wants to amend. I will be there when you need me, I will arm myself with everything you will need to protect you. I'll be your warrior, your knight, I'll defend your castle walls. I know we will finally be allowed to stand together against whatever it is we're being honed to face. Your blade is being sharpened, razor-sharp. You're being made strong as steel for a reason."

He looked around the battlefield.

"I'd kill them all over again for trying to harm you," his vow rough in his throat.

*

This was part of that honing? Giving her bliss, letting her feel this love and devotion, only to snatch it from her grasp time and again? Filling it with beautiful memories only to crush her under the heel of grief? And what about Marisha and Sophie? How unfair had this been to them?

The ringing of the telephone broke through her thoughts and she picked up her cell phone robotically, with no real interest or anything more than a compulsion to stop the sound. Sophie's best friend and former law partner, Jill, was on the other end of the line. "Marisha, honey, I've been thinking of you all day. Marnie and I want to let you know that we are here for you. Have you been eating? Are you getting outside?"

Marisha stood holding the phone and realized that she was slightly disoriented. Again, she was more Gwen. Her memories and reality had merged and she needed to bring herself back to the present. She wiped her eyes and said, "Thanks, Jill, I...I am...was just...I need to go through the closet, sort things."

"No, you do NOT need to do that! I'll do that for you. That's really the last thing you need to be doing right now. Stop this minute, and that's an order! Marnie is standing here nodding. Look, we're coming over... no, I insist, actually Marnie insists. You're thin as a rail, we can tell you haven't been eating. You're going out to eat with us if we have to DRESS you and FEED you, and we're going to come back here to our apartment and talk...and cry...and remember...and purge. We may get shit-faced drunk tonight, you and Marnie and I. I may not let you go home for a week. Lord knows there are enough memories to fill that time." She paused. "Sweetie, I miss her, too. I keep picking up the phone to call her, to share my thoughts with her. And you can help me, too...I'm just so damned lost without her." There was a catch in Jill's throat. Marisha could tell she was struggling to continue. "But she's gone. We have to take care of YOU now. She would want us to take care of YOU. You know she would."

He...she...Sophie...Marisha...Pathogent...Gwen...Jacob... Harmony...Tommy...Felix...we...they... Just names and pronouns.

*

Sacramento California, 1985

"It has been only two years ago today that Tommy was diagnosed," Felix whispered to Hester as she entered the kitchen. He was sipping his coffee while preparing a breakfast tray to take into the patient. What was once the tastefully decorated living room filled with Tommy's beautiful paintings, now served as the sickroom. The hospice nurse had suggested moving Tommy there, where he could look out the window and see neighbors passing their midtown condo, or revelers going to and from parties in the evening. Tommy had long ago rejected television as an entertainment medium. Neither of them had ever watched much television. It was all just so predictable. He was happier to watch real life pass by outside their windows. It was also much more convenient than running up and down the stairs countless times a day, Felix had to admit. But, convenience was not the issue here. The living room was more comfortable for Tommy and Felix would have torn down walls if it gave Tommy comfort. Besides, the hospital bed fit better in the larger room.

Hester moved to the stove to make herself a cup of tea. She put a hand to her aching back and looked down at her swollen belly. "Oh, please," she thought, "make it out in time, little one. He's getting so much weaker." She lovingly stroked her taut pregnant middle and turned the flame on to heat the water for her morning herbal tea. "Want me to take in the tray?" she offered.

"Oh, no, darling, I have had my breakfast. You eat and rest," Felix told her. "Sweetie, I wonder if today will be the day! It would be wonderful to erase the anniversary of such a horrible thing and replace it with such a perfect event."

"Oh, Feebug, I sure hope so," she groaned. "I loved being pregnant, but I've got to tell you, I'm so done with it now! Two weeks overdue is ridiculous! I want to serve up an eviction notice on this little freeloader!" She licked the honey off a finger and added, musing, "I was thinking the other day, I don't want to be called 'surrogate mother', that sounds so clinical, so removed. I'll always be this baby's mother."

"Yes, you certainly will. I don't like that expression either. There's nothing 'surrogatey' about you." Felix smiled at her and then stopped in his many trips around the kitchen while fixing a cheerful and elegant breakfast tray. "I made French toast...yours is in the oven, on the warming tray. The syrup is still hot; it's on the back burner." He took a few steps, then turned around, wringing a towel in his hands, his eyes shining. "Hest, I want to say this again."

"No, Feebug, you've thanked me too many times already. Now, don't go getting all soppy, I may need you in the delivery room today reminding me to breathe. You've got to get through this one day without breaking down, okay?" She smiled and hugged him and looked down at the tray. It was so like Felix to make every little detail, every single day so very special. This young man was her best friend since childhood and he had been there for her so many times over the years, through so much agony and grief; he was her angel and he was suffering. The thought of losing Tommy was too horrible for him to face and she felt helpless in the face of this inevitability.

Felix picked up the tray and moved down the hallway toward the front of the house. He stopped in the doorway and watched Tommy sleep. Tears always threatened to gather in his eyes when he compared this physically diminished Tommy to the healthy, bright, handsome, athletic, young man he had met at an office party just four years ago next month. Memories of that night would always come back to mind in years to come. Right now it was important to stay upbeat and hopeful. Smiling, Felix carried the tray over to the bed and said, softly, "Breakfast is ready, pet!"

Tommy opened pained eyes and grimaced, "Oh, love, I can't eat...please forgive me, I know you went to so much trouble."

"No, no trouble, darling, it's just that you must eat, you've got to build your strength." Felix said, brightly. He put the tray on the bedside table and went to open the sheer curtains to let more light in. He checked the IV and the catheter that the hospice nurse had told him to check often. Tommy's pneumonia was just beginning to get under control when they found his weakened system had led to herpes zoster being released by the lack of immunity. Tommy had shingles. Tommy had chicken pox as a child. The virus had come back to haunt him. The pain was the worst part. Now the pneumonia seemed to be coming back. He could hear rails in Tommy's breathing. He wrote a note for the nurse.

"What's the point?" Tommy muttered.

Felix stopped in the middle of the room and turned toward the bed. "The POINT is that I love you and want you to feel better! The POINT is that we're going to have a baby any day now and you are going to be a father! The POINT is that I can't bear to think you would ask that question!"

His lower lip quivered just slightly before he caught himself and straightened his spine to stand taller and stronger. He said, far more cheerfully than he felt, "Besides, when have you ever been able to resist my special French toast? I made it just the way you love it, with powdered sugar and just a touch of syrup. Come on, my love, just a few bites."

Tommy allowed Felix to fuss around him, tucking a napkin around his chin like a baby's bib, fluffing pillows behind him so he could sit up straighter, rearranging the tray several times and pouring fresh tea from the delicate bone china teapot. Always the very best silver and china, always the most meticulous tray, complete with a rose in a bud vase. Felix was nothing if not a perfectionist.

So, Tommy ate a few bites, if only to see Felix smile. Then he whispered, "I love you. And we love you, too, Gwen."

"Oh, Path, I was hoping you'd be gone. Are you going to see this through to the end?" Felix felt her presence and heard her answer through his lips.

"It would seem so." Then Tommy groaned and Felix pushed hard to regain control. "Do you need more morphine, love? Do you want me to call Sandy?"

"No, she'll be here later anyway," Tommy protested. "I'll wait. I want to stay clear-headed today. I want to be aware when the baby is born, today, tomorrow, soon."

Just then as if on cue, Hester called from the kitchen, "Felix, it's time. I think my water just broke." She came into the room and moved slowly to the bed, then kissed Tommy on the forehead. "I think we're going to be parents very soon, Tommy," she told him. She started pacing back and forth in front of the window, waiting for Felix to gather their things, as arranged.

Felix ran to the phone and dialed, "Mom, yes, yes, we need to leave for the hospital, it's time." He nodded, "Yes, Hester's certain. Her water broke. No, I have been coaching for weeks, I'm ready. Will you be here soon?" He looked at Tommy. "Mom's coming right over."

Tommy smiled, "GO! I will be okay, your mom will be here, don't worry! She's the best nurse in the world, are you kidding? She'll spoil me! Get this incredibly beautiful, wonderful, fabulous, best pregnant woman in the world to the hospital, my Fee!"

Felix kissed Tommy and grinned, "We're going to be fathers! I'm going to have a baby!"

Hester laughed, "I really can't wait much longer, Fee, we've really got to go, I don't want this little one to be born in your car! He or she will never get over the stigma of being born in a Volkswagen Beetle!" She blew a kiss to Tommy as Felix picked up her overnight bag and helped her to the door.

Tommy shouted after them, "You be careful with that precious cargo, Fee, don't you dare let her give birth on the way! I love you, Fee! Hessie, I fucking LOVE you, too!"

Thomas Cooper-Lesko was born only an hour after their arrival at the maternity ward. Hester's labor was surprisingly mild and she was awake and alert when her son came into the world. The baby was healthy and robust and declared absolutely perfect by her labor coach, Felix, who was beside her every moment. When they put the newborn on her chest for bonding, he smiled and broke into tears of joy. "Oh, Hester, doesn't he look just like Tommy? Isn't he beautiful?"

When he left the delivery room and they wheeled Hester to her room, he waited until she was asleep and went into the lobby to call his home. "Mom," he said, tears of joy choking his voice, "yes, but can I talk to Tommy first? I want to be the one to tell him. Thanks, Mom, I love you. Tommy? Oh, Tommy, seven pounds, thirteen ounces of beautiful baby boy. He's just incredibly beautiful! Well, of course, because he looks just like you! Oh, don't cry, yes, I know they are tears of joy. Yes, Hester is great, she did great, she's sleeping now or I'd have her tell you herself. The doctor said that he rarely sees such easy labor and such a brave momma. She was amazing, she was so strong and brave. Oh, yes, it was the one of the greatest things I've ever seen. He's perfect, absolutely perfect. Little Thomas is your image! Okay, I'll talk to her. Okay, Mom, is he okay? Mom, that cough doesn't sound good. Oh, Sandy's there? Good! Will you ask her if he can have more for the pain, this was a rough morning for him. I know you're a nurse, too. Okay, Mom, I do trust you. Yes, Tommy told you? Yes, a beautiful boy! Yes, seven pounds, thirteen ounces, twenty-one inches long. Why are those details so important to grammas? Mom, I love you, don't know what we'd do without you, thanks for being you. Hug Tommy for me."

When he returned to her room, Hester was awake. She smiled at him. "How's Tommy? Was he happy it was a boy?"

"He's deliriously happy, Hester." Tears shone in his eyes, threatening to spill over. "I could move heaven and earth and it still would never be enough to be able to thank you for what you've done for us. Hestie, when he's gone, I'll still have little Thomas. How could anyone be as unselfish as you, as giving and loving as you?"

"It's never been entirely unselfish on my part, Fee. You both gave me an opportunity I would otherwise never have had," she said, patting his hand. "I'll get to help you raise my beautiful boy. I couldn't dream of a better influence for Thomas than you and your mother and Tommy. We'll teach him so much, he'll feel so much love. Your parents will spoil him, my parents will spoil him, and we'll take him to Michigan to spend time with Tommy's...."

"No...no we won't do that..." Felix stopped her. "I will never forgive them. They know how sick he is but still they've disowned him. Still they won't even call. He's going to die soon." At this, his voice broke and he struggled to finish, "And they won't even acknowledge that they have a son who is gay and dying. They won't even give him a parting gift of their love and acceptance."

"But you said that his sister writes..." Hester protested. "Are you going to punish her for their ignorance?"

"No, I will send her plane tickets so she can visit us, visit Thomas. But I don't want those people to be part of Thomas' life, not after what they've done to Tommy. Never. I am serious."

She nodded. "I understand. Now, go home so I can sleep. You can peek into the nursery and see Thomas, but I'm going to sleep until tomorrow, go home, and spend time celebrating with Tommy."

*

Days later, Tommy held the baby so carefully, staring down at the perfect little face, the perfect little nose. At his own insistence, even though they knew that there was no risk, he wore a mask. He was openly in awe of the infant and smiled at Hester. Even though his mouth was covered, she could see the smile reached all the way to his gray eyes. "How did we create such an exquisite little boy?" he asked. "I mean, that whole insemination thing was so sterile, so clinical, it wasn't until this moment that I realized how miraculous it is that from such scientific and calculated procedures, such a tiny miracle can happen!"

Hester snorted, "What did you think I was carrying, puppies?" she laughed. "Damn, he's really not going to look anything like me, is he? He is just all you!"

Tommy choked up and struggled to speak, then cleared his throat and said, "Hessie, if this child is even one-one-hundredth as kind, self-sacrificing, forgiving, and generous as you, he will be a great man. Do you even begin to realize what a gift you've given me, what you've given Felix? Oh, I wish - I wish I were going to see him grow."

"Stop it, don't talk that way. You will always, always, ALWAYS be with us. We have you here," she looked down at the baby, "right here, we have you here in him." She smoothed the dark, downy hair on Thomas' head and smiled. "Look at those eyes. I hope they turn as soft gray as yours. He's going to break hearts!"

Suddenly, the dam broke in Tommy. "Please don't let him be gay!" Tommy cried, sobs coming out of him from so deep within that he sounded like every one of the gasps wracked him with pain. She was instantly brought to tears as her heart broke just witnessing his emotional agony. Beside her, Felix sobbed, unable to keep himself from giving in to the emotion they were all feeling.

"How can you say that?" Hester said, cupping Tommy's cheek. "I would be honored if he grew to be EXACTLY like you, including gay."

"No, no, I don't want him to go what I went through. I don't want people to hurt him, reject him, treat him like he's diseased, evil, untouchable, unlovable. I don't want him to have the childhood I had, to be treated like he's an outcast at school, like he's an abomination at church." It hurt her to hear him cry like this, his emotional pain so raw and so unguarded. He reached for Felix's hand to try to comfort his beloved, as Felix was being torn apart by his empathy.

"Honey, he's not going to church! We will take care of his spiritual growth," she assured him. "And he's going to be raised by you and Felix and me, so, sugar pie, he can be outrageously gay, if he turns out to be. He can be so damned flamboyant, rainbows can leak out of his ears! We would never be the kind of parents as those who hurt you. Thomas will never suffer like you did. None of us will let that happen to him." She moved back so that Felix could embrace Tommy, hold him, cry with him. She let them hold one another with Thomas between them and left the room so that they could have privacy for their conversation. She never dreamed it would be the last time she'd see him alive. It was as if he held on to life in order to hold Thomas just once.

BLINK

An alleyway in London in the late 1400s:

The Blink was simultaneous for them again, this time with few residual memories for them to read in the bodies they occupied. This has happened before, as if they simply pop into being, with no history, no identity but those they carry in their minds and hearts. It's as if those they Blink to inhabit are so strong that they are capable of blocking the exchange of date; or perhaps that isn't important to them, their own time and place in the world. Or, more daunting yet, their lives were so hard, their brains had kicked into denial.

It seems to happen at times and in places where it isn't necessary to have "credentials," in places where poverty crowds the poor into squalid conditions beyond belief. She looks down at her ragged dress, her petticoat and apron a threadbare gray linen, whether from age or wear is indeterminable. Sleeves pinned to her bodice which was simply a length of fabric crisscrossed over her chest and pinned or tied off at the nape of the neck. He wore loose brown pants, a loose over-shirt which would double as his nightshirt and a waistcoat of thin gray wool. Both of them grimy from head to toe. Neither of them had shoes.

"We're the poorest of poor," she nodded up to him, grimly. "I think...it seems like England, since it is obviously a city, even London..."

"I'll have to be 'industrious' then," he promised...and stepped to take her hand. In his mind, he was thinking of this not as a challenge... he loved a challenge, but as an opportunity. Perhaps they would be able to spend time together, unhindered by responsibility and the bustle of industry. "I almost think I would prefer to take us out to the country..." he began, looking around at the primitive, mean, dirty alleyway, choked with the refuge of human life. "At least in the country, we could work on a farm or find someone to shelter us in exchange for labor."

"Aren't you the one who always thinks that we're here for a reason, to learn something necessary?" she reminded him. She touched a hand to her head and found that she was wearing a simple cap of gray linen, her hair tucked inside, with strands escaping everywhere. She stood up and looked around, brushing her hands down over the coarse linen.

"Even in rags, you carry yourself so nobly, so straight," he teased. "People could take you for displaced royalty." He stepped forward to embrace her and whispered against her hair, "Don't worry, I'll find us food and shelter, I'll work."

"We'll both work!" she said, stepping back, chin held high, already mapping a course of action in her mind. "If I remember my history lessons correctly, there are Parish Houses where we can work for at least our supper. There isn't too much that I can't learn to do. Whatever is expected of us until we get our bearings...perhaps healing...we are fortunate to be strong and able-bodied," she smiled and leaned forward to kiss him.

The darkness was pierced by the sound of a sword, metal dragging against metal, leaving its sheath. "Well, well, what have we here?" Three men, dressed in uniforms of some sort, perhaps military, stood staring at them, one with his sword held full length in front of him and resting against Pathogent's chest.

"I daresay I cannot stand downwind of them," one of the men, a portly, round figure sniffed, nervously. "Shall we continue on to the tavern? What sport is here? Let us leave them to their tryst. It is obvious that they were ready to engage in some dirty, filthy act of fornication." He took a tin from his pocket and opened it, taking a powder from it, to sniff into his nostrils.

"Do you not have eyes in your head, my dear Duncan?" asked the third, a tall, thin figure who carried himself like he was a member of aristocracy. "At first glance, this seems nothing more than a scullery maid, but look at her." He smiled, an unpleasant smile, as his eyes consumed Gwen's thinly clad figure. He held out a hand and cupped her chin, turning her face from side to side. As she tried to step away from the wall, he blocked her. "Now, pretty, where do you think you might be going without our leave? Do you think it's the lad we're interested in? I am hard put for considering buggery?"

Gwen looked to see that the sword had already drawn blood as Pathogent moved toward the threat that faced them both, a red stain on his shirt growing around the sword point. She held her breath and accessed the danger they faced. The swordsman was grinning, only too eager to use his weapon, obviously well-trained, obviously skilled. What would be the risk of adding one more body of the poor lying dead in the overcrowded, filthy streets?

Pathogent stopped, waiting for a moment when the swordsman would be distracted enough to make his move. She locked eyes with him and shook her head slightly.

"Be reasonable," the man facing Gwen told her, his voice gruff with intensity, "save your young man's life by lifting those skirts and letting us take the pleasure of your wares. I would wager it would only take but a few moments of your time and we would be on our way and you would both live to face another dreary day in your ultimately dreary existence." His arrogance and poor judgment of her was obvious. He showed no pity, only contempt, in his cold, piercingly blue eyes.

She saw Pathogent tensing, ready to fight, waiting for the opportunity. She knew that he would, even barehanded against three armed men. She smiled, holding up a hand for time at the man facing her, then grimaced and lifted her apron to her face and coughed a hacking, horrible, gut-wrenching cough, pretending to spit into the fabric. Wiping her mouth vigorously before dropping the apron she said, "I'm sorry, sir, feeling no' but a bit of poorly." Coughing again, she reached for her apron. "Give me but a moment, I need to clean me lungs. But, to be sure, vicar, I can give ye' a round."

"What is wrong with you?" the man asked, his nose wrinkled by the repellant memory of that wretched sounding cough and her spittle, some of which still rested on her lower lip.

"Not but a touch o' the grip, I wager. I tend the dying over by the river, down t' the Parish House. Full house tonight, so many o' them. Mayhaps I caught a bit o' the..."

His repulsion was written on his face. "Away with you, lass, for all I know, you've got the plague! Step away!"

The stare-down between the swordsman and Pathogent was intense. She moved to place a hand against the wall, feigning dizziness, swooning.

"The damned woman's sickly," the portly man declared. He advised Pathogent, "Now, tend your lady and we will do you no harm, stand down."

For some reason, the swordsman seemed obedient to the portly gentleman, perhaps as a servant or a guard. He slowly backed away from Pathogent, but still held the sword at ready.

"I want no trouble," Path told them, his hands in the air to show them empty. "Just let me take her to find help."

"Have you money for the physician?" What they had come to think of as the round man asked. He dug a finger into a pocket in his waistcoat and pulled out a coin. "I warrant not. Here, a lass as pretty as she deserves a fighting chance." He flipped a coin to let it fall in the dust at Pathogent's feet. "Our apologies for the trouble. Get her supper, and an apothecary...and a bath. There's enough there for all that and more. Forgive me, mistress, we must take our leave." His companion scoffed at this show of charity and brushed at his sleeve.

The three men backed away from them, still guarding against Pathogent's obviously barely contained rage.

Gwen waited until they were gone, then approached, haughty over her clever ruse, to take the coin from Path's shaking hand. "Well, this will help! Let's find a place for the night since we won't need coin for 'the apothecary'."

"Gwen, damn it! We were just in grave danger and you shake it off as if nothing happened. We have to find arms, something to help us defend ourselves against thieves and people like those three. There's no magic here."

"Stop treating me like...like a little GIRL!" she shouted, thrusting him away from her. "Stop thinking you have to shield me from unpleasant things. Do you REALIZE how many unpleasant things I have faced in my lifetimes! There have been lives you were no part of in which I have lived in a sordid hell, faced excruciating trials, pain. I know through experience that a woman can not only SURVIVE rape but live a long life in spite of it. I felt that the magic wouldn't work and I would rather endure rape than lose you in a swordfight, you stupid, stupid fool." She stared at the blood on his shirt. A few more inches and his heart could have been skewered. "Harness your ego. We lived."

"Which is why I feel that when I can keep you from

enduring those pains..." he tried to reason, his face beginning to show his anger. "And I'm no fool. I did nothing to draw their swords."

"You are always telling me that you understand that the love is between us as ethereals, whatever the package, however we look. You think you have proven devotion to me, loving me when I was old and you were young, when we were poor, when you had to save me from myself and my drug addiction," she argued. "But don't try to tell me that it has nothing to do with your ego! You think you need to be stronger, to protect me. I almost watched you die tonight. Do you think I'm not shaken by that? Do you think I want a long life in this dreadful place if you're not in it? You are happiest when you are a big, brawny, fearsome man so you can shield your soft, demure woman from harm...what idiotic, romantic drivel. What a flimsy excuse to die..." She stormed, moving toward him, her face inches from his. She spat out, "Stop treating me like I need to be protected from every bad experience! You seem to think I can't handle pain? When our lives are at risk over something as temporarily damaging as rape, don't you DARE lose your life to stop it. Do you hear me? What about the pain of how many times I've had to mourn the loss of you, had to watch you take a bullet, even a sword, meant for me? How do you think it made me feel to be alive because you sacrificed that glorious self and that I am the self-same one who put us in danger! That I have been solely responsible for your death time and again...it's a heavy thing to bear. I can't even blame the enemy. Had it not been for me...there have been so many times we would have just blended in with the locals, lived a quiet life."

"What? You put us in danger by being you? Are you taking some fault, some blame upon yourself for being pretty, for being desirable? Are you saying that you are to BLAME for men wanting you? Do you think I would just stand by and allow some man to harm you simply because he wants you? I never thought you to be a rape apologist."

"Stop it! I stood there just now shaking to my core, afraid you would so something and he would run you through the heart with that sword. I won't let you take chances like that for me. I can't witness you die for such a petty..."

"That is so untrue! So unfair! Petty? I have always told you that you are the stronger of the two of us, that I think it will be you who will lead us. I have been happy to exist in your shadow, let you be the focus, the important one, the one everyone listens to, loves and supports, the one who draws others to us, the one others relate to. How OFTEN have I served you, as a servant, as a SLAVE, damn it! How many times have I given life and limb for my belief in you? Do you think this goes no deeper than a man's love for his woman, than sexual pride and possession? Think about it, how often have I died a painful and bloody death because I think the world needs you more, that you will be the one to find the answers?"

She screamed into his face, "What guilt you throw at my

feet, that I am completely and totally responsible for your pain!"

His face twisted with rage, he stumbled over the words, feeling accused, feeling betrayed. "And now you try to rob me of what I know deep within my heart, that my death meant so little so that you could live and learn, that you could survive to amass the knowledge you will need to face whatever it is this is all leading toward. That you are angered by my fighting so that you can live. There will never be a 'quiet life' for you, Gwennie. You have a mission; I don't blame you for that, it's what we are, it's what I choose to be part of...I search for you, I find you, I inject myself into your life.

"And NOW," he cut her off before she could retort, "you try to blame me for something that is completely beyond my control. We have no choice in the matter, we cannot control which body we will enter in each incarnation. I don't CHOOSE to be the man. I don't love only as a man. Being male has nothing to do with it. I have nothing to do with that part of it. And I am NOT attracted to you as a soft and demure woman. I KNOW your strength, I've felt your steel, I know its fury. Believe me, I know only too well how eviscerating even your damned TONGUE can be. Should I apologize for being physically stronger than you, for being skilled at self-defense because I have centuries and centuries of practice? And, at all times, suppressing the magic we could perform." He took deep breaths, his face red with embarrassment and anger.

She struggled to find the logic to counter his reasoning. "We also do NOT know that we don't influence it in some way, that there isn't something going on in the computer, the force, the gods, whatever it is that is sending us from place to place. You have this belief...this religion...that I simply cannot share, that I am destined from some tremendous deed, that I will end a hero. You can NOT say that there is not something out there influenced by the fact that you always prefer to be 'the man', knowing that in almost every society we find ourselves, you will have more control, more power and I will be subject to expectations of obedience, domesticity, even silence. That I will, for some reason, NEED you!"

His eyes blazed with anger at this accusation. "You think I live for your needing me? You have never been silent in ANY of your lives, you have never been controlled, nor have you ever bent knee to anyone we've met. Your obstinacy has tested the limits of law, and rule, and power. If anyone who ever met you would dream of accusing you of being soft and demure, he'd risk wearing his balls for an ornament. You can be hard, even cruel." He seemed to stop himself from continuing. He took a step back from her anger and sighed, "I may have had the strength and the power, but you have shown passion and courage enough for ten men. And, if my wanting you to need me is somehow offensive to you, I don't know what to say. I do love you enough to hope that you need me in return."

"Don't PATRONIZE me! I don't know when it happened, but even when I WAS the man, I felt the male in you...I felt your need to be in control...I pushed back, hard!" She paced the room, trying to control the strange rage filling her. "I don't NEED! I am not guilty of giving that part of myself who will fall victim to that kind of weakness." She tossed her head and walked to the other side of the alleyway, leaning against the casement of a window and staring upward, overhead at the night sky. Her body was stiff with resistance, with a barely controlled need to make him hurt. She paced back and forth along the opposite wall from him, resisting the urge to find a weapon. What was she trying to do, hurt him to the core? Torture him, thwart his love?

He wore the hurt in every muscle of his face as he fought for self-control. The pain of her stinging words caused his thoughts to escape him and he struggled to express his answer. "You, weak? You feel that love is a weakness? You are absolutely right, but not why you think. If I could have chosen, aside from the times when we were the same gender, I would ALWAYS have chosen to always be male," he stormed, then softened his voice, "but not, as you think, for ego or pride, but only for my own protection. As a male, my body is stronger, my skin seems stronger. It doesn't feel the pain."

She stopped in her tracks and turned slowly toward him but he held up a hand, weak with his own ebbing rage. "No, Gwennie. When you are male and I am female...you cause pain, you seem unable not to hurt me. I could barely take it. It sometimes...I sometimes felt that you would be barely unable to stop yourself from killing me. I don't know what it would have done to you if you had killed me in any of our lives, if you had killed me with your own hands."

She gasped as this hit her, as the memories of their times together, of their love-making came back to her. Pathogent so soft and gentle and always more concerned with her pleasure than his. Suddenly, like a bolt of lightning, it hit her that what he said was the truth, she had been capable of inflicting pain, great pain, and needed that pain for her own pleasure, not caring or aware of any of her partner's feelings. As a male, she was sadistic. This realization hit her hard, taking all the wind from the gale force of her anger. Her mind traced back over all the centuries of memories, all of her "victims" of love. She shook herself, feeling like a hideous monster faced with her own reflection.

He slid down the wall to his back and dropped to sit on the ground, weary, drawn, and unhappy. She looked at him and realized a painful truth. She went to him, weak herself, her mind spinning with her newfound knowledge and knelt before him and looked up into his eyes. "You...you are a far, far better person than I, in ALL our incarnations. I can't even dream why I would deserve to have you in my life, why you would have forgiven me time and again? Oh my god, Path, I can't understand what you see in me, why you think I hold any answers, I am unforgivable. How can you think that there is any sense that I would be some kind of 'saviour' or hero? I am villainous, detestable. I should be destroyed, never allowed to touch the lives of others. I feel so unclean...I HAVE hurt you, I am remembering more and more...."

He took her face in his hands, "No, Gwennie, don't ever think it. You know enough to know that you are not cruel. Yes, your passion carries you away in its fury, but you are good, you are meant for greater things. It may be chemical, it may be your mind's reaction to testosterone; you know enough medicine to know...perhaps it is a poison to you."

"An allergy? You think I should be forgiven because of an allergy...a reaction...like some kind of anaphylaxis?" She leaned her head against his knee, unable to process the revelation she had just absorbed, unable to screen the heinous images playing out in her brain. She saw herself, a knight, powerful, strong...a big male in armor, bending over the chained body of a young, naked victim, blood everywhere. The girl in the memory had not been Pathogent, but another innocent, not an enemy, not deserving of her fate. Did she kill innocent people in her blind rage, in the state of being male, being stronger, being invincible? Could there be lives blocked from her memory because she had been unable to process how evil she had been?

"Oh, god," she gasped, "why have we built our own legend, why do we see ourselves as having purpose, we are organic, we are animals...if anyone should be honed to save the world...it should be you and your mission should be to destroy me."

Tears shimmered in his eyes. "Never! Oh, Gwennie, I should never have told you. I truly believe that some of your memories are warped by things beyond your control. You were victim to so many things affecting mankind, warfare, drugs, alcohol, brain damage, even something as indeterminate as lead in water. You were human, you were human throughout history when things happened that never should have happened to people." He wiped a tear from her cheek but she was numb, non-responsive. "Oh, Gwen, my Gwen, fair fey, I love you so much."

"If that is so," she said, her voice choked, strangled with her tears, "how is it that I have no memory of you being anything but noble, kind, attentive?" Could he be an angel, juxtaposed against the demon within her? Could the very reason for his existence be to control her, not allow her to wreak so much damage on innocents? "Why would you allow yourself to find me, why would you even try? Why would you put yourself within my reach?"

He sighed and hung his head. Very slowly, he admitted, "I have not always sought you. I have hidden away, unable to face another occasion of meeting you, loving you, allowing you to humiliate me."

She closed her eyes and sat back on her heels away from him. "I...I cannot process this. I need to be alone, PLEASE do NOT follow me."

"Gwen," he pleaded, weakly, "please don't leave, don't make me search these mean streets...this horrible time and place."

*

She coughed into her hand and rubbed the back of her other hand across her forehead to take the sweat from her brow. Clad in wool in the summer, she felt faint but hurried to spend her ha'penny in the market. A piece of fruit would be refreshing, may make some of the dizziness pass. It had been three days since her last small sliver of bread and she knew that her body would not carry her much longer.

The dirty, decrepit buildings around her felt like walls reaching up to block the sun. It was hard to know whether to walk close to the wall and risk the filth accumulated there, excrement at nearly every step, or walk further out near the cobblestone street and risk having a chamber pot emptied onto her head from above. Choosing to step in filth rather than wear it in her hair, she moved along, less than an arm's length from the wall, putting out her arm to occasionally steady herself.

The marketplace was another place of filth and disgusting smells, rotting meat, rotting vegetables, human filth. She made her way through, ignoring all but the fruit stands, looking for a plum, perhaps a handful of cherries. She looked for Davey Carson's stall. Often he would have fruit hidden away that he had on hand from raiding the trees of the rich. He seemed to pity her and often provided her a whole apple or plum instead of just the sliver that a ha'penny would buy. Again, she braced herself against a wall to steady the dizziness.

Davey smiled as he saw her approach but she saw another look move across his face as he took in how gray her skin, how pale, how bruised she looked around the eyes and mouth.

"Wench, you are a sight bordered on blight! Y'need to get y'self to bed, needs be to rest yer head," he scolded in a cockney sing-song.

"I already spend too much time there, flat on me back," she answered, sourly. At another time, if she were still able to feel feisty, this banter would have been taken as a joke, considering her occupation. But her condition caused the shopkeeper simply to wince. He handed her an overly ripe pear and two plums and waved away her offer to pay. Thanking him with a weak smile, she bit into the pear and allowed the juice to flow down her parched throat. As she finished every bite of the pear, she started in on the plums and worked her way toward the ale houses, where she might find a trick to turn.

She had not seen him in a year. By that time she had, in her self-loathing, nearly ruined her health and her self-esteem, selling herself for a meager existence, allowing herself to be used, abused, violated in almost every way possible. And still she felt that it wasn't enough humiliation for the things she had done. She stopped in a doorway, her bosom nearly bare, leaning against the framework and waiting for a passerby to approach and offer a paltry sum. Unwashed, unhealthy, and undesirable, scarred on the outside, and just as deeply within, she reeked of neglect and starvation.

She was looking at the boardwalk as a buckled pair of shoes, shoes worn by those accustomed to comfort, came to a stop in front of her. Hose, breeches...soft material, rich fabric...clean. She kept her head down. "Tuppence for a roll..." she offered, in a soft breath.

"Gwen," he said, in a whisper.

Her knees went weak and he caught her arms, then lifted her to carry her thin, starved body. "No, leave me...I will infect you, I only hurt you." She struggled weakly against his chest.

"And where d'ya thin' y'er goin' wi' me property?" a voice challenged. She recognized the voice of her pimp, Jacko, her dirty, slimy slave-master. He stood, legs spread wide, quick to temper and quicker still with fists, blocking their way.

Path moved forward straight toward the man, their eyes locked, challenging one another. "Out of my way," Pathogent ordered, then quietly, coldly added, "do not stand in my way. I will not hesitate to have my man kill you. I will not stay his hand." He nodded to the man standing behind his challenger. The man standing behind Jacko was armed to the teeth and appeared strong enough to stop a charging bull. Jacko assessed the situation and realized that this would not be an encounter in which he held the upper hand. As with most bullies, he was a true coward.

"But gov'ner," Jacko whined, "this be me bread n' butter. At least buy the wench, she's not worth much, look a' 'er, she be cheap."

"Is the price of your life not enough?" Pathogent asked, disgusted. "I'm taking her to get medical care. If I ever see you near her, within a league of her again, I will kill you with my bare hands, do you understand?" The intensity of his glare caused Jacko to give way and step aside.

She felt herself being placed carefully into a carriage. She saw a horse, saw the man who helped Pathogent face down Jacko climb onto a bench at the front of the carriage, felt Pathogent get into the carriage beside her. He put an arm around her and pulled her to rest her head in his lap. He moved her gently, tenderly. It seemed a dream, after the year of living in the maw of Hell. He was the angel of delivery. The carriage moved forward. The rocking of the carriage seemed to go on for hours as she hung by a thread to consciousness.

She lost all memory from that point until she awakened again in a large bed. There was a canopy of sheer cloths hung around the frame of the huge platform. This was a bed fit for a king. This was the sleeping quarters of the aristocracy. The room was vast. At one far end she could see a fireplace big enough for several people to stand in. When she felt someone scurry into the room, she closed her eyes, feigning sleep. Two women talked to one another as they cleaned.

"Did you burn those rags the wench was wearing?" one of them asked.

"Aye, they reeked! What could the young Lord be thinking bringing this wretch here? What will his grandfather say when he returns?" The younger one laughed. "Of course, by then he might have her looking like a right lady. Though how he plans to pass her off as anything but a strumpet...."

"Hush now," the older woman scolded, "that tongue of yours will get you into trouble if the young Lord hears you talk such nonsense. He is just being kind, helping this poor creature. Surely he means to turn her out when she is well."

The younger woman laughed, haughtily. "Then you haven't seen the way he looks at her. He sat by her bed, holding her hand, talking softly to her. It was more than good Christian charity in his eyes, I can tell you," she sighed. "If that man ever looked at me like that, I'd be for posting the banns, I can assure you." She giggled, "Not too many of the maids in this house would turn that one down. He could put his hands up my skirt."

"Mary! How you go on! Now, enough with your nonsense. You'll be dismissed for such talk if his grandmother, the mistress, hears you say such things. She is full of worship for the young lad now that she's found him after all those years. He's been nothing but a gentleman to everyone and does not deserve to have such base talk tarnish his reputation. Now finish with the cleaning while I fetch some soup for our wee one over there, poor wretch," the older woman sighed. "She doesn't weigh more than six stones soaking wet! When I moved her about to clean her, it's like I'm moving a wee babe. I am shocked that you think him attracted to her; she's nothing but bones, that one." She grabbed clothing to take with her as she bustled from the room, efficiency in motion, not a step wasted.

The young one remained, humming to herself as she dusted and moved things around in the room. She obviously preferred working alone and slowed her own activity down, doing a perfunctory job of dusting around things instead of getting the whole surface cleaned. She picked up a glass and held it up to the light so it caught the sunlight in the pattern cut into the surface. Gwen opened her eyes and coughed, trying to sit up. "Where am I?"

"Oh, dear, you gave me a fright," Mary said, her eyes wide and innocent. "You nearly made me drop the glass! Aye, and I see you're awake, let me fetch the master."

"No, please, I don't want to talk to a 'master'. I want to place where I am, how I got here."

Mary curtsied obediently, bobbing down quickly as accustomed. "You're in the estate of Lord and Lady

Sommerville and their grandson, the young Lord. This is Highmark Manor, their home."

"London, how far from London are we?"

"Oh, but a day's ride, mayhap a little more," Mary answered. She paused and shook her head, trying to find words to explain something irrelevant to her. "I cannot know. I've never been anywhere but my own village and the manor." She moved toward the bed and began fluffing pillows, straightening the tangled sheets. "What's it like, London?"

"Dirty and dark, so little light gets in, the buildings are so close together." Gwen described the London squalor she was familiar with, west London. "Rats, chamber pots emptied into the streets, disease, dying. Constant noise, even through the night." She stopped to listen to the song of a thrush outside the open window. "And never anything as pleasant as that birdsong. How long have I been here?"

"Himself brought you here late a' night about a week ago. He woke the whole house to care for you. If you don't mind my being so bold," Mary said, in wonder, "but you do not speak like a broken street strumpet."

"MARY!" the elder maid entered the room and admonished the younger. "Listen to your prattling tongue! Our guest must feel insulted."

"No," Gwen insisted, quietly, "I hardly have the right to find fault. I was asking her questions and she was only trying to answer."

"Mary, run to fetch the master. He asked to be notified immediately upon her awakening! And why was that order not obeyed?" the older lady barked. "And mind your words, just tell him that the young woman is awake!"

Mary hurried from the room. The other maid turned toward Gwen and assured her, "Mary bathed you first thing this morn', and brushed your hair. You are presentable for his lordship." She set a cup she was carrying down on the bed table. "This is warm broth with good healing herbs within. You should try to eat something; we've scant been able to get anything down you, though we've tried. Would you like me to spoon feed you?" She reached for the cup and put it into Gwen's waiting hands.

"No, no, I can manage." Gwen held the cup to her lips but noted that her hands were shaking and that, in sitting up, she felt weak and dizzy.

The maid pushed pillows behind her. "There, there, not too fast...just take your time." She had a gentle touch, a motherly attitude. She helped move the cup to Gwen's lips, cupping her hands over Gwen's painfully thin fingers, and watched her sip a tiny mouthful of the broth. "I soaked some soft bread in it, to make it more filling. There now, that's good, swallow slowly." She watched as Gwen took another sip. "You'll get your strength back soon, if you just take a little more. Then I will suppose you'll be on your way."

"The lady won't be going anywhere for some time," came a deep voice from the doorway. They both looked up to see Pathogent moving toward the bed.

"Lord Sommerville, Sir Edward, I was just helping this young one, still weak is she," the maid told him. She curtsied and asked, "Will you be needing anything else, miss?"

Pathogent, Lord Sommerville, answered, "Thank you, Mrs. Dowling. Would you send Mary up with a fresh pitcher of water?" He dismissed her and waited until she left the room before approaching closer. "Gwen...how are you feeling? Can you talk?"

Gwen stared at him, unable to believe he had forgiven her their argument and had, once again, rescued her from an ugly fate. How was she ever going to set him free from this sense of duty toward her?

As if he could read her thoughts, he went on, "I searched for you, oh, Gwen, how I searched."

"How did you end up here?" she asked. "How are you...a...a lord?"

"It seems I am the grandson of Lord and Lady Sommerville. It seems that my father was quite the cad and I was the result of his wild ways. At least that is what they think, at least that is what they have told me, after they found me. I am told I am his image. When I told them I was orphaned, they were not surprised. But this good, kind man and his wife are convinced that I am the son of their errant scoundrel son and they have taken me into their home and they treat me as such. They have given me a history, a name, a title."

"How?" She tried to speak, tried to find words.

"How which?" he smiled. "How did they find me or how did I find you?" He came to the side of the bed and looked down at her and put a hand gently to her forehead, smoothing her hair back from her face. "Your fever is finally gone." He moved to the chair and sat. "They found me when I was working as a stable hand."

He continued, "After you ran away, I found work at a livery. Nights, I went searching the streets for you," he sighed. "Lord Sommerville is very fond of horses and seeks their company wherever he travels. While on a visit to London, his mount had thrown a shoe and he came to the stable to see the farrier. When he saw me walking the horses, his face went white, like he'd seen a ghost. He explained to me that I was the image of his son at my age. The next day he brought his wife to meet me. They put things together in their mind, my age, my lack of parentage. They asked a lot of questions about my mother, what she looked like, where she worked. It seems that they had reports of their son's activity while he was studying in London and my story fit. They knew that he had a son. They remain convinced that I am he and who am I to say that I'm not? They asked me to move here with them." He smiled and continued, "And have treated me like family ever since. They are the kindest people I've ever met, full of love and charity. My father had died in a duel when he was very young, right after I was born, I gather. It seems he was in love with my mother and the duel was over her. I think it's much like having him with them, having me here."

"Better," Gwen said, "You're not a thoughtless cad who would leave a pregnant woman to bear his illegitimate son."

"But for all we know that didn't happen...we don't have much memory before the Blink. I don't even know where I got the history I gave them. It came from somewhere but nothing like lives we've lived before."

"That doesn't mean it didn't happen; it just means that we didn't find the residual information in the way we're accustomed. There may have been a young couple standing in that alley and we may have Blinked into their lives and they Blinked out without them giving up any of their own memories. It doesn't always fit the pattern, we both know that," she answered. "Path, why didn't you just let me go, leave me to die? I would have been dead within no time if you hadn't found me."

"Shhhh, don't say that. I was meant to find you then. I needed to find you," he said, softly, not so much to keep his words from being heard by servants, but to soften his tone with her. "Gwen, I have relived the argument we had so many times...so many things I should not have said. I should not have let my anger control me." Tears shimmered in his gray eyes. "Forgive me, Gwen. I hate what happened between us in that alley. I hate what was said between us."

"You said nothing wrong," she sighed. "I have nothing to forgive. You simply told me an ugly truth, made me face my demons. I have given it a lot of thought," she told him. "Granted, I have tried to drown my memories in drink and drug but I have faced a lot of those demons, and I'm not sure I want to live with the possibility of my hurting more people...my hurting you. I don't know how you have continued to love me, how you could ever have forgiven me. I am tainted, so much evil in me."

"You have to see that you have no choice in the matter. You never have had a choice."

"I could have committed suicide!" she countered.

"You did! All too many times, that's exactly what you did," he whispered. "And what did that solve? Nothing. Instead, gather up the times you saved lives, you sacrificed your own happiness, even your own life, so that others could be safe, could live out theirs." He kept his voice low, aware that servants could be listening in. "I have been beside you through many of these occasions, my love. You have been on the side of right so many more times than...."

"That doesn't buy me penance," she moaned. "I started remembering things I had done, people I had hurt. The most tortured memories were those when I hurt you. You, who have been nothing but loving and supportive and giving...even in those memories, you were the one who tried to patiently guide me back to the light."

"Shhhh, hush now," he comforted. "You need your rest, you need to recover. Gwen, you've done a damned good job of trying to destroy this lithe body that you are within. My love, you don't eat, your sleep is haunted and restless. I think, no, I know, that you are going through this to conquer the urges, to battle with yourself, but don't kill the vessel!" He bent his head close to hers, hoping for a reunion kiss.

She turned her head away. A feeling of revulsion for herself, for being unworthy of his undying love and forgiveness filled her. She surrendered herself to tears and unconsciousness.

*

In the weeks since he had found her, he needled her, urged and pleaded with her to regain her health. She began to take the liquids, working her way back toward solid food, and started to feel strength return to her body. Her muscles ached with the neglect she had put them through and she was still deathly pale and thin. Little by little, she was able to keep more broth down. He practically lived by her side, and she, knowing the servants would speculate, would talk, urged him to leave her, to continue about his day as if she were not present.

"That's hardly necessary," he smiled. "This estate practically runs itself in my grandfather's absence. He has built a well-oiled machine of efficient operation. He allows me to use much of my time with the horses knowing my love for and experience with them. His stables are impeccable, run by a good man. The horses are treated well, healthy, good stock. He knows his skill, our stable master."

"I'm sure your years as a veterinarian will come in handy when the foals are coming." She smiled weakly. "Ah, you and your horses. I used to call you centaur. Remember Rome? Remember Animus?"

"Ah, he was the finest horse, full of strength, courage, heart. Built for battle." He smiled at the memory, his handsome face lit with the joy of revisiting this moment in time. "Animus saved me with his power and speed so many times."

"Saved us both! Remember when he outran that entire enemy troop? It felt like flying as his mighty hooves made thunder on the beach." She entered the memory with him. "And with two fully-armored Sagittari on his back," she laughed. "Listen to us, like two geriatric soldiers, sharing memories of battles fought and won." She loved to see this light in his eyes. The way his face moved through the memories almost brought them back to life. She wanted to reach to touch the deep dimple in his cheek as he smiled.

His eyes locked on hers and he held them. "Gwennie, don't reject me. That look you gave me when I tried to kiss you..."

"It was revulsion for myself, not for you," she tried to explain. "How can I tell you how dirty I feel, without and within? How can I even begin to express my need to protect you from the monster in me?"

"You are what and who you are. I have loved you collectively for thousands of memories and probably thousands more that neither of us remembers," he said. "I have lived lives without you and those are the lives I so gladly and happily forget, even those other loves. And that may be horribly unfair to them. I love and accept and need all of you, not just the part of you that you embrace, but also the part of you that you are trying to purge. Give it up, Gwennie, it's just another aspect of you, another piece of the puzzle. Perhaps it is what makes you strong and independent.

"But...but when you look at me and move away from me," he continued, "whether it be self-revulsion or not, it takes a piece of me with you every time. I live for the memory of your laughter, of the times you were light-hearted and funny and clever. We've seen too much of death and destruction and we know the darkness we face ahead of us. We need to let the light in, for our souls, for our preservation." He paused, knowing that she barely had the strength to answer, which gave him the upper hand. "You are part of me, beyond any doubt. We are connected, intrinsically. I am not fully me without you, and I think that's the reason we have followed one another through time and space. The romantics want to call it star-crossed. I tend to think that we really are two very important pieces of a plan, a work in progress. I think we need to experience the taste of blood, the fragility of life."

"You are the good part, I am the evil," she said, tears marking a pathway down her sunken cheeks.

"I could not love you as completely and deeply as I do if I believed that of you. I have known you, Gwennie, and it seems I know you better than yourself. I saw you collapse in surgery moments after heroic and ground-breaking work, saving the life of a young boy. I saw the tears you shed as you held a dying baby in your arms in a long-ago delivery. I've seen you tender and gentle, vulnerable and weak. You wear your empathy so wide open, you have taken on the pain of others just to shield them. What you did for me when I was dying of that painful and god-forsaken illness will live in the forefront of my memory forever, the sacrifices you have made for me and for others. I love you, and that won't end. I won't, I can't watch as you destroy yourself. You can't destroy what is immortal, my love. Live this life with me, Gwen, this is our opportunity for happiness, laughter, the light we need to have shining within us."

He sat back, drained from his speech, staring down at her. Then, leaning forward, he took her hand and pulled her arm from beneath the covers, slowly and gently massaging her arm, her muscles screaming from atrophy. He worked his experienced fingers over the tendons and veins, trying to force life back into her, hoping to awaken her will to thrive. Those fingers had healed many, man as well as animal.

"You did this while I was unconscious, didn't you?" She breathed slowly, his hand warm, his touch gentle.

He grinned. "At great risk to my reputation as a gentleman. Maids were in and out and they wondered at the privileges I was taking with you, massaging your limbs. Mrs. Dowling, well, I enlisted her help, taught her how to move your limbs to breathe life back into them. She came to understand and I know she defends my 'honor' among the servants. How long do you think you've been here?"

"Several days...a week?" she offered, closing her eyes as the massaging continued. It felt so good to have his familiar hands working on her. It felt so good to know his gentle touch again.

He scoffed, "Days? We've had you more than two months! You have rolled in and out of consciousness for days at a time. Gwen, you've done a really good job trying to kill this little vessel but you've forgotten who I am, what I'm made of. I am not about to let that happen." He reached into a steaming bowl that a maid had brought into the room and placed on the bedside and wrung out a cloth, wrapping her arm with the moist heat, so that the muscles would not seize up. "Remember, I'm also a doctor, a formidable adversary to your attempt to stop living."

When he was certain the maid had left the room, he leaned in close. This time, as he bent over to kiss her, she did not turn away. Those familiar lips closing over hers stirred all the memories of a binding and eternal flame within. Were she only not so weak.

*

As she gained strength, she slowly began to walk. First around the room, a trip to the window alone exhausting her, spending her strength; days later, she was able, with help, to descend the stairs to the floor below. Mrs. Dowling helped her to the door so she could look out at the surrounding estate that she had only seen from her window.

Within another week, she was walking, slowly and painfully, but gaining strength daily and she found herself at the stable, watching Pathogent painstakingly groom an enormous and beautiful horse.

"Percheron?" she asked.

"Ancestor, perhaps," he told her, smiling. "And this horse's ancestors might have been friends of my Animus. Isn't he nearly as noble and strong? My grandfather and his stable master are excellent judges of horse flesh. I could learn a lot from them." He brushed the horse as he talked, his hands moving masterfully over the huge muscles, making soft noises in his throat, in a communication between him and the equine mind he soothed. He continued, "Isn't it funny how we've witnessed these circles of 'connection'...this horse and Animus, time and again meeting relatives of people we've known in other lives, standing in places we've talked about in a far, distant place and time? Our Shawnee friends believed in the connectedness of it all, the hoop, the circle that life...that the centuries bring back to fold in on another. We are caught in that hoop, Gwen, and given the gift of memory of all those lives, however good, however bad. Don't you feel that the good has far outweighed the bad?"

She leaned against the top rail of the paddock fence watching him, nearly mesmerized by the way his hands moved of their own volition, feeling the quiver of muscle beneath the hide. She smiled at the pleasant memories those hands evoked playing through her mind. She leaned back and let the sun warm her face and inhaled deeply of the fresh country air.

"Your grandparents, have they been gone all this time?" she asked.

"They summer in the north, they told me. Summer's a hard time for my grandfather. He cannot take the humidity, the heat. They wanted me to go with them but I hadn't found you yet, so I declined. They have a cottage in Glasgow. Some of my grandmother's ancestors are Scots. They should return as autumn approaches; when the cold sets into the Highlands, they'll want to be here, for certain." He worked the withers, massaging comfort into the horse's back.

"You do that all day, then massage my arms and legs," she observed. "Don't your hands get tired?"

"This is work," he grinned. "Massaging you is pleasure." He winked and stopped, turning toward her. "Let her come back, Gwen, let the fun, happy, blithe, and spirited woman I love...set her free again. Relax your guard, come back to me. Don't let me grieve that our argument changed you forever, that my careless words, hurled in anger, made me lose you forever by revealing what I revealed. Embrace that you have affected so many lives for the better, MY life for the better...doctor, surgeon, healer, friend, lover."

"I...I am trying."

He smiled. This smile lit his face like sunshine. "Good! Let it come. Walk in the light with me." He put the currycomb down and smiled. "And now I mean that literally, come with me, I've something to show you." He led the horse into the barn and came back to her, taking her hand and gently leading her to the back of the barn where it rested in the lee of a high hill.

He took it slowly, particularly the climb uphill, supporting her more than she realized. They seemed to have been climbing for an hour and she felt weak and shaky. When they reached the top of the hill, she stood and looked at him, wondering why he had brought her here. Then he took her by the arms and slowly, one careful step at a time, turned her in a full one-hundred-and-eighty-degree turn to face a vista so green and beautiful, it was hard to believe it real. She gasped at the beauty that surrounded them. Rolling hills, unspoiled nature, the manor, and the grounds so neatly kept, so naturally comfortable in place it seemed the buildings embraced their setting. This was a vast and beautiful pastoral tableau laid before her.

"Breathe deep, Gwennie, breathe it in, this beauty, this earth, before it is despoiled, before it needs human intervention to save it from humans. This, this is what your destiny is about. You know this as I know it. The tiny interactions we've had through time were all leading up to the realization that we owe this glorious planet our greatest efforts, our concentrated strength."

"What if it has already gone too far? What if there is nothing anyone can do to reverse the damage?"

"What if we were meant to start it all again but to start it with our knowledge intact, with the things we have gleaned throughout the stories of our lives to teach the children, to keep things from going so wrong again?" he countered.

She smiled and filled her lungs with the cool air. She could smell the ocean in it. She could taste the clarity of it. She sent a message of thanks to the trees in the valley for cleaning it, for giving off their precious gift of oxygen to the air so that it tasted so sweet, like mountain air, like air cleaned and snow-laden. Tears filled her eyes for the love she felt for this thing identified by such a simple word as nature. She loved every blade of grass, ever creature moving through it, every cloud in the sky, every bird on wing.

He had been giving this great thought while she had buried herself in her own psyche. He had been thinking so far beyond their daily lives that she was utterly and completely amazed that he thought her to be the one who had vision and purpose.

As she felt weak, he held her. They stood, breathing in and out, feeling the breeze on their faces, their feet firmly planted on the hilltop, the heartbeat of the land beneath their feet. He kissed her hair and wrapped his arms around her to keep her from falling, feeling her lean completely into him. "This is what it's all about, Gwen, it's so much bigger than we are; it's bigger than the culmination of any of our thoughts or actions. When we face the future, we will face it together and we will use all that we have learned and all that we can teach to make a future for the children, for the people who remain...to bring this back." He waved his hand in front of the surrounding beauty. He kissed her neck, "My lady, my life...I am nothing, I am lost without you. Don't ever think to turn from me. You may as well kill me, then and there."

She smiled at the warmth of his breath against her skin. She thought about what he said, about the fact that she had been looking for answers internally when all of this had surrounded her, called to her, offering her purpose. They had been witnessing the growth of mankind, had watched the encroachment of humanity but had also been involved with those people, people with no ill intent, people just trying to live, honestly, at one with the world. They had lived through the Renaissance, the Industrial Revolution, the Electronic age, revolutions, evolutions, growth. They had been standing in open fields where cities would once grow, had stood on fertile soil that would one day be covered with concrete, iron, and other representations of civilization and progress. The earth was part of their story. The earth was their story.

She turned in his arms and looked up into his eyes. "I love you, I love you....oh, my god, how I love you." Her face wet with tears. She buried herself in his warmth, but she wasn't done yet. "I love you as a man, I love you as a woman, I love the nature of you, your scent, your heartbeat, every atom of your body. I love the roots you give me, the fact that you anchor me to keep me from floating off into oblivion. You are my breath, my life. I want to die in your arms, walk with you in the stars, sleep with you in the moonlight. I want thousands upon thousands more lives with you."

His face, also wet with tears, smiled down at her, his fingers in her hair, one arm holding her weight as she sank slowly into unconsciousness again. Concerned that he had caused this by forcing her overexertion, he frowned. He lifted her, gently kissed her lips, and laid his face against hers. He carried her carefully back to the manor. But this time his heart was lighter, his step not heavy with regret and loss, his joy filling him, buoying his spirit.

*

She grew stronger each day and it was becoming more and more difficult to keep their trysts and time alone from the servants. Although he had already established bedside devotion to her regaining health, there were times when the door to her chamber was locked and the sounds within were stifled. She knew that she could not care less if servants knew, if the family knew, if the whole world knew, or what they knew, but that this was a different time and reputation was important. Were they to Blink out of these two people, she wanted to leave them the best chance to continue their betrothal, should that be the decision they sought.

It wasn't until the return of his grandparents, though, that she would learn that these two, dear people loved their new grandson with such devotion that they embraced her presence instead of finding her to be a "problem" to be dealt with. The grandmother was particularly accepting of the situation as it unfolded and insisted that only the finest clothing be made for the young woman, who was gaining her health back and was revealing far more beauty than one would have expected, had they seen her months earlier. She was determined that the world should see her grandson's lady as someone befitting his new station in life.

"My dear," Lady Sommerville told her as she watched Gwen being measured for gowns, "you have such an elegant carriage, your posture is perfect. One would think that you, too, had lineage and title. Is there a possibility?" She sipped her tea and wondered if she were pushing the girl to talk. So far they had learned very little about this woman that their grandson had brought to their home. She had inquired of the servants and had learned about the ragged and horrible condition of the little creature upon arrival and how the servants had not expected her to survive. But her grandson was very tight-lipped about everything, beyond letting them know that he intended for the young lady to stay.

"No, I remember my parents and our hovel," Gwen told her. "They were quite ordinary and not the least aristocratic, nor the least kind," she sighed. "Mean and coarse, they both buried their sorrows in drink and wasted their lives." Though it hurt her to relate these sordid details, she had come to love the kind woman attending her and allowed Lady Sommerville insight into the woman she was sheltering. "I'm afraid that I have no 'Cinderella' tale to tell."

"Cinderella tale?" the older woman inquired.

It had been a very long time since Gwen had made such a mistake. How on earth would these people know the fairy tale she was referring to? She covered by adding, "Oh, a tale my neighbor lady would tell the children, in which a wretched step-child is given finery by a fairy godmother to attend a ball. A 'rags to riches' story, you see, something to give those of us poor children hope."

"Oh, do tell me more someday!" Lady Sommerville thrilled. "I would love to hear the tales you were told. Mine, too, is a rags to riches story, so to speak. My family was very ordinary. I was extremely surprised when my husband pled troth to me." She smiled and turned to address the seamstress. "A full wardrobe, my dear Rachel. You are so gifted, you probably already have a vision of what I have in mind. I would also like a gown for any coming soirée. I want the whole family to attend the next one together. Make certain the gown is befitting the lady on my grandson's arm. What do you think, a lovely green silk or perhaps a brocade with a rich green throughout to bring out the color of her eyes?" She smiled at Gwen, "Would you like green?"

"Oh, I can't ask that much of you, that is more than..."

Lady Sommerville raised a gloved hand and stopped her, "Now, dear, do not deny me this pleasure. I have seen the way he looks at you. I know love when I see it. I may be old, dear, but I do remember love." She smiled.

"You have done so much already, how will I ever repay you?" Gwen asked.

"By being good to my treasured grandson." The lady's eyes sparkled with tears. "You cannot know how precious he is to us. My husband found a will to live when he laid eyes on the lad, and I, too, feel reborn! We feel that we can rest comfortably knowing that our estate will be in such capable hands when we are gone. That young man is so kind and attentive, we could not be more pleased. He has given us hope for the continuation of our name and title. We've seen to everything with our solicitor; do not worry about the future, my dear."

"I would never assume that I am part of the future. What if he should change his mind?" Gwen asked her, preparing the elderly lady for the possible reaction of the woman within, should she Blink out of this body soon. "What if he were to meet someone more befitting his station?"

"My dear, his devotion to you is steadfast, I can assure you. As I said, I do know love when I see it. Besides, you have something within you that no other woman could give him."

At that moment, Mrs. Dowling entered the room and curtsied before her mistress. "His lordship, well, both lordships are requesting your presence, well, both of your presences in the parlor. His lordship seems to have a surprise for the young miss."

Lady Sommerville smiled, knowingly. "Well, if all the measurements are done, we'd better attend, my dear. I do love surprises, don't you?"

Gwen dressed in a light summer shift and joined Lady Sommerville at the top of the stairs. "Not yet," the older lady told her, "we don't want to appear TOO eager." She smiled and confided, "You want to allow them to wait; one does not want to appear to be at the husband's beck and call. They become too complacent. Keep him waiting occasionally, my dear, so that he learns to anticipate more."

"I like the way you think!" Gwen told her. "Shall we go to the back stairs, through the kitchens, so that it looks as though we were distracted by duty before rushing to their beckoning?"

The Lady smiled, "And I like the way YOU think!" she admitted, linking her arm through that of the young woman's. Conspirators, they walked the long hallway to the back staircase.

They chatted a while with the cook and Mrs. Dowling, sitting in the kitchen and enjoying hot tea and biscuits with the servants. Gwen laughed as they gossiped amongst themselves, comfortable to entertain the mistress of the house. She looked around the warm and cozy stone kitchen, happy finally to have an opportunity to explore this part of the home. It was a trip back through the history books: the giant, open hearth; the ironwork for hanging pots over the flame; the rough wooden tables; the bustle of the women as they worked and talked. Not at all like the kitchens of the future but warmer, somehow more inviting, more conducive to friendship, and the invitation to linger. Lady Sommerville was obviously at home with her kitchen workers and was not the type of highborn person who would keep their lives separate and ignorant of the ways of their staff. She giggled at a story Mrs. Dowling was sharing about a granddaughter and a local farmer, blushing at some of the coarse details but leaning forward to listen to every sordid word. She obviously came from simpler folk in simpler times, though she had become a grand lady. She could still relate to those who worked for her and their lives with their families. Gwen found that she liked Lady Sommerville very much.

"Oh, I've nearly forgotten that we were to meet the men in the parlor!" Lady Sommerville laughed, blushing and breathless from the excitement, and took Gwen's hand. "Come, dear, they may have given up on us and we may have to summon them from the stables. You really should have reminded me."

"We were having a good time, and, as you said, we don't want to appear to be at beck and call," Gwen smiled, and winked.

They walked together into the parlor, continuing to chat about Mrs. Dowling's tale, as Lady Sommerville added, "And after all he is the parson's son. Can you imagine their shock to find that their son has feet of clay? That should bring that snooty couple down a peg. When they came to call, they were both such snobs, I could barely find anything in common with them."

Lord Sommerville and Pathogent rose to their feet as the women entered the room. Path smiled at the vision of his Gwen and grandmother sharing such intimacies like old friends. He put his glass down on a table and went to kiss them both on the cheek. He offered his elbow to his grandmother and led her to her armchair, then returned to guide Gwen to a seat beside him.

"Oh, Edward," Lady Sommerville addressed her grandson, using the name he had given them, "this Guinevere of yours is such a delight! Talking to her makes me feel young again." She looked at her husband. "Shall you tell them or I?"

"Well, it involves all of us," the elder Lord Sommerville announced. "Knowing that Gwen can handle her own, we are going to London for the season. Gwen is going to come out to society as a distant cousin of the family. If she chooses to do so, that is. By the time she charms our peers as she has charmed us, Edward may gain competition for her hand. At any rate, our young ones are going to be seen as peers so that when Edward inherits, none will question his right. I've had a solicitor draw up all the papers. He will legally be declared, not only our heir apparent, but the legal grandson we know him to be. What say you, Lady Guinevere?"

Gwen smiled and nodded, "I will do as you wish, my lord," she told him, respectfully. "I owe you all my life."

"It's not about debt, my dear," Lady Sommerville insisted, smiling and straightening her gown. "It's about the legacy we wish to leave you and Edward, and any children you may have."

Gwen wondered if she could beg off by telling them that she hadn't been feeling well lately. Although recovering from her starvation and her damaged system, she had felt in the last few days a bit of a relapse. She had felt queasy and light-headed. She gathered her strength and realized that she wanted to do this for them, to lend an air of legitimacy to her affair with "Edward." She smiled and nodded. "I will certainly try to make the right impression."

"Oh, they will love you, my dear. You're a vision!" Lady Sommerville assured her. "And YOU, Edward," she turned toward Pathogent, "yes, there will probably be other suitors, but NO duels, my love. I won't have you dueling and risking your life. We will simply announce the engagement shortly after we allow her to come out in London and that should be the end of it! You have already made your intentions clear enough to your grandfather and me. Now, there's no time to waste. We already have the servants preparing our trunks."

Gwen smiled. It seemed the elder couple had it all figured out.

BLINK

It was night and a full moon seemed close enough to the earth that they could but reach up and touch it. Illuminated by moonlight, they stood together, letting the waves of dizziness pass. He reached to steady her and she was grateful for his gesture. She felt as though the blood had completely rushed from her head and she struggled to retain consciousness. She anchored herself by reaching for him with both hands, but sagged slightly as her knees tried to give way. He caught her and held her up. As the dizziness subsided, she looked up at him and they smiled at one another in recognition and celebration.

The fact that they were facing one another and completely aware that these two bodies were a representation of how they often thought of themselves was stunning to them both. She recognized him immediately: he was a mixture of so many of his past personas, the black hair now was touched with gray at his temples, and those pale gray eyes arresting and breathtaking. Taller than she ever really imagined, he was straight and thin and, though aging, as handsome as she had ever dreamed. "So I finally meet THE Pathogent, unveiled, almost as you looked in my mind's eye when we were between Blinks," she said, smiling. "Hello...you."

Then, conscious of the fact that he was staring at her and smiling and taking her in like a breathless teen seeing his prom date transformed by gown and glamor, she put a hand to her hair. "Am I gray and old?" she worried

"You are beautiful, you are incredible, woman...my Sidhe, my fey one," he told her, reaching to hold her upper arms, to steady her dizziness as well as his own. "This is Sabd, this is you as I always remember you in my mind...you're older, sure, but so am I! Your hair is tousled and untamed, those green eyes so familiar to me. And, you still make me feel like a giant, you tiny creature! Whatever the time, whatever the plan for us here, I am just glad to have finally Blinked into what feels like my own body, my own self-awareness. And we'll deal with the rest later.

Gwennie, right now we deserve this. Nothing is going to take this away from me now."

Gently he pulled her toward him and found her lips with his own, bending down to wrap his arms around her and lifting her to bring her closer to his own height. She felt his teeth as he smiled against her lips, then he returned to the task at hand, their kiss. He held her as the kiss gained intensity. She buried her hands in his black hair, feeling the thick texture of it in her fingers, feeling the familiar softness. Her kiss matched his with an intensity that was ripping from her soul. Only too often they had been torn apart at this moment, when they were finally able to be alone, to be lovers, to allow themselves the feelings that they shared. Her heart was pounding in her chest, her own chest, not the chest of someone she occupied. Her heart, her mind were completely and totally captured in this moment. This seemed a reward for all the lives they had touched, all the times they had loved but then been forced to part.

Gentler still, he bent to place her on the grass. Nothing would stop them from consummating this reunion once this fire had been lit. He undressed her slowly, his hands moving over her skin as if she were made of Braille and he were reading her. He was determined to make this last, to give this time with her the luxury they deserved. His lips followed his fingers in their exploration of her skin. When she tried to move to touch him, he smiled and held her back. "Later," he whispered, "you first." Faces and images blended in her mind as he made love to her, bringing her to orgasm with his touch, then later with tongue. They all visited her in his movements: Edward, Sophie, Nuadu, Tommy, Jacob and all the rest. It was surreal, her mind concentrating only on the intense sensations and the feeling of his skin, his breath, his whispers of endearment. Just a slight moan from him enhanced her own pleasure tenfold. She moved through the long, intense waves of pleasure, every pore of her skin responsive, every movement like riding a wave on the ocean, a pulsing sensation that lifted her out of her own body. She felt that she floated on silken threads above herself, removed but feeling everything he was doing to her, every shiver of feeling his breath on her skin. She was driven near madness, to the edge of consciousness with emotion, desire, fulfillment, pleasure. This, this was it. It was because of him, because it was with him, because of love, the depth of their love.

She rolled with him to put herself on top and knelt above him. "Now, my love...your turn." Her smile was full of promise to chase pleasure beyond all boundaries, full of a latent wickedness to find his weaknesses and exploit them fully. She gave him everything she had, finding erotic places to explore, wanting to make him feel everything as intensely as she had felt it. She kissed a tear at the corner of his eye and smiled as she moved him to a peak of intense pleasure. The sound of him, the scent of him, filled her and drove her to want to please him as she never had before and yet, she knew that they had been here on this zenith, had ridden these intense emotions, had explored these depths. This was why they were eternally pledged to one another, this feeling that their souls entwined, that they reached great heights as one entity, that there was one beautiful creation that formed of their two bodies combined. She was amazed that she was given enough energy to continue past the point of true and complete exhaustion, as was he. They laughed together as the night moved on toward morning.

After the lovemaking, he rose above her and looked down on her face, happy to see her in the afterglow, he kissed the corner of her mouth. "I hate to tell you this, but this must be the future, the landscape seems pretty grim." He took in the dawning of the day and described the mountain they found themselves on.

She rubbed a hand on his chest. "I noticed," she whispered, "But I can do it; I can face this if I'm really going to be spending it with you. Even if this is our final life, our final Blink, I can do this." Her heart swelled again as she spoke, "It's like a reward...or perhaps an apology."

He smiled, just one corner of his mouth lifting. "So, you've begun to believe?" His brow arched in anticipation of her admission.

"Perhaps, so long as we aren't ripped apart again, I could almost believe that we are here for a purpose, and I'm willing to take on the challenge, if we are going to be allowed to face this together. We've never been here together. This time is different."

"Wait!" He looked around in alarm. "Wait, where, where are all the insects? We should be lying on them, covered by them."

She smiled, "You're not complaining, are you?"

"No, seriously, what would have happened, is it so bad that the insects have died off, too?"

"It feels like we're at a pretty high altitude. Perhaps it's not all that insect friendly here."

"We can hope," he said, smiling. He raised himself up onto both elbows, his hair tousled and thick. He took in the scenery which, actually, looked better than first glance. Though there was desolation far below them, this mountain was grass-covered, not barren. There were trees below them, so they were above the tree-line, but there were living trees, not scorched and barren skeletons that were once trees. "Gwennie, wherever we are, we are farther from the destruction and horror than I've ever been. I've never seen a place look so promising on any of my trips to the future. I had seen the remnants of a completely destroyed New York City, small pieces of travel through desolate landscapes I had assumed to be parts of Kentucky by the road signs, and it was grim, fire and brimstone grim. I talked to other survivors who said that the South was completely gone and the Northwest had been destroyed by volcanic activity. But this, this doesn't look anything like I expected."

She sat up to join him. "Look at these mountains! Are we in the Sierras? No, no, that's impossible, the weather doesn't feel right. How did those trees survive? We have to find out where we are!"

"There's a town down there." He was looking at the valley stretching from the base of the mountain. "Let's go see if we can find food. And we're going to need jackets," he shivered. "The air...the air doesn't even smell right...it's clean and clear...sweet." He helped her to her feet. "Once we get moving it won't feel so cold."

"I didn't even feel the cold last night," she smiled. "Must have been the vigorous activity." She shivered and cuddled against him, flirting and happy. "Why are we here together, I mean, REALLY together, laid bare...it's you and me, we're not occupying any host? I'm sincerely beginning to think that you've been right all along, that it has all been leading up to this, whatever this 'mission' is."

"I know," he agreed. "I've been here so many times but always in a host, always for just a few hours, like a witness, like news bytes of time. I can't even remember every time I've been here. Fifty? Sixty? And I know you've been here just about as many. This feels different, boosts my hope."

She laid a hand on his arm, "We need to find out where we are, then we really need to think long and hard where we want to go, after all we've learned from our 'visits' here, where would we be safe?"

"Actually, this feels pretty good, I mean, we are sitting on grass. I didn't think that there was grass in this time and place. Look, the sky is blue and the clouds are almost white. Do you remember seeing a blue sky, white clouds before?"

"Do you think this is years from the other futures we've been in? It was always 2062 in each of my other flashes of this future. Could it be later than that? Could nature have started to come back from all the damage?" She pulled a handful of grass and brought it to her nose.

"I don't know why, but I feel this is close to the same year we usually Blink into, just a different place. Come on, let's walk down to that town, see what we can find."

*

"We're in Florence, Colorado, according to this flyer and we just missed the airshow at the county airport by only two years!" Path joked as he read the yellowing poster taped to the window, "Well, I mean, that is, if it's really 2062. He blew dust off the counter to read the newspaper under a sheet of plexiglass. "And," he added, "it doesn't seem likely that it is. This paper is pretty old and the date on it is July 17th, 2062."

"Why is there still so much food here?" Gwen asked, as she looked through the cans on the shelf. "I mean, it's as if the people just disappeared! Didn't they think to take supplies? I would have expected the entire town to be wiped out of canned goods." She opened a jar of olives and held it out to him. He took a few of the olives and popped them into his mouth. They had already found a clothing store and helped themselves to jackets, parkas, and backpacks and now were in the process of filling those with as much as they could carry.

"Ah, good, this is what I was looking for," he announced, turning a revolving stand full of maps, "let's see where we are and where we might be able to go." He opened a map of Colorado, searched the eastern side of the mountains, and was able to locate Florence. Gwen walked over to the rack and found a brochure about Florence and began to read.

"Omigod, Path," she gasped.

He looked up in alarm and realized that her reaction was to something she read so he peered over her shoulder. She continued, "There is a prison here, three prisons, to be more precise, and one of them is called a Supermax facility, 'a Supermax facility which holds the most dangerous inmates in the federal prison system with an adjacent satellite prison camp for minimum-security inmates.'" She turned to look at him. "There are almost more inmates in that prison than the entire population of Florence. If all the people are gone, where are the inmates?"

"Would they have released them when everything started to go bad?" Path pondered aloud. He traced his finger over the map toward the prison facilities. "We have to go there.

We have to know. This could be a very dangerous place to linger."

A bicycle shop awarded them with bikes and two trailers so they were able to load up with blankets, food, and pharmaceuticals that they found at the deserted local drugstore. "I've never seen so many antique shops in a small town like this. That must have been their claim to fame, that and the prison, that is," Gwen said. She was trying to keep her mind busy and avoided thinking too much about the prison. Something told her that it wasn't going to be a pleasant visit. But what if some of the prisoners had been released? What if they were still nearby? She and Path had already decided to head toward Denver or, in the very least, Colorado Springs.

"Path, I've been thinking," she began.

"Dangerous!" he teased.

"No, seriously, what is the one consistent thing about your memories of your visits here, to this time?" she asked. She was checking to see if the hitch was tight enough on her bike so that there would be no chance of her trailer swinging loose and possibly causing her to wreck. It had been a long time since she was on a bike and she didn't want to take any chances.

"Crushing bugs under my boots," he offered. He saw her struggle and came over with tools he had found to tighten her hitch and checked the bolts all over the trailer to make certain they were tight and would not shake loose.

"No, I mean, other than that. What were the memories of encountering others, of seeing other humans while you were hiking?"

"I always felt like I was swimming upstream, like a salmon. Like I was going the wrong way and everyone else knew something I didn't," he said matter-of-factly, remembering the feeling as he walked. He remembered being determined that he was going the right way but had to wonder if he was just being foolish for not following all the others.

"But you kept going in the direction you were going, right? And, those other people, where were they heading in such masses?" She knew the answer. She wanted him to verify her thoughts.

"They all seemed to be headed toward the coast. I even had people try to convince me to join them. I was determined to keep my momentum and when I was with others, it seemed we had a common goal in mind."

"The center of the continent," she supplied the answer. "We were being drawn to the center of the continent when all the others were convinced that they would be safer and better off near the coast. I think they were hoping for help to come from elsewhere, that other countries would send ships or help."

"And yet, the other countries probably don't exist, or they aren't in any better shape than this one," he nodded.

"I don't think it was an accident that we were transported here. I think we are supposed to set up camp somewhere close by, somewhere that might draw others like us. Someplace that might be seen as a mecca or a place to go, something familiar about it, something that might give people a destination. I mean, Colorado isn't the dead center of the country, but it's pretty darn close, and it's not lowland and in danger of becoming a dustbowl or, the opposite, flooding. We may actually see even more vegetation higher up into the mountains."

"Denver might be our destination?" he queried.

She nodded, "Or somewhere close to Denver, close enough to keep secret but close enough to be able to leave signs in Denver, a place for people to meet."

"Well, it's pretty obvious that winter is just starting to let go here and it will probably take us a good while to work our way to Denver, so we'd better begin this trip. We're still at a pretty high altitude, about the same as Denver, here, but we'll be going up and downhill. Are those wings on your back up to it?"

"That was another question I was going to ask you," Gwen said, grinning. "How's your magic?"

"Funny you would ask. I honestly haven't tested it, but it feels pretty strong." He caught her eyes. "It feels very strong. Why?"

"Because we might need to turbo-charge our speed, if there are any inhabitants of that prison still hanging around, is why. And, besides, I really get the feeling that we need to find our safe zone quickly. There are many on their way to meet us and we have to be there before them to ready everything, to prepare to colonize."

He didn't question her statement nor her power of knowing. There were too many times throughout the centuries when he learned to trust her premonitions and feelings. He swung a leg over his bike and mounted the seat, adjusted his sunglasses and smiled at her. "Lead the way, my Sidhe," he invited.

*

The prison was worse than anything she could have imagined. The fact that men had been left in cells to die a slow, tortured death was heinous beyond understanding, though she realized that they would have also had to think long and hard about releasing dangerous felons, even with the continental disasters and bombings. But what she and Pathogent found at the Florence Federal Correctional Institution was a nightmare. She knew that she would never forget the stench, the horror, the revelation that mankind could truly be unforgiving in every way.

Path had steeled himself against the horror, after searching the facility and finding no life but so much death. He found the keys in the central guard's quarters and located the munitions room. He was able to find weapons that made their rifles and handguns look like children's toys. "I really want these stun guns," he told her. "Something in me doesn't want to shoot to kill if there's a chance that a person might be help to us. We don't need them, of course, but those who are coming might." He readjusted both of their trailers to allow him to take the things he deemed more important to them, wrapping some of the weapons in blankets to hide them.

They had separated to search for supplies and information. He found her standing in the high security yard that was dusty, desolate, and empty. The inmates hadn't even been let out of their cells to face death together in the yard. They didn't even get the humanity to die with others. They each died alone or with their cell mates. He came quietly behind her and held her. "Are you going to be able to go on?" he asked, his breath in her hair.

"I have to," she answered. She wanted nothing more than to put many miles between her and this concrete hell.

They walked away from the prison and went to their bikes. She looked at him and took his hand, her other hand firm on the handlebars to make certain that it went with her. "Path, I need to use my magic. I need to get us out of here. I need to fold space. I hope I can estimate this right in my mind but I want to take us northwest of Colorado Springs. I have to. I haven't done this for a long time; concentrate with me." She saw the map in her mind. She saw the mountains to her left and faced North. She felt a buzzing sensation building in her head and it traveled down through her body, causing it to feel warm, then hot as she folded time and space between them and their goal.

*

They hadn't needed the bikes, nor the trailers, nor most of the supplies. Only the weapons were not duplicated. Much of Denver had been deserted as though people had just walked away from their lives, their businesses, their families. Non-perishables were everywhere for the taking. However, on their arrival, the urgent need she had felt was revealed to her. They were here for a reason and the reason was soon to become known to them.

They were transported to Lakewood and had dismounted their bikes to sit on a bench in the Commons to let their heads clear of the dizziness. Path even voiced the opinion that they might want to find something for altitude sickness, more for the way they had gotten here than for the fact that they were now feeling as though they'd ridden through a hurricane. They sat there, catching their breath and trying to shake the spinning feeling in their brains when Gwen suddenly sat forward. "I heard a voice!" she insisted.

Path sat forward and their eyes met. "I heard it, too. It came from this direction."

"I heard a loud voice and then children crying," she said, and allowed him to lead her across the green toward a huge parking lot still filled with cars.

He led her down a strip of green cutting through the parking lot until they came to a large park-like oval situated right before a mall. In the center of the grass stood a man who was waving something above his head and yelling loudly. They recognized his speech as being a passage from the Bible: "Then Abraham reached out his hand and took the knife to slaughter his son. But the angel of the LORD called to him from heaven and said, 'Abraham, Abraham!' And he said, 'Here I am.' He said, 'Do not lay your hand on the boy or do anything to him, for now I know that you fear God, seeing you have not withheld your son, your only son, from me.'" A woman lay at his feet, fresh blood pooling around her. Two small children, holding on to one another and crying, stood just a few feet away from the man.

The man waved the knife above his head. It was a vicious-looking weapon, long and shining in the setting sunlight. He looked at the children and took a step toward them, "And Abraham lifted up his eyes and looked, and behold, behind him was a ram, caught in a thicket by his horns. And Abraham went and took the ram and offered it up as a burnt offering instead of his son. So Abraham called the name of that place, 'The LORD will provide' as it is said to this day, 'On the mount of the LORD it shall be provided.'"

He raised the knife to bring it down on the nearer of the two children when Path bent forward and raised his own hand and stopped the motion. The speaker was frozen in place, gray, like a statue.

"Is he still alive?" Gwen breathed against his ear, her heart in her throat.

"No," Path admitted, "no, he's not."

"How will they ever forget this horror?" she asked, already walking toward the children. There was a boy, perhaps about five years old and his younger sister, not more than a year younger. She went down on her knees in front of them, strategically blocking their view of the dead woman. Neither child moved toward the woman, or away from Gwen and Path. They stared at the man frozen in front of them.

"Your father," Gwen began.

"He is not my father," the little boy stated, matter-of-factly. "He's the scary man. We didn't run fast enough this time. David told us to stay far away from the scary man but Raven was hungry and I wasn't watching. He snuck up on us. David's going to be so mad at me."

"Was that your mother?" Gwen asked him.

"No. We don't have a mother. We just have David," he told her.

Path knelt down, checking the little girl for shock, holding a hand against her temple. "Dehydrated and thin, but otherwise okay. She actually seems okay." He was surprised to find living children this far from the coast. This strange tableau had them both shocked and uncertain where to begin.

"Can you show us where David is?" Gwen asked.

The little boy nodded over her shoulder, his gaze intense and he smiled. "There he is!"

A boy of about twelve approached, a bow and arrow in his hands, the arrow aimed directly between Path and Gwen. They both froze and watched as the young boy walked toward them, tense and poised to strike.

"Let them go!" he demanded.

"They're free to go," Gwen said softly. "We just stopped him," she nodded toward their scary man, "from killing them."

"They did!" the little boy they had saved agreed. "That man," he pointed at Path, "he raised his hand and scary man died."

"I'm not stupid!" the older boy said, looking firmly at Path and Gwen. "You can't kill a man just by raising your hand. Did you shoot him?"

"No," Path told him, "I did not shoot him, there wasn't time. I have a gun in my holster here. See it? I didn't have time to draw my gun."

"I'm not stupid!" David repeated.

"We know that you're not stupid; you seem very capable," Gwen reasoned. "Listen, you have the upper hand here, we don't have an arrow pointed at you. Can we just talk? Can we help these little ones get away from this body?"

"We have to make you forget what you saw," Path said. Gently, he reached to touch the little boy on his forehead.

"What are you doing?" David yelled. In his shock at the sudden movement, he let the arrow fly. Path caught it in midair just inches from Gwen's face. Gwen did not even flinch. She had readied her own defenses, should Path have missed his catch. "How...how did you..." David, his voice now a hoarse whisper asked, faintly. He sat down on the ground, unsteadily, his mind fighting against what he had just witnessed. With all the horror he had already seen, he could not process magic.

Gwen hurried to his side and pressed fingers against his forehead, helping him to forget what his eyes witnessed and, fortunately, his mind was already rejecting. She gently smoothed his hair back on his brow and met his eyes. "David, you are a very brave boy and you were protecting your friends. Are there any others?"

He nodded, slowly. Tears shimmered in his eyes at her touch, a motherly touch. It had been so long since he had felt a motherly touch. She smiled at him, this woman who looked and touched like an angel and he smiled back at her. "Can you show us where they are, David? We've got to find them and take them someplace safer. There may be other crazy men coming."

Pathogent picked Raven up and carried her and the original little boy reached up and took his hand. Path smiled down at him, "What's your name, tough stuff?" he asked.

"I'm Tyler," was the response. And Tyler followed where Gwen, Path, and David led them. David entered through a construction zone into the mall and then took them deeper into the maze and led them through a warren of passageways into the center of the former food court. He stopped in front of a Spencer's Gifts and grinned. "We live here. There are toys and stuff."

Within the store there were two more children, a girl just slightly younger than David, and another boy, who announced that he was Geoffrey, "Spelled G-E-O-double F-R-E-Y and I'm five!" David introduced them to the girl, Cassie who, as the oldest girl, seemed to mother the younger children, particularly Raven.

"Is this everyone?" Gwen asked. Cassie assured her that the only people alive in the world were the five of them, scary man, and screamy lady. Gwen assumed that screamy lady might have been scary man's victim, but didn't want to revisit that memory in the children's minds. They sat with the children and talked, Pathogent urgent to get back to their bikes and the weapons. But Gwen delayed him to earn the children's trust, assuring him that there was time.

"We are going to the woods, all of us," Gwen told them. "We're going to camp and be safe in the woods. Scary men don't live there. We can learn to camp, play in the creeks and streams, and get muddy, and have campfires. There might even be deer and rabbits! How would you like that, to come with us and we will keep you safe? No more scary men, no more screamy ladies."

She had them at "woods" and "deer" and "rabbits," though she could not be sure they'd ever see any of the latter again. They were all locals. The older ones had gone on field trips into the mountains or on little junkets with parents in the long ago. Even David was warming up to the two adults. He knew that there was something strange about them. He remembered pointing an arrow at them but didn't remember anything after that but Gwen's soft touch and warm eyes.

"Besides," Path added, "we could use someone as good with bow and arrow as David. He can be the teacher and teach all of us how to shoot."

"I can teach you how to make popcorn!" Cassie offered.

Gwen smiled and nodded, "I'll hold you to that one. We need to find a store, fill up on popcorn."

They found so much more; they found a four-wheel-drive SUV, standard, that Path easily hot-wired and laughed with pleasure when it started up, a powerful engine beneath the hood. It already had a trailer hitch, so they "borrowed" a U-Haul trailer conveniently located adjacent to the mall, to tow. They looted stores in the concrete box stores surrounding them and found backpacks, bedrolls, pillows, clothing, food, and medicine to add to the supplies they already had. "With this truck, we can always come back for more," he assured Gwen. "When you were feeding the kids, I was reading the maps and tourist info in that booth over there and I think I might have found just the camp you're looking for. There's a town west of here, closer to the mountains, on Interstate 70, called Golden, home of the former Coors Brewery and the former School of Mines. Resources. There's a camp there used by scouts and groups. Plenty of accommodations, very private and hidden." He grinned at her smile. "C'mon, milady, you navigate, I steer, and the kids sing *'The Bear Went Over the Mountain'*." Cassie giggled and helped to load the children into the roomy vehicle.

"This is a luxury mobile. I put gas cans in the trailer, after teaching David how to siphon and with both of us working the mall parking lot, we've got enough to get us halfway across the country," he bragged. "My dear, I think we're on our way."

"Cassie?" he asked, looking in the rearview mirror into the back seat.

Her face appeared in the mirror. She was already warming up to the funny guy who teased and acted like a kid himself.

"Do you know what year it is?" he asked, sincerely.

She thought for a long while, consternation showing on her face. "It's hard to keep track, I really tried. I know that I just turned seven when everyone disappeared. I know I'm nine now. I think it's April, so I turned nine this month! I was born in 2054. I can't do that math. I used to know how to add but I forgot."

"That's good enough math for me, my sweetie!" Path grinned. He reached across the console and took Gwen's hand, bringing it to his lips. "A year has passed since either of us was last here. What could have happened within that year? And, good Zeus, these kids have survived for two years? I am more than just impressed with their toughness! That means that Raven was just a baby when they found her, and Tyler was a toddler. Holy crap, it seems impossible."

"Tough kids...but sleepy ones." She looked into the back seat and lowered her voice, smiled. "Only the two oldest are still awake and we haven't even driven more than a couple miles. Gotta love auto-cradles. I was thinking. You know how we drove around and posted notes throughout the city to meet us at the Commons?"

"Mmm-hmm, that was another good idea of yours, love," he said, watching the road as he worked his way toward the highway, detouring around deserted cars, sometimes driving up through lawns.

"What if we attract the wrong type of people?" she worried.

"We won't be taking the kids, well, maybe David, cuz he's the man!" He looked into the rearview and winked at David. "And we won't be unarmed and stupid about it. Once they start arriving, these people that you seem to know are coming, I think we'll know them by some common denominator, something we'll all have in common, something to look for."

"Kids," David declared, without doubt, "they'll all have kids with them, and they won't be mean or hurting those kids. They'll be good people, saving kids."

Gwen and Path looked at one another and she whispered, "Out of the mouths of babes." She snuggled back into her seat and smiled. The plan was working so far. Why worry about the worst instead of anticipating the best? She had to begin thinking with the mind of a child, with the faith of a child again.

"What did you feed Tyler and Raven when they were babies?" she asked David.

"Boxed milk and cereal and stuff like that. There's still food in the grocery stores. Boxes are easier than opening cans but sometimes I did that, too. I like the cans with the rings you just pull. We ate peaches and pears and applesauce. Sometimes we just had to walk farther to another grocery store, is all. Cassie made us all take vitamins, like her mom did," David told them, matter-of-factly. "We all like gummy vitamins best." He paused. "Before she was screamy lady, and turned screamy all the time, she used to bring us food and stuff. But then she tried to hurt Cassie so we stayed away from her."

"Two years," Path repeated, incredulously.

*

The campground was better than Gwen had dared to hope. There were ten dormitory style cabins with eight bunks each, six small cabins, probably used for troop leaders or staff, and further away from the rest, down the hill toward a fire road, were the privies and more small cabins. There was a big central dining cabin with a well-equipped kitchen, complete with wood stove with burners on the top. The camp had been set up for relatively primitive camping, much to their delight. Little good a gas or electric stove would have done them. They found lanterns filled with oil, extra wicks, a large supply of candles for trips to the privies at night. The mattresses on the beds did not look too old, nor had they been invaded by rodents or insects, much to Path's amazement. But they would gradually be replaced with better ones from Denver. Gwen began to make lists of things they would need to bring up from Denver from their trips to the city.

They saw no sign of others for the first two weeks as they set up sleeping arrangements in the dormitory cabins. Gwen and Path took a small room at the back of first dormitory for now, to make the children feel safer. They worked on stocking the already well-stocked dining cabin with the trailer full of food they had brought from Denver. Path and David returned to Denver every third day to see if anyone was waiting at or near the designated spot and each trip saw them return with more supplies. But it wasn't until their fourth trip that they came back with five more children who had seen the posters and cautiously approached David. There were three boys and two girls, ranging in ages from eight to fourteen, bringing the total children to ten. Gwen and Path could not begin to fathom what might have happened to the parents of the ten children found in Denver. Nothing made sense. Surely people would not have left without their kids, their cars. How had Denver emptied of so many people, people who seemed to have just walked away, taking no supplies with them, leaving their cars in mall parking lots, at banks? A couple of the kids remembered that their parents had been very sick. Could there have been thousands of deaths in Denver? If so, why had the children not encountered more bodies? How had the children survived whatever had decimated the entire population of eight hundred thousand people? How had they found one another?

Unwilling to use precious time searching houses in the city, Path and Gwen decided to let this mystery ride until others had found their way to the city, until there were enough adults to make such an excursion reasonable.

Gwen told the children that they were welcome to decide whether to split into other cabins. She was not surprised that they chose to stay together for now. Exploring the cabins, she was able to find a crib and told herself to remember to supply it with a mattress and sheets, just in case someone came in with a very young one. Cassie was continuing to mother the younger children but she now had another child closer to her own age, Christine, and the two of them were proving to be wonderful with the kids. But they were also given freedom to be children again since Gwen and Path did most of the caretaking. Even so, Gwen was able to free enough time to explore and plan and supervise when children were napping or Path took over the watch.

Fourteen-year-old Brad and thirteen-year-old Jason were quick to learn how to build fires and to teach the other children about gathering kindling for the cook stove. They made a game of it for the younger children. It felt so good to run through the forest and play that the children quickly gathered enough twigs and sticks to keep the fire going for a very long time. While Path knew that they would eventually have to chop wood and there was plenty of equipment available, he was happy to find that a large supply of cut wood was piled in the forest, near the dining cabin.

In the third week, Path and David returned with another vehicle behind them and a very large group of travelers. Five adults and nine children had traveled from as far away as Virginia and Ohio. She was happy to meet five strong adults and they were introduced as Conner Sommerville, an English literature professor; Shawnee Youngblood, a teacher and an activist for Native American rights; Clint Jones, a mechanic and electrician; Mary Anderson, a university student studying biology; and the oldest of the group, Layla Johnson, who told Gwen that she had been many things in life, none of them lazy, to which Gwen responded with delight, "We need a whole lot of you here, then!"

The newcomers were amazed at the set-up that Path, Gwen, and the kids had already initiated and were happy for the woods. And, as Clint so aptly put it, "Not looking over our shoulder every second to make sure we aren't going to be someone's next meal." During the next few days, after the kids had been put to bed and they sat around the campfire sharing theories and speculations, they also shared a lot of tales about some of the nightmares that they had encountered. All agreed that they were happy to work at putting the camp in order and having somewhere to feel more rooted.

Conner, Shawnee, Mary, Clint, and Path decided to begin searching a few houses in Denver when they went to check the meeting place to see if there were other arrivals. They did find a lot of skeletons, more skeletons than they ever imagined, implying some disease or malady had actually struck many of the people of Denver. Conner told Path that there must have also been a mass exodus, as well, probably more out of fear of disease rather than the things going on elsewhere in the country. The highways leading in to the city from the east had been log-jammed by the cars of people trying to leave. Impatient that the east-bound lanes had been clogged, they had even moved to the westbound lanes, using them to travel east, until those, too, were impassable. The four of them witnessed most of this with binoculars, since it was impossible to get onto those highways except on foot. Even some of the city streets were impassable. But they detoured up and around, sometimes on sidewalks to get through, and were careful not to go too deep into the city. Not many people seemed to have left Denver west-bound into the mountains. They must have considered the sheer height of the Rockies, risk of quakes and volcanic activity to the west too great a risk. Conner assured Path that he had been only too happy to be heading west against the huge tide of refugees heading east, toward the coast. From the news he'd been able to gather, the east coast had been bombed, as had the south. The people heading east would be wading over bodies.

"When we get a chance, we could come in here and clear some of these roads," Clint suggested. "I'll find a wrecker and tow cars. We can fill parking lots and get a lot of the cars off the streets, make it more passable."

"What are we going to do about all the bodies?" Mary asked.

"They'll stay where they lay," Conner said. "We don't need those homes for anything and I think it's fit that they rest in their homes for now. At least they've already pretty much decomposed so there isn't a great risk to us. Eventually, if we begin to see a population build, we could organize burial details. We just don't have the manpower right now." He smiled sympathetically as she winced. "Sorry, Mary, it's a continent of death. But we've got to concentrate on the living. Right now we've got to post some more of these." He held up posters that Gwen and Layla had the children making. "Hopefully we are only attracting harmless people, people like us."

"David gave us a good indicator," Path told him. "We watch from hiding. David said that they will have children with them and the children will be protected and happy, not bound, not frightened. Pretty good thinking for a little kid, I think."

"Sounds like a plan," Conner nodded.

Shawnee, who rarely spoke unless spoken to, added, "His vision might be the safest rule of thumb to follow at this point."

Three days later they found another group that had come in from the east and were waiting nervously at the Commons, led by a ginger-haired, gregarious leprechaun of an Irishman named Declan Donnelly. With him were three women: Melody Coen Dunning, Lisa Coleman, Brittin Peterson, and a brawny, strong lad named Randy Stanley. This group of adults had seven children with them, five girls and two boys, all of them protected and happy, especially happy to see other children and the camp.

"Are any of the children related to one another or are they all solitary finds?" Layla had asked at the campfire several nights later.

"We know that Tyler and Raven are siblings," Gwen offered.

"Fawn and Coyote are cousins," Shawnee said, "But no siblings. Most of the kids were found in different places in our group."

"Ours, too!" Melody nodded. "And, believe me, we searched."

"Josh is brother to Haylie and there was another sibling," Conner said, quietly. "I want to tell you while he's sleeping, because I'm not sure that he's still not affected by his horrible tragedy but, Josh, the oldest in our group, lost a little brother to cannibals. We almost lost him, too. Fortunately for us, Clint is one strong, well-armed mo-fo and he came out of nowhere and saved us all. Several fewer cannibals alive. Good riddance. My whole group owes Clint our lives."

Mary shivered at the memory and buried her face in her hands. Gwen reached a hand to comfort the girl. "You've been through so much. It's okay to let go now; it's natural." She had seen much of the same kinds of horrors through several of her hosts. One of those hosts was here in the camp. She had been seeing some of their travels through Shawnee's eyes. She remembered the short Blink of a vision she had when she saw Conner and recognized him as the man behind the pharmacy counter in a Target store. Path had told her that he had the same experience with Declan, that he had been a host for one of Path's views of the future.

It was becoming apparent to them that those who had hosted their visions were now the same ones who were finding their way to Colorado. Whether Gwen or Path had somehow implanted that thought before it had even occurred to them to voice this goal was a mystery.

Two weeks later, Path and Declan encountered a well-armed, well-stocked group coming in to Denver from the south. The strong young woman who the group seemed to defer to as the leader drove a pick-up and hauled a camper overflowing with kids. Gayle Cooper-Lesko was a serious quiet woman who remained suspicious and cautious, unable to relax even when assured that Path and Declan were leading them to safety. She had come from California, as had a couple of the children in her group. The adults with her were Lily Shupe and Dave Carson from Provo, Utah. And Stephanie Lann was found in Pueblo, Colorado. When sixteen children and two adults tumbled out of the camper, Path offered to split the load and the older children, along with Dave Carson, piled into the SUV with him and Declan, after assuring Gayle that there were many more children back at the camp. They told the newcomers to follow them and, once again, headed up Interstate 70 to the area near Golden where the hidden camp was.

By now, the group had organized four of the dormitories for the children and had assigned sleeping arrangements. Gwen and Path had taken one of the small, staff cabins, as had some of the other adults. The new group brought the population to nearly sixty, with only sixteen being adults. Adults monitored the children to make certain that they were comfortable and unafraid. Keeping them busy was no easy task. There were just so many chores to be done, so several of the adults organized play groups and offered to watch the smaller children as the older children learned how to cook, use tools, and help set the camp to rights.

When Gwen saw Gayle, she recognized the girl she had seen in the mirror back in Santa Rosa, California. So, the strong one survived. She was so happy to see that Gayle had not only survived but led the largest group assembled so far. The young woman was formidable and they were fortunate to have people like her coming into the camp. They would need all the strength they could find, strength, and organizers, and teachers, physicians, mechanics, builders, farmers.

*

They sat around the campfire after the children had all been fed and sent to their cabins. The fire was much smaller than the earlier blaze used for teaching and telling stories to eager young ears. Now the adults were winding down toward their own rest and slumber.

Most of them were seated on the logs around the fire. Path smiled as Gwen came from tucking in the youngest children and from feeding baby Constance, to sit at his feet. That crib had been perfect for the little one and she was safely down for the night. Gwen sighed and snuggled into her blanket. She sat on the ground with her head against Path's knee and stared into the flames. Something about the open blaze always took her back to another, simpler, happier time. "I would give anything to hear wolves right now," she sighed. "When I was young, there were wolves howling several miles away; their songs were so filled with a celebration of the night...and freedom...and their sense of family and belonging to a clan. I could sleep peacefully knowing that I was sharing the world with such wonderful families. I wonder if everything is gone, no owls, no wonderful night sounds. Where are the frogs?"

Path smiled and let his hand move through her hair. He allowed himself to be pulled into her memory.

"As Rachel Carson told us in 'Silent Spring', the frogs would have been the first to go. Where go the frogs...." Shawnee Youngblood stared at Gwen as she shared the memory, then nodded. "I didn't get to hear wolves. They were gone from our area since I was very young, but the song of the coyote is similar and I always enjoyed their chorus. Although my father would grimace and call them scavengers and pests, I admired their cunning and patience. I thought him too ruined by the ways of the twentieth century." She paused, always serious, always thinking. "We are going to have to be able to find food in the forest. Perhaps we can find some books identifying different plants that I am not familiar with. The forest is still pretty lush. The food in Denver, the canned goods, won't last forever. Besides, it is mostly processed food, not healthy, not the kind of nutrition we need. I found seeds in our last excursion and Conner helped me plot out a small garden. We will all have to become farmers again, just like we will all be called upon to teach or guide in some way. Conner suggested I plant the three sisters, and use it as a way to teach the children about the ancestors...I appreciated the suggestion. There were no fish for the holes." She let her voice wander off. She picked at grass on her jeans, distractedly.

She looked into the fire, seeming to focus on visions within it as she was drawn back to the previous conversation. She leaned back and looked at the canopy of stars above them. The earth may have spun out of control as Mother Nature tried to claim back what man had ruined but the stars were still above, the same constellations, the same twinkling eternity.

"Tell us your story, Shawnee," Gwen urged, "I can tell you're on the verge...that memories are pouring through your head."

Shawnee nodded, "I often think about my ancestors and how different their lives must have been. How they would have looked up at the same stars as those above my head. I am named for the tribe of my grandparents, my mother's people, many times removed. They had come to join the Lakota people, by choice, when their way of life had been forever altered by the white encroachment."

Gwen stiffened and reached up to take Pathogent's hand. She looked back over her shoulder and caught his eyes, then turned back to Shawnee and encouraged her. "Tell us about your life and the life of your ancestors. We can all learn from one another by taking the best from our pasts and sharing it with the children. We can't allow ourselves to make the same mistakes that this culture made. We need to, we must, learn from the past."

Shawnee turned toward Gwen, trying to consider whether or not to share her story. Something about this older woman was compelling. Something about her gave off great strength and power. But, none of these people gathered around the fire was Native American. None of them shared the Lakota traditions and heritage. How would she make them understand that it was difficult for her to feel light-hearted and anything but serious with what she had witnessed, with what she had studied?

Gwen's open smile charmed her and, for some reason, Shawnee found herself wanting to open up to her. "My parents were already gone long before the troubles started. My father died an alcoholic and my mother, as well. My grandmother finished the job they started, raising me. She was a great improvement; my grandmother was a better parent than the two of them together. While my father was alive, we had lived on Redbud for a while, the reservation. But my mother's people were from Pine Ridge, so we moved there when I was little. My grandmother lived there, near Wounded Knee, and that is where I grew to adulthood. Have you ever been there?"

At this, only Melody nodded. Sadly, Shawnee continued, "It is pretty desolate on that reservation, very poor, very sad, dusty land, that close to Wounded Knee and the Badlands. When I grew up, I taught at the school, trying to work in traditional skills between teaching mathematics and history." She paused, her voice choked. "I just realized that I don't know if any of those children survived. I can't help but think of them."

She sighed. "I had been visiting family in Oklahoma when the earthquakes and eruptions began. No flights, highways congested and impassable, I was basically trapped to ride it out. I never dreamed I would not see South Dakota again. I am glad that five of the children from the Oklahoma reservations survived. It was no difficult task to lead them away from Oklahoma but I was hearing stories of death and destruction to the north. I was headed for South Dakota. I still don't understand how or why we came here instead but we just seemed to all agree. I met up with Conner, Clint, Mary, and Layla. The children were safer with a larger group."

Conner stoked the fire, making no sound of distraction, listening intently to Shawnee's story. He noted the strength, the nobility in her profile, her wonderful way of weaving a tale with her native accent. He loved the long pauses, the way her voice was modulated, no dramatic rises and falls that fit the speech pattern of so many hysterical, attention-starved young women; Shawnee displayed no drama, just quiet and thoughtful reflection. He smiled encouragement for her to continue.

"You moved through the details so fast," Pathogent said softly, not wanting to seem critical, but interested in knowing more about his newfound grandchild. "I hope that, in time, we will learn more about life on Pine Ridge from you, things we may use to teach the children survival skills. I am sure it wasn't easy, that you learned so much you could share."

Shawnee nodded. "Another time about my life. Let me talk about my ancestors, it is so much easier. Their history has always been with me, part of my storytelling. Let me go back to the beginning of my story, the oral tradition that was given to me by my grandmother and my aunts." She took a deep breath and entered right into her familiar oral history. "Long ago, a Shawnee man and his woman, my ancestors, fought against the westward expansion of the whites. They had fought in the Ohio lands, following war chiefs like Black Hoof and Blue Jacket, their villages threatened by the whites coming down the Ohio into the Can-tuck-ee lands, and threatened by the campaign of George Rogers Clark as he led troops through Ohio to subdue the Shawnee, the Delaware and the Wyandot. They, my family, then moved to Tippecanoe to follow the great leader, Tecumseh. Perhaps you have heard of Tecumseh. There was much more to him than simply inspiring the middle name of General William Tecumseh Sherman. You see, he was actually the greater of the two men. He was, perhaps, the greatest leader of my people."

She was giving a history lesson that she had often given students on the reservation. "My grandmother speaks of Tecumseh as if he could move mountains. I think many of my people have felt that way about him, as well as about Crazy Horse and other prophets. History speaks of him as a great thinker and orator and that he could move others to follow him with his speeches and his logic. Even his sworn enemy, William Henry Harrison, said of Tecumseh that, had he been born at another time and place, he could have been a Caesar. My ancestors were drawn to follow him from the Ohio territories to his new village in what would come to be known as Indiana. At Tippecanoe, my grandparents were happy to be beyond the reach of most whites, but soon there were more and more, pushing ever westward. Tecumseh was trying to gather the tribes from the south, the north, and the west to join his forces to fight a resistance against the Europeans moving into this land. The land that soon became the state of Indiana, named for 'Indians' land', but the whites kept coming, moving on, pushing through Ohio and beyond." She smiled apologetically at Declan and Conner. "I am sorry. I am just relating it as it was told to me." The fire lit her face and she carried sadness in her eyes.

"No, go on," Declan encouraged. "We certainly understand how they must have felt...remember, I am Scotch/Irish...the British have been pushing us both for centuries."

"Ouch!" laughed Conner. "No, it's okay, I do understand that as well; we Brits can be bastardly eager to try to force colonization on the unwilling. Please do go on, Shawnee."

She seemed deep within the confines of her own story as she continued. "Tecumseh was visiting tribes in the south and had left his brother, Tenskwatawa, known as 'the Prophet', in charge of Tippecanoe. Tenskwatawa was a zealot who completely hated the whites, preached the old ways, shamed anyone embracing anything to do with white people. Unfortunately, the Prophet gave the whites led by William Henry Harrison an excuse to attack by aggravating the men of the fort, sending his men to steal cattle. You may know that part of history. Tippecanoe was soundly defeated and Tecumseh's plans for united tribes were dashed." She paused and stoked the fire, her face lit by the glow. Gwen smiled at the realization that this strong, noble, beautiful young woman was of her own blood.

"He and my ancestor went on to join the British forces against the colonial whites during the war of 1812. When Tecumseh was killed at the Battle of the Thames, in modern day Canada," she paused and sighed, "I wonder if Canada still exists." Then shook her head and continued, "My ancestors were disheartened. They had moved to a small settlement on the Ohio River but felt threatened almost every day by the proximity of more and more whites. My grandmother, my ancestor, wanted to move farther west away from encroachment, toward a life filled with respect for nature and an understanding of the hoop, the circle of life that is affected by every other living thing. They were accepted into a band of the Lakota and completely assimilated into the Lakota way. I am supposed to have gotten my green eyes from the grandmother, they say. But let me continue their tale. Unfortunately for them, the encroachment never really stopped. But they were able to spend the last of their years in freedom. It wasn't until the next generation that many members of my family were killed when following Crazy Horse."

Pathogent squeezed Gwen's shoulder as Shawnee related their story, their history. This was almost too much to process. What was obvious to them both, and neither of them could barely trust themselves to breathe, was that they had just met their own great-granddaughter, many times removed. Gwen thought, *I can't even imagine what is going through Path's mind...but I want to hug her, I want to know my granddaughter better. How could this possibly have happened if we never were able to give birth?* Then she realized that she might have left the body of her host before the birth took place, that the Blink may have happened each time to them and yet their seed was sown. "This amazing opportunity being laid at our feet is almost too much to believe," Path whispered against her ear. "We had children after all; we just weren't present to know..."

"They were at Wounded Knee?" Melody asked, saddened by her memories of traveling to that desolate place in what seemed another lifetime now, and witnessing the mass grave atop a lonely hill. "When I went there, I could not help but think of how cold, desolate, and forbidding that place must have been on that day, frozen bodies everywhere. Oh, Shawnee, I'm so sorry."

"No, don't feel that way. There is no reason for all whites to carry the guilt of what was done by some very evil men. I do not hate all whites because of Tecumseh, nor because of Wounded Knee. I am not like the Prophet, Tenskwatawa. I do not see it that way. Our elders speak to us, tell us that in each of us, there live two wolves, one good and one evil, and we could all choose to be good or bad. It is our own journey to choose which wolf to be."

She shook her head. "Fortunately for me, much of my family was in hiding and they were not there on that fateful day." She sighed and stared into the fire. "Generations of our people were forbidden to talk of it as a massacre. We heard it taught in our schools as a battle, a victory battle for the whites. How can it have been a battle when people without arms were slaughtered as they tried to run away from confrontation, not toward it? Women, children. Later, on reservations, my elders were sent away to Indian schools. We were forbidden to wear our hair long, forbidden to follow our traditions." She stared into the fire.

She explained, "I heard enough hatred from my family and their extended families. I saw it passed from generation to generation. It is no way to raise children, saturated with hatred and dismay from the day they are born. As a teacher, I saw the hatred and resentment as a poison that had infected our entire nation. Hatred in them for us, hatred in us for them. I tried hard to steel my mind and heart against 'inherited hatred'; I turned to books...and learning. It was in my mind to teach the children a better way." She sighed. Her knuckles were white where she was gripping the log she sat on as her memories ebbed. "Too much utter and total dismay, too many suicides...and now it may all be gone...."

Conner, stirred by her tale, spoke. "I do carry that inherited guilt and I realized in college that it had made me open my empathy to the point where it was causing harm to my soul. I worked elbow to elbow with the activists, the reactionaries, the feminists, those who protested British rule and the very ideals of colonialism. I tried to escape some of that guilt by coming to America but, by then, it was the America of open bigotry, intolerance for any religion but the one of the majority, open contempt and lack of understanding for gays and lesbians. Women's rights that had been gained were reversed and taken away. I had chosen the wrong place and the wrong time to be born, I sometimes think."

"Tell us your story," Shawnee urged, eager to take her own mind off the sadness she was feeling, sadness for her lost way of life, sadness for her people. She trusted her new friend, Conner, saw courage and hope in him and wanted to know him better. Whenever there was something she wanted to explore, some project she thought might help, she sought out Conner who never questioned, who was always willing to help her, often simply trusting her earth-knowledge, her survival instincts.

Conner nodded. "It's nowhere near as noble as yours, even though my family had title and lineage which they considered to be inherent, inherited, and validating. It is very strange to be raised knowing the lineage and rumors and genealogy of your family as if something about those details and facts could possibly make you better than the man standing next to you, like purebred dogs with a royal pedigree. Rebel that I am, it always made me think that my fellow Lords, Ladies, Earls, and Countesses would rather die than lose their titles as if those prefixes somehow gave them the rights of superior consideration, and passes for misbehavior and cruelty. My family tree was known to me from a very young age, with all its twists and turns and broken links and is full to the brim with scoundrels, knaves, and blackguards. You see, the name Sommerville comes down to me from a history that can be traced back to when the word 'noble' had lost its truest meaning." He smiled.

Pathogent leaned forward at the mention of the name. Gwen suppressed a gasp and felt his body tense behind her. What was happening to them, what could this possibly mean? The name Sommerville seemed to hang in the air in front of them. Could this possibly be another birth tied to their former life in England? Were those lives that they had affected now able to sense some kind of genetic gravitational pull, being drawn to them without their awareness that it was so?

"There were scoundrels but there were also great romances and tales told about those conceived on the 'other side of the sheets'; I think that's the expression used to look down their noble noses at illegitimacy."

"We've heard so much sadness, we need some smiles, give us the romance!" urged Melody. "Give us swashbuckling, dangerous, unnatural liaisons filled with intrigue and daring do!" she demanded, smiling.

Conner grinned, and nodded, "Lord knows there is enough of that in the generations of stories. Governesses and history tutors would give us the nobility. We had to dig up the skeletons in the closets from other sources. My father had stumbled upon a tale that he related to my mother and me in great detail. My mother, you see, was a writer...a romance writer...I blush to admit, and she wanted to use the family's secrets to enhance a story of hers. We sat one night and listened to my father's tale of a 15th century ancestor, and his being pulled from the gutter to claim his rightful place in the family manor. His grandfather had found him in a stable on the outskirts of London and took him to the family manor near Essex."

As Conner went on to relate the story of the young stable boy and his "whore," Pathogent massaged Gwen's shoulders to keep her from tensing up. Hearing the tale of their love and their challenges made it very difficult not to amend the parts of the legend that were wrong and give answers where there remained mysteries. To hear the life one lived related as a close substitute for romantic fiction was not the easiest thing to endure.

"...And imagine their horror to return from their summer lodgings in Scotland to find what would normally have been thought of as a 'gutter tripe' by the snobs in their own circle, in the guest chambers. Simply scandalous beyond belief! The grandmother urged him to abandon plans to turn the duckling into a swan but, when she realized that her urging and nagging were beginning to alienate her newfound and greatly treasured grandson, she took on that very challenge herself. And, she was to have told friends, it was not the difficult task she anticipated. The duckling, ragged, wretched, and starved to the point of frightful emaciation, carried herself with noble conformation and turned out to be a stunning beauty. She was able to walk through a room filled with the bluest of bloods and turn heads everywhere."

He smiled, "I was told that she went from being a mere skeleton, to fleshing into one of the finest ladies in all of the London society of the time. Of course, to make this story a good romance, could it have turned out any other way? And, of course, the new Lord Sommerville was tall, dark, handsome, and dashing. I could see, in my mind, the fluttering of the ladies' fans when he passed, the heaving breasts, the classic descriptions my mother filled her books with when she was at her peak. The family paintings proved that the couple in question was an extremely handsome pair.

"Nothing could deter the new Lord from his mission to save the young woman and watch her flourish. He allowed nothing to get in his way, until he was finding himself fighting off other suitors among the self-same aristocracy that would have rejected her out of hand, had they known her story." He shook his head. "You see, I am willing to admit, that many were insufferable snobs and could be very scathing and unrepentant in their attempt to elevate themselves in their own esteem.

"To go on with their story, their first child was a son, striking and strong as his father and filled with the true grit of his mother. His grandmother wrote in a letter that my father had found that, shortly before the birth of their son, they changed, settled, became country squire and wife. For a while they were thought to be ill. They both seemed distant, out-of-sorts, but that didn't last long. After becoming parents, they seemed subdued and happy to live a quieter life, away from the parties, the public life. They went on to have seven fine, noble children and the question of their legitimacy was lost in the ravages of time. There was never a real question that I was a descendant of this little detour from aristocracy. I've seen all three paintings and I must declare here, upon my oath, there were no exaggerations about her notable beauty nor his nobility and stature. They were striking creatures and I would be, no, am happy to bear even a little of their genetics in my countenance."

"I'm sure that you do," Gwen told him, looking into the gray eyes of the speaker. Why had she not noticed them before, his pale gray eyes, so like those of his ancestor? Gwen suddenly remembered the conversation in which Lady Sommerville told her, "You have something within you that no other woman could give him." Gwen had thought that Lady Sommerville was referring to her personality; she had not dreamed that the Lady was hinting that she knew that Gwen was pregnant at the time…because Gwen herself had never suspected.

Conner smiled and demurred, "It was with the greatest relief I have ever felt to leave that life behind me and simply become a simple itinerant English professor. Of course, the English accent was often times a trump card when you realize that, all too often, people mistake the posh accent for refinement. I went to college with mates who were far from refined in their habits and practices. I did try to keep a low profile and wanted to be accepted for what I had to offer, not for a mere heritage. I was teaching at a small college in Virginia when the coast began to be hit by the first storms."

"When earthquakes and other natural disasters followed, I thought about moving further inland. When diseases started to spread, and huge segments of the population died, I simply began moving westward, a little at a time, first Tennessee, then onward. It seemed like things escalated in my travels. Death, diseases, hatred, mistrust, until the rebellion, the overthrow of the government, military coups, and nuclear blasts laid waste the entire continent. I went north into Ohio for a while. I met few along the way who were still sane. I don't even remember when Clint, Layla, Mary, and I began gathering children. Then we met up with this amazing Native American warrior in Kansas," he nodded toward Shawnee, "with her own troop of children, and, Shawnee, I must say, you kept us all from going off the deep end. We talked her into changing her direction. She was headed toward the Great Lakes after finding out that South Dakota was suicide. Layla assured her that the Lakes were poisoned and barren."

There was silence for a short while as they all absorbed what they had learned about two of their new companions. The silence stretched out as each of them realized how exhausted they were from the day's activities. Declan yawned and poked at the fire. "Can we agree to continue this tomorrow night, where we left off? I truly have enjoyed learning a little of the background of Conner and Shawnee and eagerly await getting to know the others."

"So long as we begin with your story tomorrow night," Melody agreed. "I don't want to lead off the revelations. My story isn't half as compelling and historically breathtaking as Shawnee's, nor as romantic as Conner's."

"I seriously doubt you've lived a boring life," Conner assured her. "Besides, this is not about trying to outdo one another. It's just a breaking of the ice and a little self-reflection. Believe me, there is so much more to me than my heritage and lineage, just as Shawnee has not been defined by her blood." He grinned. "We are going to have years to get to know one another, I am certain of that."

"How can you be certain? We don't know if we'll even be able to find more food, if anything in your garden will grow, if we will have a tomorrow," Gayle contested bitterly. "How can we keep the children safe from those out there actually hunting children? Not for the future they ensure but for their tender..." her voice broke at the horror behind what she was seeing in her mind's eye, the terror she had experienced on her trip from the west coast, the drive and exhaustion of working to keep the children in her group safe. How many times had they come so very close to being central to the terrors they had hidden from? How often had they been the hunted?

All eyes turned toward her. The undercurrent of frustration and despair was evident in her voice and in her comment. She voiced what many of them had felt at one time or another, but each adult knew that they could never share these fears with the children and expect those children to grow happy and strong, untainted.

Conner met her eyes and smiled a wry smile, "My apologies, Gayle, believe me, I do know what you mean. I'm just such a hopelessly optimistic soul, not much of a realist. But I have not forgotten. I have not put aside the times when I was fortunate to be better armed than my adversaries."

Gayle looked down into the fire, "No, really I am sorry, believe me, I wish I hadn't spoken. It's just that I've seen more than enough ugly, and too much horror. If I hadn't found this place, I don't think I would have wanted to live very many more days. I'm sure we've all witnessed horror out there on the road. I think I just let it get to me and allowed it to invade this perfectly wonderful evening."

"No, Gayle," Path assured her, "you simply have a very strong sense of the gravity of our situation. We are taking on a very dangerous and challenging role here, to teach and protect these children...to try to assure the survival of a species that perhaps, quite frankly, shouldn't survive. We are breaking new ground here and we cannot know what will happen tomorrow, if we will remain hidden and safe. We can hope, we can plan...but I, too, have been wondering if there is more that we can do to assure the safety of the children."

He squeezed Gwen's hand. It would not do to tell these perfectly grounded people that there was already magic at work, that he and Gwen had combined theirs to make this place unknown to others, invisible to those who might cause harm or death. They had found this campground near Golden, Colorado, and felt it a perfect place to shelter with the original five children they had found. Not only was there a dining cabin, but several large cabins with dormitory style sleeping arrangements. They had found a bicycle shop and bike trailers in Denver as well as a grocery store that had barely been touched, almost as if the population of Denver had simply ceased to exist and no one was left to loot.

After loading up on food and bedding and storing supplies that would even get them through the winter, including sleeping bags and down comforters, and making certain that every bunk was clean and neat, they found a gun shop and loaded a trailer full of guns and ammunition as well, along with the weapons they had found at the Florence Federal Prison. They had an arsenal. Those were safely locked away in what Pathogent now thought of as the armory. Neither of them carried weapons. They really felt no need now that they knew that their magic was stronger than ever. So far, it seemed to them that most survivors were traveling toward coasts. That had never been their agenda. They wanted the woods, not only for cover but for the fact that, due to the forest canopy, there was hope that there still might be living animals. So far they had not heard any evidence or seen any scat, but the mountainous area was vast. The Rockies had once been teeming with wildlife.

No one had found this spot. They had met every one of the new people in Denver while scavenging for supplies or in answer to their posts. There was no way to test their shield, but so far it seemed to be holding.

*

Declan sighed and grinned, then rose to his feet. "I cannot suppress my inner thespian," he told them as he walked around the fire and smiled at each and every one of them. "Nor can I take my turn sitting down. It's in my blood, performance art, that is. I also warn you, I can't tell a short story. Snuggle on down. We'll be here a while...this may be the only tale told tonight. Now you will all have to bear with me for all that you know I'm Irish, and have some Scot sprinkled into the mix. I didn't have these auburn curls and green eyes for nothing that doesn't prove my heritage. But I will warn you, the first to call me Leprechaun will feel my wrath, for sure and all. I don't know if you are aware, but we Irish not only tell our pub tales, but we feel inclined to act them out, complete with different voices and props. I will spare you my antics, if at all possible, and try hard to rein them in but you can't say that you haven't been warned. I, too, could wax poetic over the romance and intrigue I found when studying my genealogy charts and, believe me, we've had some incredible characters in the Donnelly tree and, as with Conner, on both sides o' the sheets." He waggled his brow to add emphasis to this.

He paused for dramatic effect and drew them in with his aside, "Now, I've never been one to think that 'bastardy' was an insult as such, for that 'shameful secret', that unspoken truth, was part of what I am made of and I am too proud and stubborn to find fault with that, I can assure you. There just isn't many a northern family who won't find unwedded romance if they shake their tree hard enough, for all its craggy, hard life to survive, for all the toughness one must develop. Northern Ireland, that is. I always forget that that reference may mean nothing to Americans. To wax romantic about forbidden love is ingrained in all the people of the Isle, north and south. Ireland gave the world Jonathan Swift, James Joyce, William Butler Yeats, Patrick Kavanaugh, Seamus Heaney, Sean O'Casey, Edna O'Brien, and on and on..." He tipped an invisible hat and held it over his heart to show respect for the names he had just listed and walked around the fire. "I give you my freedom-fighting gran and grandad from Ulster. Ah, Kaitlyn Donnelly, if she wasn't a fine hard-headed lass, it was she who was the leader of their cell, not her man, Brendan, and I've heard the tales that she was the fiercest and most deadly fighter among them. There are rumors that she might have been a little too eager to spill blood, a little too violent toward the opposition. But, alas, those were violent times and she was struggling to survive against insurmountable odds; it was brave, or foolish given your perspective, of her to even fight against the might of the powers that be. And, oh, did she love her Brendan Donnelly with a fierceness of any Celtic warrior. Word had it that they weren't wed but she took the name of Donnelly and woe to the man who tried to take it from her. And, were it not for that banshee, I'd not be standing here today telling this tale."

Pathogent's hand again found Gwen's and he squeezed...so, they had survived the rebellion...or at least SHE had survived and gone on to bear the father, or grandfather of this brilliant and compelling young man.

Declan tapped his head and grinned, "But I've a mind to take you farther back into the past than we've been before for my family roots run deep and wide and we've shared stories for more centuries than many people can hope to trace their blood. Let your mind travel back with me to the wearing of skins and the settlements of villages in what we refer to as the Dark Ages. We're going to the coast of Northern Ireland, somewhere between Torr and Ballycastle, where you can nearly look across the Strait and see Scotland. On that craggy land, high above the sea, in villages that bore names lost to history, is where my story begins. My heroine is a lovely Scottish lass, bonny as the day is long, beauty so stunning it could nigh on to stop a man's heart in his chest just to see her auburn corkscrew curls caught in the wind and sunlight." For comic effect, he flounced his own curls, then pointed to his rare, bright green eyes, "Dare he look into her emerald green eyes, he would find himself as lost as he would be to any forest Fir Darrig, the water fairie, the undines who could tempt a man to give himself to drown in them.

"Mourning the loss of her mother and fearing her father would die of grief if not given purpose, she agreed to go with him to return to the land of his own people, the Irish. This was a fearsome trip for anyone who isn't used to the sea, narrow though the strait may be, it cuts a deep channel and the waters can be treacherous. They crossed the channel with some of the fishermen who to this day ply trade with their Irish neighbors across the strait. Now, picture this, the fair maid is making a journey she never dared dream, afloat on the water, leaving the only world she has ever known behind. Picture the fires of her village disappearing in the night as the waves take her further and further from the people of her mother and the familiar Scottish highlands."

The one who lived it closed her eyes, remembering. It was as he had described it, the boat moving further and further from her Highland home toward an uncertain future. However, what Declan did not know, had no way of knowing, was that she was also going toward her own ancient roots, toward the Isle of the Tuatha. The small rowboat that took them to the fishing vessel had rocked hard on the choppy waves and her hands had gripped the sides, her knuckles white. Because she and he alone knew the beginning and the end of this story, as had the young girl in the boat, she knew that this very sea, this strait between the two countries, would give her both life and sustenance, and heart-rending grief.

"They arrived in the village of her Da's family during the autumn harvest and her da' was able to make himself useful to his sisters and their husbands by helping in the fields. This village stood close to a rocky eyrie overlooking the sea where women could watch their men take to their boats to harvest the gifts of the mighty waves. Fishermen were to be seen down near the water, mending their nets, preparing to put them up for winter. Crops to be gathered, nets to be mended, no idle hands in the village while all were preparing for the cold weather to come.

"The young lass, Sabd, found her own niche in the village, and not just for her beauty and grace. She would soon become invaluable to her new family for sharing the knowledge her mother, a great healer, had taught her. And the village quickly embraced her as she helped them with maladies that would have been far worse, if not for her gentle and caring touch." Declan's face was lit by the fire as he paced and leaned down to emphasize passages of his story. He had warned them of his physical drama and he had not been exaggerating about his air of theatrics. He used the clearing around the fire as a stage. He paused, letting them enter the setting he had laid for them. He took a drink from his canteen and let that moment stretch for dramatic effect.

Gwen had closed her eyes, remembering this life she had lived. She opened them and leaned her head back to catch Path's smile. They waited for Declan to proceed with the story of their longest life together, the life that they both cherished in their hearts. However sad, however tragic, it had been a life they both treasured and it was amazing to hear Declan tell it in such great detail, getting so little wrong. Anything he had added for drama must accidentally have led him to enhance it truthfully and embellish with enough knowledge of the past to make it work.

Declan smiled, "Ah, and so, as the harvest is taken in and the approach of winter enters their minds, their greatest and most beloved festival is fair coming upon them. Samhain. You may already know that Samhain was practiced by the ancient people to celebrate the harvest, the work that villages accomplished as one, the assurance of survival through another winter's freeze. Great fires would burn across the green Isle as in the days of the Druids, the days of remembrance, the days of dancing. Pagan celebrations had not yet been driven into secrecy. No church would forbid these practices for many years to come. Samhain, just the brisk winds and the promise of mystery and darkness make the hair on my arms stand as I say it again, Samhain. The day when the veil between living and dead, between fairy and mankind, between Tuatha de Danaan and the rough hands of warriors, farmers and fisherman would fade and all things, strange things, uninvited things could happen. Many villagers would be too superstitious to leave the ring of light cast by the fire without others for protection against the night. This was where spirits abided; this was the night when miracles could be witnessed. Halloween as we know it was born then. Tales of the crypt were born then but not given flight. Superstition and fear were set aside by celebration and laughter and sharing, the warmth of being in a village full of your own, a village where everyone knew you, cared for you."

Melody drew her blanket tighter around her and looked at the darkness of the forest outside their own ring of fire. Declan had drawn her so deeply into the story, she could almost smell the threat of snow in the air; she could almost feel the approach of winter, despite the fact that it was early spring here and she was in Colorado, not ancient Ireland. She smiled and shook her head to bring herself back to the story as his voice continued in his soft, Irish accent, lulling her gently, captivating in tone and timbre. She felt her breath quicken as he talked and, when his eyes met hers, she knew that she blushed. She hoped that no one could tell how he affected her.

His voice softened, almost a whisper, "Many a babe is conceived on that night, that night of danger and romance, out of the feeling of closeness, the feeling of roots, and history and family. Such a stirring of emotions by that great fire, the celebrations, the closeness felt by those warming themselves with ale, mead, and merriment. Many a couple would leave off dancing, filled with the rhythm of the dancing feet, the music, filled with the laughter and smiles, to find their own little hideaway to consummate their own fire, that inner, burning fire of attraction and lust. Drunk with mead and their homemade wines, drunk with life and the ends of their hard labors, drunk with the love of life, they would be caught up in it, the rhythms moving them." He caught himself drifting too far from his story and grinned an impish grin, "But our heroine was not bedded on that night and I'm getting away from the story." He took a deep breath and continued, fanning himself for comic relief, which made everyone around the fire smile in response.

"She, too, was enjoying the revelry, the camaraderie, the happy festivities. So full of life and so young, so unaware that many pairs of eyes were on her, she was unaware that many a man would watch her, hoping only to draw her eye. She was a vision, dancing in the firelight, like a pagan goddess, her wild auburn tresses framing her lovely face, her figure so pleasing to the eye, so ripe, so full of promise." Declan took a deep breath, "And as it was there that himself saw her, this vision, this goddess of womanhood. It was said that, at the very moment, my ancestor with no name but Nuadu, saw her through the flames, he thought her a fairy that had escaped the veil. He thought he was witnessing a member of the folk themselves, joining the humans in their celebration. He stood and watched her, drinking her in like a man dying of thirst."

Shawnee spoke. "I'm so, so sorry. Speaking of dying of thirst, please wait while I go to the cabin to bring a drink. I am parched but don't want to miss a moment of this." Shawnee rose to her feet. "Does anyone else need water?" At the raising of several hands, she nodded. "I'll bring a jug! Keep that vision in your mind, everyone!" She moved toward the cabins.

Patiently, Declan paused his story and grinned. "I did warn you, did I not? I told you I'd be carried away and my story would fill the evening."

"Don't apologize," Gayle said, stretching and smiling. "I'm enjoying it, even when you talk of dancing, you dance...you are an actor, after all, my friend! But," she admitted, "I'm glad you're on hold for a moment...I have to pee." She laughed and disappeared into the darkness.

Conner watched Shawnee as she walked to the cabins. Assured that she reached them safely, he smiled, and leaned to address Gwen across the fire. "I've been watching you, Gwen. You really are enjoying these stories, aren't you?" he asked the older woman they all seemed to defer to for opinions and advice.

She nodded, "You have no idea how wonderful it is getting to know you all better, getting to know where you come from, what kind of history you can bring to our children, what has formed you and what you can share. Trusting the accumulated knowledge around this fire will help us to survive and I can't help but smile when," she paused, her throat closing, hardly able to breathe around the tears she was choking back. "I now have hope...I now can see a future."

Melody showed surprise. "Gwen, I never would have dreamed that you didn't think we stood a chance. You've been my inspiration when I faltered and thought, 'Why are we doing this?' I thought you firmly believed in our mission to begin this human population all over again, to start a new society for these children, a feeling of the birth of a society where we can teach them and keep them safe."

Gwen reached to take her hand. "I believe NOW! Path never faltered in his belief that we would survive and that we could actually sustain life. He has always had this unshakeable faith...not so much a religious faith, just an ingrained faith in the will to survive. I never shared that...never. He thought me a pessimist. I thought myself a realist."

"I think you were a realist," Gayle said, rejoining the group. "If the seeds we've planted don't become crops, if we don't find animal life, well, hell, let's cut to the chase, we can't live off the canned goods of Denver forever."

"Can we just not go there tonight, please?" Melody pleaded.

"I know I annoy you," Gayle admitted. "I know I annoy everyone with my negativity but it's part of me to see things rationally, to need proof, to have to see something tangible. I am not metaphysical in any way, shape or form. I want to see it through a magnifying glass and then hear each theory debunked and torn apart...that's just me...and I know I'm raining on the party."

"No, you're not!" Shawnee's voice assured her as she approached. "You are bringing us back to earth, to the gravity of our situation. We can escape it momentarily but we will all need to keep it in the forefront of our minds if we stand a chance." Shawnee entered the light around the fire, put cups down on the ground, and poured water from the jug into each cup. She handed them around to those who hadn't brought their canteens to the circle. "We seem to be a pretty balanced group. There are those who exude joy and confidence, like Melody, Declan, and Path. And those who keep the danger in mind and keep us grounded. You are one of them."

"I agree," Gwen said. "I hate to tell you this, Gayle, but you are more like me than you may want to admit. I didn't begin to believe in our chances until we found the spring."

Six days earlier, while exploring, Conner and Shawnee had found water trickling from a rock higher up the side of the mountain. Shawnee had tasted it and found it to be sweet and unspoiled. There was no chemical smell that most surface water gave off. They dug into the soil surrounding the rock and found that the water came from a crevasse between two very large buried boulders. Shawnee knew that they had found a spring. She looked up at the high mountain above them and realized that this water could be coming from a source almost a mile beneath the surface of the mountain. The adults spent a day putting a pipe into the fissure and gathering enough water to fill every empty container they could find. If there was a spring, un-poisoned, unspoiled, there could be more life. Afraid to allow themselves too much hope, they clung to this tiny revelation.

"No, listen, I'm going to be the one to apologize to the group," Gayle said, taking her seat. "This is Declan's story. I will hate myself if I have infected the magic he has spun."

"Don't be sorry, Gayle. The shaking of the earth could never put an Irishman from his tale," Declan laughed and bowed. "I could pick it up tomorrow, if everyone is tired of my voice."

"I could never be tired of your voice!" Melody said, aloud. Realizing she had voiced it, she blushed, embarrassed to have revealed too much.

Conner smiled and decided to save her. "No, Declan, it's still early and your story is great. I want to know about Nuadu and Sabd. And, thank YOU for finally verifying to AMERICANS that 'SAM HANE' is really pronounced 'Sow when'; you've validated what I profess to be true but, after years of hearing people mispronounce, I began to doubt myself."

"We have to remember to add a Samhain celebration to our agenda," Gayle noted. She smiled at Melody, hoping to help cover the embarrassment the girl was feeling, as if it wasn't obvious to them all that Melody was finding herself attracted to Declan. Could the girl lean any farther forward when he was talking? Could she smile any brighter when he was near? Gayle wondered how anyone could allow themselves to think about connecting with anyone in that way with the hopelessness of their situation. But then, there were Gwen and Path and their obvious devotion to one another.

"Right then!" Declan declared and collected himself, obviously thinking back over what he had told them, wondering if any details were missing that he should fill in before continuing. "Now, where was I? Oh, the fire, the dancing. And imagine the man's delight when he was to find that the wife of his own best friend was related to the fairy! And, to add to that delight, the wife was only too happy to play match-maker and introduce the two young people.

"Now, let me describe our hero. He was a strange one, that one. He could never much abide the company of others, preferring to live far up-coast in his own hut. Some knew in their hearts from the time he was a wee babe, that he was destined to become a strange one, a hermit, anti-social and yet kind. I always thought that he was just one of those soft-spoken lads who preferred their own company, to dream, to think, to consider life. A man alone, away from the village, he kept himself busy making a hut, fishing, creating. His talent was that he could take a stick and fashion it into an instrument or a log and create a grand table. What a craftsman he was said to have been, fashioning his own tools and creating valuables out of wood. Many a fishwife wanted to own a stool, a chair, a comb made by those hands." He paused and chuckled before adding, "Many a fishwife kept their dreams about other things those hands could do, to them, daring not to tell their husbands of those dreams. Tall and slender, handsome to a fault, but shaggy and wild, he made many a lass want to catch his piercing glance. But to no one had he declared more than a passing interest.

"And then there was Sabd. Never had the village known him to stay more than a brief visit of an hour or so with his sister and her twelve, yes, TWELVE children. But, in the coming weeks, they saw more of Nuadu than they had seen in all his years as he made it his intention to court the woman who had stolen his heart with one glance. Sabd's father saw good things in this man, as he watched Nuadu put his sister's cabin to right for the winter, helped her husband with laying up firewood and changing the bedding of straw in the loft for the children to sleep better. He walked through the village with a trail of nieces and nephews attending him like ducklings. Sabd's father warmed to him quickly and they say that Sabd had not hesitated to let her father know that this was the man she was going to call her very own. The courtship was quick and the marriage was accomplished just before winter's end. Through the cold, the two trudged her belongings to his hut. She delighted in the new home that would be hers. And they were both happy, feeling very fulfilled.

"No time throughout time could have more happy than the life they shared together. He could hardly allow himself leave of his lovely young bride, even to go to sea. He hated the sea, anyway, a fisherman only from need, not desire. The man admitted to anyone that he could not swim, his fear of deep water a handicap for anyone taking a small fishing boat to sea to spread nets. He was only too happy to stay home with his new and beautiful wife, exploring, planting their garden in the spring, getting to know one another. Sabd would tell her father on his visits that she could not have found a greater happiness, nor a greater man to share that happiness with. I have pictured, in my mind's eye, this joyful young couple, walking the crags and moors of their home, braving nature and life together. Their first years of marriage were a testament to the institution. He felt that his hut had been made a home simply by her presence. Life for them was so happy for a time. There wasn't a villager who didn't love to visit just to take away a little of the beauty of the relationship they shared. 'T'would have been happier for them both if they could have made a child, try as they might. And I'm sure they tried often."

Every day, Pathogent thought, nodding. These memories surged over him, like a wave, like THE wave.

The sadness in Declan's face was apparent and those around the fire could sense that the end of his tale was near, and was not as pleasant as the rest. "He was, after all, a fisherman, though he hated being on the water. Every trip out on the waves was filled with dread. He had been out to sea for only two days. A huge storm blew in suddenly. She feared the worst and watched the bay all day every day for his return. As you might have already guessed, he never did, though she stood watch, steadfast in her hope."

Melody spoke through tears. "How sad...how romantic

and sad. I cannot imagine her grief...cannot imagine not being able to see him again."

Gwen's lower lip quivered as she, too, relived the thoughts, the hurt, the slow shattering of hope. She remembered days lost standing on that craggy knoll, the sea wind whipping her, her rough woolen shawl wrapped tight around her as she stared out across the waves, hoping only to see a boat come in sight. When the men found the broken remains of Nuadu's fishing boat, she continued to hope, simply because she could not live without him.

Declan held up a finger... his long pause to give them time to feel this overbearing sadness pass over their minds. "But that is not the end of my tale, my friends. For, you see, there was a child growing within the belly of Sabd and months after Nuadu disappeared, she gave birth to a strong, beautiful girl, the belle of the Isle. Combining the beauty of both parents she was dark-haired like her father but with the emerald eyes of her ma'. My ancestor raised her daughter in that hut on the craggy hill. People came to them for healing and Sabd lived many years. The daughter, Nuadine, grew up strong and beautiful and married another of my ancestors, the first to bear the name Donnelly. Our family traces its roots so far back, to both Ireland and Scotland. And the story of Sabd and Nuadu, and the beauty Nuadine, live in our hearts and minds." A deep, theatrical bow ended his story.

Gwen took a deep breath and remembered that she had Blinked from Sabd shortly after Nuadu disappeared, so that is why she did not know about the birth of their child. This had possibly happened each time, so she and Pathogent had never known that they had produced children after all. And now the descendants of their children were finding their way to join them. Path had been right all along, there had been a reason for the detours of their lives, there had been purpose to the Blinks. It was almost too much to process. How many more of them were out there?

"And to bring this tale, I came here from New York City, where I was an actor and a part-time teacher. Fortunately, I had already moved west before the barrage of warfare. I was living in Virginia, teaching for a time before everything started to go bad. By the time my group passed Frankfort, Kentucky, we had grown to a tribe of five adults and four unrelated children we had found. We saw a lot, we learned a lot, we lost a lot, including two of our adults and one child, and gained a lot when we found the four more children when we passed through Missouri. But, I'm here to tell you, it's a relief to be here. And that's the most condensed tale I've ever told. To give you my personal history, we'll wait for another night."

"May I go next?" Melody asked, smiling. She took a deep breath and looked around the fire at the people she was beginning to know better, beginning to trust. Trust was coming hard to those who had been through so many tragedies and witnessed so many frightening scenarios. She let herself remember the only "set" of actual parents she had met as she walked west from Ohio. A couple who had desperately begged her to go their hiding place and find their children, to save their children. They were both mortally wounded when she had found them; there was not a chance that either of them would survive what had happened to them when they had been set upon by thieves. The woman hung by a thin thread to life. The man had not been spared and was not in much better condition. They told her of the copse of trees where they had left their children. When she found the three little ones, they were Casey, a girl of about nine, perhaps ten; a boy who was gaunt, thin, perhaps four, Kyle; and a thin, quiet, starving baby who never cried, who would never cry. The baby had not survived. Melody shook her head, trying to push aside the haunting memories. She needed moments free of this kind of remembering. She needed to put her own story together as she told it.

"I've been wondering what part of my genealogy to cover and decided that I do best talking about what I know best. I am most fortunate because my great-grandfather wrote a book about my great-great-grandparents. He was born shortly after the death of his father. His parents, though never married, had every intention of doing so, engaged, in love, devoted. His father was killed in a car accident, eight-and-a-half months before he was born. His mother, at the request of the father's parents, gave the baby their last name, so he grew up Jake Coen, instead of Jake Tipton, her maiden name. It caused some confusion when the book came out. There were people who didn't seem capable of connecting the dots, even though it was spelled out quite clearly in the first chapter. His mother was often on tour to promote a new album. Motherhood did not 'become her' nor did it fit in with her life, and he would stay with the Coens, his grandparents, or his mother's parents, the Tiptons. He really hardly knew his mother." She sighed.

Gwen closed her eyes...it hurt to know that the woman she left behind when she Blinked out of Harmony Tipton was capable of neglecting a child that should have been so very precious to her. Her heart hurt for little Jake Coen, Pathogent's son, her son! Harmony had never seemed so self-involved. Had she allowed her grief to blind her to her own child's needs or had she felt removed from the child because it had been Gwen and Path who conceived it? Or, and this was the most painful possibility, had her time in Harmony's body stolen something from the woman, had she not experienced enough of her own life to know how to be a mother? Had Gwen stolen her childhood from her? Had she been within the host but resentful of the other presence she felt? It hurt to know that little Jacob Coen felt rejection and loneliness. She found it hard not to be angry at Harmony. With all the losses she had faced through her many lives, she still managed to give her children all the love and attention they needed.

"Your grandfather was Jake Coen, Junior?" Gayle asked, in wonder. "I read that book...his mother was the late, great Harmony? My god, I had all of her albums! I loved her voice!" Gayle smiled and said, "I'm sorry to interrupt your story but didn't she also put out an album of remixes of tapes they found after Jacob Coen died? He made his saxophone do things I didn't realize the instrument could do."

"Yes! Her father, my great-grandfather several times removed, Max Tipton, helped her to get the record released. Max Tipton's own band played on the re-mix but they featured Jacob's original sax solos." Melody nodded, "And Harmony sang on it. It was my favorite recording. I loved *'Jacob's Heart'* more than her more commercial releases. There was a song he wrote called *'Our Lives Together'* that just raked my heart. It made me believe in an everlasting and eternal love."

Gwen looked up at Path to see the shimmer of tears in his eyes. It was her turn to squeeze his hand.

Conner looked amazed and nodded. "My blues record collection would not have been complete without that one. My favorite was her *'Roses on the Baby Grand.'* I think I still had that on all of my electronic devices when the destruction began. And your name...I didn't put it together until this moment...what a sense of irony to call you Melody. I want you to know that Jacob Coen was one of my favorite axemen of all time. I'd have given anything to have seen him perform live...blues and jazz inspired me."

"The real irony is that I couldn't carry a tune if you gave me a bucket!" Melody laughed, then continued. "You may already know much of this story," Melody said, smiling.

Everyone around the fire urged her to the contrary and she settled into telling them how her great-great grandparents had fallen in love, with music playing a huge part of the connection between them. She related their short courtship, complete with the frustration of being separated by time and distance, followed by their engagement. She told them all about the night of their engagement, about the romantic surprise of having him flown in from New York for her show. She described his looks from photos she had seen of them, her tall, dark, and handsome Jacob Coen. And everyone already knew what his red-haired, green-eyed fiancée, Harmony Tipton, who would go on to be known to the world as simply 'Harmony', looked like from album covers and magazines. Nearly everyone around the fire had seen the photos, had heard the story, yet it was touching to hear it from the grandchild of that tragic couple. The tragedy of his short life made the story a sad one as she told them about Harmony's struggle after losing Jacob.

"She raised her son with the help of four loving and doting grandparents. Of course, music was destined to be a big part of Jake's life, but he also had his Coen grandparents, highly educated and successful people. Jacob's life could have been seen as charmed as he grew, treasured. But he wasn't always happy. His book was hard to read because he did talk about how he basically grew up without not only a father but a mother as well. Harmony was away more than she was present for most of his life and he felt her absence even when they were in the same room. It wasn't that he was complaining or feeling sorry for himself. He just used his loneliness to inspire the way he wanted to live his own life. He wanted to be a family man, not a musician; he wanted to spend time with his children. My grandfather said that he was the best father anyone could ever have asked for. My mother was a Coen. My father's last name is Dunning. I carry the hyphenation because I love both families.

"I'm sorry, I'm afraid I'm not very good at this story-telling thing." Melody stopped. "I really rush through it, I don't breathe life into it, like Declan. My characters fall flat. I don't do them justice."

"One thing we're going to have to work on, lovely lass," Declan told her, "is your self-debasement. We're all sitting here in awe of the fact that you can be so matter-of-fact about having such famous family and you're putting yourself down. Girl, you enthralled us!"

"I was listening to the modulation of your voice, Melody," Conner told her. "You may not be able to sing but when you read or tell a story, your voice is pleasant to listen to and you will make a wonderful teacher for the children. Are you not the least musically inclined?"

"Oh, no, I didn't say that. I just said that I can't SING," she laughed. "I can play nearly any instrument given a few moments alone with it! But, seriously, I play stringed instruments best. My favorite is the violin because it can be the voice of elegance on one hand and a toe-tapping, let your hair down fiddle on the other." Her eyes sparkled.

"The violin can reduce me to tears or make me want to dance."

"Does this mean we might have a round of fiddle music some night around the fire?" Declan asked, hopefully. "If it's a fiddle you need, we'll be sure to find one on our next trip to Denver."

"I'd love that!" Gwen said. "Maybe we can play instruments and sing and begin teaching the children guitar, perhaps drums, some woodwinds."

Pathogent smiled. "And Gwen is now planning our music curriculum. I'm all for music. When we're sure it's safe."

They all realized what he meant. Music would be heard for miles in these hills and they wanted to do nothing to draw the wrong kind of people to them. Until they knew it was safe, the music lessons might have to wait.

"Gayle," Conner said, "you haven't told us your story yet."

"Oh, it's late...let's save mine until another night. I am going to warn you, the story I've going to give you isn't pretty."

"We're not after pretty; we're just sharing to give a little piece of ourselves to the group."

*

The next day was the day they went into Denver to look for more survivors and Declan and Path again offered to take the trip. Declan wanted to find a library to do a little research in hopes of finding out more about the mystery of Denver's last days. Clint rode with them. He had already begun his project of clearing some of the streets and moving cars to parking lots. They marked cars that they had emptied of gasoline and he was beginning to tow them to fill lots around the shopping areas. Waiting for them at the Commons was another group, three adults and five children. As Pathogent explained what the others were doing, he offered them food that had been prepared back at the camp. Before taking people back to the camp, he liked to get to know them better, to assure himself that no one was troubled or even mentally unstable. He was delighted to find out that two of the three adults, one woman and one man, had been gardeners and knew a lot about plants. They went together to a feed store that Path had discovered on the edge of town and they went through seed sacks to find good things to grow.

"Can't go wrong growing greens," Zeke told Path. "They are easy to grow and provide better nutrition than nearly anything you can plant."

When they went to the library to pick up Declan, he was happy to meet more survivors, particularly those who could help them with their growing garden. After the introductions, he asked Path, "If you don't mind, can we make one more stop before going to get Clint?"

Path nodded and shrugged, "Sure, where to?"

"There's a music store about four blocks to the east," Declan told him.

Path smiled. "This wouldn't be a violin we're seeking, would it?"

"Of course! That and other instruments, let's face it, however dangerous it may be to give away our position, music would surely lift spirits, now, wouldn't it?"

They loaded the already crowded trailer with their finds. One of the newcomers, Janice, suggested that they take all of the recorders to introduce the children to music. She told them that she could play both guitar and banjo so they took several of each and Declan cradled a beautiful violin case in his arms rather than leave it to the elements.

Clint greeted the new arrivals and smiled, reporting the progress he had made. The other new arrival, Darren, expressed interest in helping him with this project and told them that he had operated heavy machinery in his "former life." He also suggested that he would be able to operate the machinery required for the burial detail, when they felt the time was right. Pathogent had explained to them their discoveries of bodies throughout Denver and they told him that every house they had entered as they came into Denver had the same yield, people who had died in their beds as if they had some terrible illness.

"It was a strange flu," Declan told them. "The newspapers at the library said that, because of isolation and relief efforts stretched to impossible limits, no medicines were developed to combat it and it swept through the city like wildfire. The elderly were hard hit and were the first to die from the disease. Others died from the complications, pneumonia, weakened hearts, and lungs. People who fled the city were dying en route to nowhere. The highways were clogged with those trying to get to somewhere safe when they heard of the bombings. I would wager they helped to spread that flu and that might account for many of the empty cities we encountered. At least we have a partial answer. We still don't know what happened to the parents of the children we found."

"We can only assume that the children were somehow immune or had survived being ill and had parents who did not," Path pondered. "We may never know."

On their arrival back at the camp, Declan presented Melody with the violin when she came to help unload the trailer. She was speechless at his thoughtfulness. She opened the velvet-lined Musafia case and picked up the rich, well-crafted, tone-wood violin, putting it to her shoulder and testing the strings with the bow. "Oh, it's beautiful!" she exclaimed. "The sound is so pure, this is a Strad...such a nice instrument! How did you know to choose this one?"

Declan smiled and said, "I just looked for the one that seemed the most like something you would play." He grinned. "And Janice said that this is smaller than most, more fitting for a young woman. Besides, the wood just looked so good, so rich."

"Rich is right, this violin is a gem!" Melody put her chin on the rest and tested the strings. She tapped the bow on each string to test the sound.

"Please give us a song!" Gwen urged.

To their amazement, after a few adjustments and a run through the scales, she gave them an impeccable and sweet solo version of Mendelssohn's *"Violin Concerto E Minor"* that brought tears to more than a few eyes. She played it without ego, unselfconsciously, strong and certain. She played for the music, in love with the sound, and completely transformed from the shy, awkward girl they were becoming used to. The sweet notes nearly burst into flame, they rose so high. It was like a special kind of magic to hear it here in the woods, in the middle of the day, instead of in front of a symphony orchestra. They watched in awe as the playing transformed the shy girl into a passionate and consummate performer. She smiled as she drew gasps from her newfound friends...then gave a sly wink, began to tap her foot and went from this powerful performance into a rousing and incredible *"Cliffs of Moher,"* enough to set any Irish foot to dance. Declan rewarded her with a huge grin and he pounded his arm across his chest in a salute to show her that she'd won his heart with this choice.

She played on, the children following her like a string version of a pied piper, and she led them to dance reels and bluegrass tunes. Many of those children would hold the memory of that day in their hearts forever, the day that their music lessons began with a dark-haired, gray-eyed sprite of a girl and a solitary violin that sounded for all the world like it filled the forest with rich trilling. They all danced around in circles, skipping, and hopping, and making up their own steps, filling the clearing with laughter and delight.

"I thought I was good on banjo," Janice declared, "but I'm nowhere near bein' in that gal's league."

Gwen watched with tears in her eyes. Yes, it was about the children...but it was also about the children of her children's children, her descendants, these beautiful adults who had managed to find her and fill her heart with hope, joy, and a sense of family. Path came up behind her and wrapped his arms around her, whispering in her ear, "Look at what we did, Gwennie! Look at them! Could you feel more proud? Could we be more fortunate? It was all about this, my love, and I could die happy now."

"There are so many more coming," she told him, "so many more talents and dreams and inspirations." She smiled, "Yes, this is happiness we were denied, but we have it now, my magician, we have it now."

*

The very next campfire, they encouraged Gayle to share. She had been a strong leader for the last group to come in from the west and they all wanted to know more about her background. "I've thought long and hard about how to tell my story. I decided to start a couple generations back, like the others, and then tell you about how our cross-country trip happened. Would I ever go back to the west? Not after what I have seen. You would have to carry me to get me to go there now. But, let me begin with the story of my choice. My story could be called a love triangle. I know it sounds crazy that I love putting it that way about the three most important people in my family tree, but were it not for that triangle, I would not be here today. Tommy Cooper and Felix Lesko fell madly in love in the late 1980s, having met in San Francisco at a party given by a mutual friend. Hester had been Felix's best friend since childhood. They had grown up together, gone to school together, and shared successes and heartaches. She adored Tommy because he made her best friend in all the world so happy. She pretty much dedicated her life to them because she had no real interest in pursuing her own heterosexual lifestyle after her own nightmare childhood of rape and molestation. She was pretty open about this, even wrote a book in an attempt to help other survivors. I had a copy in my library back home. It was so inspirational and well-written. Back home," she paused, thinking of all the things she had left behind in her struggle to survive.

"Tommy added color in more ways than just his racial identity. And his bright spirit added so much more to their lives when he moved into a Sacramento apartment with Felix. Hester rented the apartment above them to help them afford the payments on their condo. The three were inseparable, enjoying Sacramento nightlife, making many excursions to San Francisco, even taking vacations together. Planning and hoping for a future family together, the two men had donated sperm when they had met and fallen in love. The plan was to eventually find a surrogate for their future child. But, being wild, happy, and young, they decided to wait for a few years before having that perfect child. Then because of a horrible argument and misunderstanding, and rumors of cheating, they broke up for more than six months, and, guilt-ridden and heartbroken that he had hurt Felix so deeply, Tommy returned to his parents' home in Michigan.

"However, as most people who were meant to be together, they reunited when Felix flew to Michigan, urged to do so by Hester, of course, to see if he could convince Tommy to come back to California. They realized how deep their love was and how much they had missed one another. They buried their anger and pain and realized that they loved one another much too much to let go of their relationship. It was just shortly after this reunion that Tommy was physically brought down by what they thought was flu and pneumonia, nearly losing his job as they waited for him to feel well enough to return to work. Because Felix was an amazing provider, he wasn't as fearful about the loss of job as he was the toll it was taking on Tommy's body.

"At that time, all gay couples were aware of the epidemic proportions of the illness known as AIDS but they never really dreamed that it could be this that was making Tommy so ill. After tests were run, they found out that Tommy tested positive for HIV. It was frightening to the three of them how quickly his illness went from flu symptoms to full blown AIDS. And, yes, he deteriorated very quickly.

"You probably have already guessed that Hester came to them with an offer to bear their child, to be their surrogate. She honestly felt this was one way to show her love and devotion for her two best friends. And, she also saw this as an opportunity. Though she never wanted a sexual relationship with a man, she realized that she really had always wanted to be a mother. She was not doing this for entirely selfish reasons, don't get me wrong, she was doing this mostly for Felix, afraid that he would not be able to bear the loss of Tommy. Of course, because he was losing his beloved, Felix decided that it would be Tommy's sperm that they would use so that he would always have a little piece of his love with him. The three of them were over the moon when they found that Hester became pregnant.

"My grandfather, Thomas Cooper-Lesko, was born just before Tommy died and they had already decided to give him both last names. They couldn't ask for a better mother for their child than Hester. She was attentive, intelligent, capable, and gave their little boy as much love and guidance as any mother could give. Her determination to keep him safe from suffering a childhood wrought with fear and betrayal like her own, made her fiercely devoted to his happiness and joy. By that time, Hester had moved into the spare room with the baby so she could help Felix care for his beloved and so that Tommy could spend his last days with his son. The three of them had been by his side when Tommy gave up the fight. By that time, he was skeletal, completely wasted away. Photos of Tommy at that time broke my heart when I saw them. He looked like a Holocaust survivor, thin, wasted, skeletal, and in pain."

Pathogent touched Gwen's hair and rubbed her scalp gently. He knew that they were sharing the memories. That life was one of their most tragic together. Path had not Blinked out until Tommy's body died, able to stay with him until the end. Felix had been the model of devotion and love and he knew that these memories were hurting Gwen deeply to relive them.

"My grandfather once told me that his childhood was more like he had two mothers. Felix and Hester were both that involved in his childhood. They married to give him a sense of legitimacy. He was raised by two intellectuals, and was given the advantage of the best education, both outside and inside his home. If the stories and photos of Tommy affected me two generations later, imagine how they drove his career. He was accepted at Stanford and worked diligently to go into medical research. Growing up with full knowledge of the story of his father's suffering and pain, he was driven to eradicate any similar infection or disease. After his graduate studies, he joined the staff at Stanford and his team made ground-breaking advances into the study of auto-immune deficiencies and diseases. My father, his only child, was raised to think that the laboratory was his second home and followed closely in his own father's footsteps. He was interested in studies that postulated that there were links to brain injuries or trauma and auto-immune diseases and worked tirelessly to not only eliminate the effects of AIDS but to help those infected with HIV/AIDS to live normal lives with slight changes in diet, exercise and medications. We spent a lot of time in Africa, when I was a child. He believed that going to the source and even studying primates infected would help him to learn so much more about the spread of the virus. He was right and I learned so much at his elbow.

"Of course, my path was already pretty much laid out for me and I studied medicine. After witnessing my future first-hand, I started long-distance running in high school. It was my escape from the pressures that I knew faced me. I was prepared to commit my life to the studies that he started," Gayle told them, "but I saw what it did to him because he devoted his entire self to it. And I was determined to make sure that my body was not neglected by giving my mind to scientific study." She smiled. "And the running sure came in handy when crossing California and those mountains. I had entered Iron Man contests that were far worse than running along I-80 through the Sierras. However, having to run into the forest when encountering others made it a longer journey. And, there were times that I was literally running for my life as I crossed from the coast to the mountains.

"Another wry observation. Living on peanut butter for my protein made my muscles scream but I was glad to have it, despite how goddamn heavy those four jars were! Just before I hit the mountains, I found a Whole Foods store just off the highway in Roseville and, while it had already been hit pretty hard by looters, I was able to score the peanut butter and two coconuts, found a box of almond milk in the rubble, and the bulk food honey tin still had honey in it. I drained that into two of their nice, convenient plastic containers and that store is where I found Abi. She was hiding in the shipping and receiving area of the store where I went to look to see if there was any food in the storage rooms in the back."

She sighed, "Poor skinny little thing, she's only eleven but her poor young mind has seen too much and she is mentally seventy. After I convinced her that I had no plans to eat her, she told me her story: both parents succumbed to the outbreak of flu that hit after the first big quakes. Roseville was pretty much wiped out by the flu and the poisoning of their ground water because of the quakes and earlier fracking, a hideous practice by gas companies to force more gas from the ground. I read about that outbreak of the flu; when the coast also began to suffer, that virus decimated what was left of Oakland. But, back to Abi. She had been homeless for some time, which might have contributed to her survival. She definitely wasn't soft and helpless. Rummaging together, we found an entire box of unhusked coconuts. Now, I figured that they were just too much trouble for the average person to want to mess with, since they are hard to open. Most people don't even begin to know how. And coconuts can keep for a very long time until they are broken open. They can float in the ocean for years and still have fresh, clean milk within. They are filled with electrolytes, so this was better than finding canned food! I had a bicycle cart I was using as a wagon, easily done if you find a belt loose enough, so we loaded the trailer with coconuts and the peanut butter and a few other canned foods we could salvage. It was the most food I had seen in weeks and I assumed that people walking toward the coast out on 80 hadn't seen it from the highway. I only knew it was there because we had gone shopping at the nearby mall in Roseville, whenever we took trips up into the Sierras, so Roseville was a familiar stop to me.

"Anyway, we made it through the Sierras and that was treacherous, believe me, so many people walking west on that highway, so many detours into the forest. There were times I wanted to ditch the cart because we were travelling uphill at such a sharp incline. Abi wouldn't let me do that. She pulled it herself and I couldn't bear to see that little thing work so hard to save our lives. Cars and semis blocking the highway were just a tiny drawback compared to the climb and the people walking in the other direction. We saw no one else heading east. People were all heading the opposite direction. It seemed everyone thought that the coast would offer some answers. I had seen the coast and I knew that it was only going to steal their hope: death everywhere, a dead ocean. However, those walkers didn't seem as aggressive as the ones I had encountered in California. Perhaps they hadn't been as well-armed or desperate but I was happy that they left us alone for the most part. I wish I had had the courage to warn them about the danger they were headed toward. I did warn some of them but they assured me that I was equally crazy if I thought life would be better in the east.

"Winter was approaching and I was desperate to get us out of those mountains before the snow so I paced us pretty hard, and felt so very bad for poor Abi. We picked up Toby as we passed Tahoe, or rather, he picked us up...he followed us for about four miles before we were aware of his presence. He might have broken away from one of the groups heading west, or maybe his group had been killed. He never really told us and he doesn't communicate very well, for all his bright attitude. When I realized we were being followed, I sent Abi forward and I circled back. Imagine my surprise to find a seven-year-old boy tagging behind us. It was Abi who convinced him that he had nothing to fear from us. She did it with direct and forward brutality. 'If we had wanted to eat you, you'd already be dead.' He grinned at her and shot back, 'You don't know how fast I am!' So now we were three and we made it out of the mountains before the first major snowfall.

"The Cabela's outside of Reno had been hit pretty hard by looters but I found ammunition for my gun and found a small gun for Abi. We also found three knives and some canteens. That poor little bike trailer was getting pretty heavy to haul. I wish we could have found a bike but all the bikes and camping equipment were gone, nearly everything stripped. We only found the ammunition because we looked in a shoebox in the shipping area and, for some reason, someone had put ammunition in that box. Thank you, employee of the month!

"In Reno we found three more children, hiding together in what I first thought was a vacant house. Toby saw them watching us from a window...those sharp little eyes don't miss a thing. I learned to trust him when he scouted for us. Believe me, his vision is a phenomenon, seriously, he's like an eagle or a hawk! The three kids were terrified but Abi and Toby quickly calmed them down. I felt that the youngest was too small for the journey; she was just a baby, and I actually am ashamed that I found myself thinking about the burden and not wanting to take her with us. Abi stared at me for a long time. It seemed she could read my mind. She fashioned a sling out of a shawl she had found in a woman's closet, possibly the mother of the youngsters, and tied the baby to herself. Defiantly, she glared at me, daring an argument. The other children were seven and five. Crystal and Caleb. They told us that the baby was Constance. We gave the baby coconut milk and she downed it like it was ambrosia and the electrolytes revived her. That house was stocked full of canned goods by someone who was obviously expecting a second Great Depression, but the children were too small to know how to use anything but an electric can-opener, so they were literally starving in a house full of food.

"We stayed there two weeks, gaining back some of our strength. I buried Crystal's, Caleb's, and Constance's mother in the back yard. We found a family Bible in which their ancestry had been recorded in minute detail.

That mother wrote everything down for her kids, so we packed that in with their meager possessions for them to have in the future.

"I looked at the maps and decided that it was too risky to travel on I-80. People were still traveling west, despite the onset of winter. I knew that many of them would die in the mountains, as the Donner party had long ago. I chose to drop down to Carson City, then take 50 across Nevada. I never really had a destination in mind, but it was the best decision I could have made. We found Lily," she nodded at a woman across the fire from her, who smiled encouragement back at her, "and three more children, just west of Carson City in Silver Springs. Lily had been traveling west from Provo, Utah, and had picked up the kids along the way. Silver Springs was empty but gave us a great chance to rest and drink clean water from a deep underground well at a farmhouse, a well with an old-fashioned hand pump. I was never so happy to see technology shunned as I was when I stared at that old, rusty pump. And, that is where we found a truck with a full tank of gas, attached to a camper, parked in a barn behind the farmhouse. That barn was so well-supplied, we found portable gas cans, oil, spare parts and that damned, wonderful truck was sitting on brand- spanking-new tires! In honor of the gift they had given us, we buried the elderly couple who had once farmed that land. They died sleeping together, or perhaps had chosen to die that way, so we buried them together. It was the least we could do for pay them back for that precious truck and all the supplies they afforded us. Their pantry was stocked with canned goods. The old woman had canned her own and there were jars of delicious fruits, vegetables, and jams. It was a gold mine. We loaded every nook and cranny of the camper with food. Traveling was great from that point on. We siphoned gas from stalled and abandoned cars, sometimes having to leave the road to detour around logjams of cars on the highway, but it was a lot better than some of the other major highways...and the children were able to sleep and play in the camper. It was a luxury. I never let the tank get low. We became experts at siphoning gas. We kept three full gas cans in the back of the truck, just in case. We had learned to be expert hoarders."

"Thank goodness!" Gwen declared. "The back of your truck was a treasure trove when you arrived here. You had medicine, bandages, canned goods, guns...how on earth did you avoid being hijacked?"

"Lily was infantry in the army and learned to fire any number of weapons during the wars. She is deadly with a rifle, even more deadly with a high-powered semi-automatic. That is one very tough survivor," she smiled, and nodded at Lily, who blushed. "There were fire-fights. I learned a lot from her...not that we didn't suffer losses," Gayle said, struggling to keep her voice steady. "We buried two along the way.

"Crossing the Rockies was tough. I thought we were going to lose the truck four or five times, hauling that load, but it got us through. I'm almost as attached to that truck as any human. It saved our lives, I truly believe that. I don't know what made us head north at that point but, on the downhill slide of the Rockies, we were already talking about Boulder, maybe even Denver."

"You said you lost two, and I assumed they were two of the children...but you arrived here with sixteen children and four adults...."

"Yeah, I know...we were like the pied piper...children found us because of the other children, they trusted us because the children with us looked far healthier than any of us. We rescued three kids from a group of...um, you know...cannibals. But it was so deadly frightening, traveling through the flatlands. There were those who looked at our trailer full of children like it was a stock truck." She closed her eyes at the memory of being pursued for such an evil purpose. "The camper and the truck allowed us to keep on the move and we took turns sleeping while the other drove.

"Luckily we had found Dave back when we passed through Provo, Utah. Lily had known him from when she lived there. She had encountered him many times in the Provo park and she already considered him a friend and trusted him and was overjoyed to find he'd survived. He had been homeless since his return from the war, was skilled at survival, as well as guns, and had no desire, whatsoever, to allow anyone to steal the kids. One of the first places he took us to was a gun shop where we loaded up with more ammunition and weapons. His prime directive has become a mission to protect those children." She smiled at Dave, who was sitting a little aside from the rest. "I love you, Dave." She turned toward the others. "He's been like an adoptive grandfather to them. I don't know what we would have done without him, he's a genius at calming down panicked children and a dead shot with a gun. Stephanie was our last adult find. She came to us in Pueblo, Colorado. Found her sitting all alone at the bus station as if she was waiting on a bus. She's a pediatric nurse...talk about luck, huh?" Stephanie smiled, embarrassed by the description of her futile waiting on a bus, alone in a dead city, alone and defeated.

"When we met up with Declan and Path in Denver, I thought we were dreaming when they told us about this place. When I got here, I pretty much collapsed with joy, it's so beautiful here and there are more good people and children every day. It was so wonderful to be able to relax for the first time in months," she said, smiling. "But I still jump at every sound out there." She nodded toward the woods.

"What sounds out there?" Path asked softly.

"For the last five, ten minutes, I've been hearing sounds...soft ones...thought it might have been one of you guys returning from relieving yourselves."

"No one has left the campfire," Dave whispered. "And the kids are all in that direction," he nodded toward the cabins. Dave slowly stood and, his hand on his pistol, quietly melted into the forest. Everyone was tense as Path followed Dave into the darkness surrounding them. The two men returned moments later with huge smiles on their faces. "Bat ears." Dave turned to Gayle and he grinned like a child on Christmas morning. "What you heard may save us all...deer...a whole herd of them...sneaking quietly through the woods."

Everyone around the fire gave a huge sigh of relief, relieved that there was no intruder or threat, and relieved that animals had, indeed survived.

"The canopy of forest must have protected them from the fall-out," Dave announced. "And if they were protected, there may be other species...elk, mountain goats...what lives in the Rockies? Hell, the Rockies have so many different kinds of mammals, Gwen may get to hear wolves again, yet. I heard that there were some on the northern Rockies that had broken away from the Yellowstone packs. Don't know if it's true, but it would be great if they found their way here." At the thought of one of the most famous of America's parks, he added, sadly, shaking his head, "I doubt much is left in Yellowstone. That eruption was pretty damned decimating. The forests melted down."

"I wonder if people are moving north from Mexico?" Melody wondered aloud.

"Honey, didn't you hear?" Stephanie told her, with a voice full of anger and frustration. "That goddamned religious zealot in the White House destroyed South America and Mexico with nukes. Why? Because of the 'sinfulness and debauchery' in Rio de Janeiro and drug cartels in Mexico. Apparently that creep was so freakin' bad at geography, not to mention common sense, that he didn't realize that Rio is just one city on an entire continent full of good people and the cartels did not make up the entirety of Central America. I think his warped brain actually believed that he was put here to cleanse the earth of sin and start it all over with his holy seed. When he went off the deep end, he just started pushing buttons. By then, there was nothing anyone could do. The military protected him. Of course, as a Texan, his 'excuse' was that he was really just looking for a way to stop immigration and please his hateful constituency. And that monster's solution was pretty fucking permanent." She grimaced. "For all we know that maniac is still alive down there in his bunker pressing buttons and sending nuclear warheads all over the world. At least most of his 'constituency' took the fallout." Melody reached to take Stephanie's hand to calm her down. At first, Stephanie resisted. She had her own trust issues. Then she allowed the gentle touch and smile of reassurance.

"The Middle East had already ceased to exist before the first major quakes and floods. And that, too, was his fault," Conner nodded in agreement. "He killed our own, HIS own, troops over there when he dropped those bombs. He hit the Muslims because he hated Muslims, but he wasn't any kinder to Israel. He wiped it off the map before they could respond with their own nukes."

"Who nuked us, then?" Stephanie asked. "I mean, we know that there were bombs dropped on the east coast and down south. If the Middle East didn't do it...we stopped getting news right about then.

"I thought it was wise of those who wanted to impeach him and bring sanity back to the situation, but, by then, Congress was already as evangelistic and crazy as he was and he held the strings that controlled the Pentagon. The response came from China or what was left of China, and the backlash was brutal, countries that weren't even involved were laid waste. For all we know, there are really only parts of Europe and parts of this country with life remaining. He would have had no reason to bomb Europe...well, I shouldn't say that, after all, he did bomb Canada...when communication ended, when television, even the internet went blank, I actually felt that it was because his 'government' didn't want us to know just how far he had gone. I would not doubt that he has pretty much destroyed much of the world...and the earth fighting back with quakes, floods, and volcanic activity has destroyed even more."

"Africa, I think Africa may still be there, there may still be life there," Gwen added. "I don't think they ever really saw Africa as a threat. They had already caused mass killings in that country when their missionaries went there preaching hatred and intolerance. I think Congress thought of Africa as a winning situation, their evangelistic success story. Africa was becoming more evangelical than states in the southern United States, and that is going some. Africa may still be intact. I hope the animals come back."

"I hope the animals come back strong and kill most of the people!" Stephanie declared, then put her head down. She couldn't control her anger, had tried very hard to control it, since meeting Gayle and her group may have saved her from certain death, but she wasn't quite sure that they had saved her sanity in time. Every day was a struggle not to break into rage in front of the children. Dave often took her aside to talk to her, to calm her and keep her from frightening the children. Gayle had given her sedatives but even those didn't hold the anger at bay.

"I was afraid of this," Gayle admitted. "I knew that my story would bring us down, and now we are here talking about the recent past and every time I think of it, my hope starts to drain away."

Lily got up from her place and went to console Gayle. She wrapped her arms around her and soothed her like a child.

"Yes, let's change the subject and talk about our strengths," Gwen agreed. "During your story, Gayle, I couldn't help but think about a couple of those children I see as pillars of strength, already showing signs of being leaders among the children: Abi and Toby and maybe even Crystal, so that would make three. With all that they have seen and witnessed, those kids have really shown strength and intelligence that makes me feel that they have strong potential as future teachers."

Lily nodded, "Abi has been amazing, even when we lost two of the children, she kept the others from hysteria, and told them stories and tended them so that we could concentrate on burials and finding food, water, and shelter. I don't know what that girl has in her, but she's got the mettle of a soldier!" Dave nodded vigorously in agreement. She continued, "And Toby and Crystal both act so much older than they are. Crystal, perhaps, because of her elder child status, but Toby is a clever little monkey, very mechanically inclined, and like a sponge. If you have anyone who could work with him, he could probably learn to take an engine apart and put it back together after seeing it done just once. He has a communication problem. Perhaps he's got a touch of Asperger's, but he only needs to see things once to understand how they work. There's genius in that."

Shawnee chimed in, "Yellow Feather is the leader of our group of children. All the others defer to him; he's been a great help. But the most amazing thing about that child is what appears to me to be ancient wisdom that he carries with him. It's as if he has lived before."

Path looked into Gwen's eyes and just the corner of his mouth lifted. They communicated silently, but Path made a mental note to talk to Yellow Feather to see if there were a chance that he was a traveler. He nodded at their silent agreement and added, "David and Cassie kept the other three children in their group alive for two years. They practically raised Tyler, Geoffrey, and Raven. I see great strength in them. This group of children has some true survivors."

Melody smiled and told them, "Our strong one is Jenna. She is like an old spirit as well. She kept them all in line crossing the country. I was so glad that she was among the first that Declan had found. As we added more children, she seemed to just take charge, keeping them from hysteria, already beginning to teach them."

Conner turned to the youngest adult around the fire, seated to his left, "And Josh here has proven himself time and again. You sure seem a lot older than I felt at thirteen, Josh." He smiled and nodded approval. The young man in question smiled, poking the fire with a stick. He blushed, but kept his ugly memories at bay, not wanting to bring up the un-pleasantries that had aged him. He squelched the memory of almost falling into the hands of cannibals in Cincinnati, Ohio. Had it not been for Conner and Clint...but, it had been too late for his brother, Todd.

Dave noticed how uncomfortable Josh seemed under scrutiny. Empathetically, he grinned, "I'm with you there, Josh, I don't want to talk about my past either. Don't think you're going to get a story out of me. I am the happiest I've ever been in my whole, entire, sorry life right here and now. I don't ever want to look back over my shoulder to relive the life I've led, and I never really knew my parents so I don't have an ancestor tale. There is something I wanted to bring up, however. I have been a loner for a long time and I don't want you to think I'm rejecting y'all's company by sleeping off by myself. It was just a habit hard-learned by being homeless in an increasingly violent world. I trust the people here, but I feel more alert and more useful when I'm out there...away from the cabins."

"Our first line of defense," Gayle grinned at Dave. "Your habits saved my life, and I will give my life to defend your right to them."

"Speaking of sleeping arrangements," Path smiled and rose to his feet, then helped Gwen to hers, "I think we'd better turn in, or at least those of us who are on the breakfast team in the morning. We've got a lot of pancakes to prepare! And, those kids rise with the dawn."

"Ooooo, don't forget about those jars of pear juice we found," Melody said, smiling, "a good dose of fruit with breakfast will strengthen us for the day ahead of us! We've got a garden to enlarge and I want the children to do much of the gardening. It is, after all, something they need for the future. I think we should make it like...you know...part of the curriculum."

As everyone left the fire, few noticed that Declan had reached up to take Melody's hand as she was leaving. She turned in surprise, then sat back down at his bidding. "Let's talk about this attraction everyone seems to think you have for me," he whispered. As she started to protest, he put a finger over her lips and added, "Because I wanted to let you know that it is entirely reciprocated."

Her huge pale gray eyes showed surprise and, behind his finger, her smile grew. "Really?" she breathed, her heart pounding. She stared into his eyes and her own eyes told him everything that he needed to know. She tried hard to work up courage not to seem nervous. Why couldn't she be confident and collected like Shawnee? Why did she have to be so goofy?

"Entirely," he assured her. "I know it's too soon, after all we've been through. I just wanted to let you know that I'm hoping we can spend more time together, get to know one another." He rubbed his thumb around her palm and turned it over to kiss the back of her hand. "You have such an air of sweet, sweet innocence about you."

She snorted, "And here I was just wishing that I could be more calm and sophisticated. I feel clumsy and self-conscious all the time...it's so annoying."

He grinned. "I find it charming, refreshing. You remind me more of the girls back home in Ireland, if there still is an Ireland. I have a problem with sarcastic, sophisticated, modern girls. They intimidate me. I hope you don't sincerely want to change. I adore the way you blush, the way you sometimes hold back...you're sweet, unspoiled, the world needs that now, everyone is so serious...we have a mission to teach the children to have fun, to play, to blush, to feel awkward yet accepted. You and I are more child-like in our demeanor. We can relate to them and teach them to leave the ugly past behind and be children again. Even if I'm only acting, I'm going to pretend that the world is safe and good and fun, so that they can have fun."

"Thank you for saying that. I was thinking about that just today. The children are becoming robotic, afraid to explore, watchful, and wary. We need to provide them with enough security to begin to play again, to stop acting so hunted. They need to be children. We need to take them out into the woods, let them turn over rocks, pretend to be pioneers, cowboys, Indians. They may never lose that haunted and hunted feeling, but we have to give them some 'safe space' surrounded by adults to protect them. They need to be able to let loose their regained energy."

"Now, I know that you're sleepy. I was watching you almost nod off during the stories," he teased, "but I would really like to kiss you. I'd dare not without asking."

She leaned forward and her lips stopped his final words. The kiss was sweet and good and felt right to them both. He smiled and cupped her face in his hands, then helped her to her feet and they walked together toward the cabins, both feeling lighter in the heart than they had in months, even years. Hope can be a healer.

Before she entered the cabin she shared with Mary and Lisa, she turned to him. "Wait," she put a hand on his chest, "I never really got the chance to tell you just how much your remembering about the violin meant to me. I, I can't even begin to express what music does for my soul, just holding that beautiful instrument in my hands restores me."

He pushed a stray strand of hair back from her face and lifted her chin, "And just seeing and hearing you play, watching the grace with which you handle that violin, seeing the magic of your being able to pull those notes out of the air. Lass, I was already falling in love. That moment sealed my fate." As he talked, he leaned closer toward her lips. "It was restorative to me, too, and I became more your slave with each note." His lips moved gently against hers and he put his hands on her waist and pulled her close against him.

Melody's mind was spinning. She had been in love with this man since the first week that she joined his group back in Kentucky. It had seemed a dream to hope that he felt the same way. Their struggles for survival put all other thoughts on hold but she always felt that to expose her feelings about him would make him feel obligated or would make things awkward between them. Now her spirits soared. He loved her, he returned her love in kind. For the first time in several years, she was filled to the brim with a new sense of hope and purpose. She would make him happy. They would find a way to make every moment filled with joy.

He smiled and started to leave her to go to his cabin.

"Wait!" she whispered. "Maybe it's time to claim a cabin of our own."

*

In their own cabin, Path confided in Gwen, "I have to talk to you about this, my mind is still spinning from what I have discovered this week. Dave got me alone to talk a couple days ago. He let me know that he's a traveler, too. He has known us in many of our lives. He said that he was a fruit vendor in London in the 1400s and sold fruit to a starving young woman who was your spitting image. He had grinned. He knew it was you. He also was a paramedic who watched you die in an auto accident. He attended the Tiptons' wedding anniversary celebration, as one of Max's best friends, when you sang and I proposed. Gwennie, he was my best friend back in Michigan when I was Tommy. He knew where he was in each of the stories being told around the fire, including his time as a Scottish fisherman who took a father and his bonny daughter across the strait to Ireland."

He sat on the bed and watched her as she combed her hair, then rose to his feet, took the brush from her and brushed those beloved red locks.

She stared at him in the mirror and smiled, then sighed, "And I was waiting to tell you about Layla. You may have known her as Mrs. Dowling, Edward's favorite head housekeeper. She was also my aunt in Ireland and she was Jill, Sophie's partner....oh, Path, she has been so very close to us both! She was Hester. She gave birth for Tommy and Felix; she ran the pub where Kaitlynn and Brendan Donnelly often celebrated, sometimes hid out. She said she was the Coens' maid and watched you grow into a handsome young man...AND, she was your attending nurse in Kenya."

"I don't know about you, my love, but I am beginning to see that our lives were all intertwined with others, much more than we knew. Perhaps we were always recognizable to one another because we were, at once, in the bodies of ancestors or descendants. It boggles the mind, but I kept another discovery for last. Yellow Feather...we have known him before." He paused, knowing that she would guess correctly.

"Tecumseh?" she breathed in awe. "Omigod, she found him in Oklahoma."

"Yes, he was, indeed, reborn Shawnee, just as his people thought he would be. We may get the privilege of watching him grow. You do not have to worry about the future, our little community, our tribe...will have its leader."

"How on earth did you find out?" She had to know. "How do you begin a conversation that ends with such an earth-shaking revelation?"

"He came to me and asked if we could talk far away from the others. We took a long walk through the woods, saw where the deer had passed the other night. He showed me scat and we decided that it was probably raccoon, then he found the tracks and verified it. We walked for a long while and followed a river up the mountain. There is life here, Gwennie! We saw fresh water, fish; we saw rabbits.

The canopy did protect the wildlife here. The earth will regenerate if the volcanic activity levels off. We talked about many things and I know that I was gaining his trust. We sat deep in the woods and he drew it out of me: I talked to him of former lives. I have never told anyone about the Blink, never revealed to anyone aside from you that we traveled through time, yet, somehow I was telling him bits and pieces of my past. He listened, not like a boy, not like a boy who is barely ten, but like a man, a thoughtful, insightful, wise man. He told me of his 'travels'. He remembered ancient times, truly ancient, like Paleolithic times. He remembers hunting mammoth. He could remember the sounds they made, the steam of their breath as they ran. He had traveled to the future, was a writer of fiction in the late 1970s; he had lived in Los Angeles. I'd even been in the neighborhood he described. He then started talking about Tippecanoe and the Ohio lands near the Scioto...he said the Shawnee word for the Ohio River, do you remember it?"

She breathed it, "Spaylaywitheepi." She closed her eyes. How long it had been since she had spoken Shawnee? But it came back to her like a long-forgotten friend.

He smiled. "Then he said, 'but you know this because you were there with me.' And I realized that we had stopped speaking English to one another and were conversing in Shawnee. Gwen, he told me about his many lives but when we talked about that time, we talked as old friends. It was an experience that shook me to the core. I knew, I knew then who I was talking to and the smile we shared was so full of understanding and our deep connection, the friendship we had always shared during our life together.

"Now, he and I have talked about this and you must remember, we have to allow him his childhood. We have to treat him no differently than the other children. They will grow with him and trust him but he does not want us to set him apart, to make something special of him."

"It will be so hard, when he could lead us right now," she nodded. "But I understand what he is saying. Oh my god, Path, this is amazing, it's like all of our lives and those we've known are crisscrossing one another."

"He explained to me that it is part of the wheel, part of the continuity of things, that our pasts may cross our futures many times, that the circle is not just a hoop, but concentric circles joined to the lives of others who are living their hoop. It's complicated, but for some strange reason, in light of what we have discovered, it makes sense. It finally all makes sense to me: we were the ancestors of so many of these people with us today and possibly many of the children, but the children wouldn't have the memories or the research to have established that. That is why so many of them have our features, our looks...and that is why so many of those we 'occupied' were so like us."

He brought his head down to kiss her forehead as she leaned back. "We can go into the forest with him occasionally to talk, but we did discuss telling the others about the hoop, about the regeneration of life, the traveling, whatever we want to call it. He discussed this with me. We were both worried about the establishment of religion and what it had done to his people, meaning the Shawnee...remember what a zealot his brother had become? And we talked about the government in this country leading up to the bombings and holocaust it became, and we all know where a lot of that began, the zealotry of evangelism. Religion invading government to the point that Congress and the White House were filled with zealots who justified their evil deeds as God's direction. We wonder if we should tell our complete tale to the young adults, let them know that we know of their roots."

"Some of them may believe that we made it up after hearing their own legacies," she suggested.

"Then we give them details that we could not have known, describe their grandparents' houses, something to make them believe. Details that we will pull from our memories. With David and Layla's help, we should be able to convince them. By the way, he doesn't want us to worry about the children. He's going to work on it within their ranks. He wants us to teach them things they will need: music, reading, math, science, mechanics...with more children coming in each day, he'll have his hands full."

"Why is he so worried about religion? What if it gives motivation, comfort?" She sighed.

"Am I talking to Gwen, the eternal atheist?" Path teased.

She smiled up at him, taking his hand and rising to her feet. "My lack of faith was always a problem for you before. Don't you remember how often we had philosophical discussions about your faith that this hoop...this 'traveling'...the Blinks had purpose, reason, a system?"

"And I still believe that," he laughed. "Why is it that when I'm talking to him, I can see this so clearly, but when you and I discuss it..."

She smiled, "Because I'm the skeptic who had a true awakening when this entire thing started to unravel. Perhaps that's the wrong word. To 'reveal itself' to me, the connections, the fact that something deep, something within their DNA was bringing them to us. He's not suggesting we use magic tricks to convince them?"

He grinned, "After what they've been through, he doesn't think that will be necessary. I don't think it will be necessary. They believe in us. They think of us as the core, the reason they came here. The very fact that we were preparing for their arrival."

"We were, weren't we? We were preparing bunks for a hundred or so, not just for our small group. We were packing away supplies for an army, not just a handful of children."

He yawned, "We'll sleep on this and talk more about it later. Right now we need the comfort of one another and some really good sleep."

As he wrapped his arms around her to embrace her, she winced over his shoulder where he could not see her pain. She felt fragile right now and tried to tell herself that the electrical charges in the atmosphere were because of the elevation. But she knew better in her heart.

*

Three days later, just before dawn was breaking, the boy came to walk with her. She went into the forest to see if she could find any sign of animals other than the deer, the fish, and the rabbits that Path reported. She was not surprised that he had joined her but she didn't see how he was able to slip away from the other children without any of them following, since so many of them shadowed him everywhere he went. Suddenly he was beside her and returned her smile as they climbed beyond the spring, beyond their normal boundaries.

They walked farther than she had been before in her explorations, following a stream up the mountain. Both of them were almost deliriously happy when they worked their way up over a high rocky ledge near a small waterfall and came upon a pretty sizeable lake. The sun had not yet cleared the horizon and a mist hung over the water. It seemed surreal, almost as if they were having a simultaneous dream. The water sparkled diamonds off the surface as sunlight hit the still water.

They stood and stared at it for a long time, neither of them moving, both of them scarcely able to believe their eyes.

His smile to her told her what she was daring to hope, that the water was clear and clean, that the lake was not poisoned by pollution, or the atmosphere. He pointed to the opposite side where a forest of Aspen came almost to the water's edge. There was a deer drinking.

"It's absurd...but do you want to know the first thought that went through my mind as soon as we saw that it was clear and sizable?" she asked.

"Tell me," he said, quietly, his eyes exploring for sign of beaver, muskrat, water birds. He knelt in the mud to see if he could find signs of life.

"No more sponge bathing!" she said, embarrassed and shook her head. "I want all the children to come and play and swim and wash their hair!"

He laughed. "I don't find that absurd. You are always thinking of us, how to make things better for us. Our hygiene has always been a concern of yours. I also think it wise that all the children learn how to swim and swim well. Could you talk to some of the adults about that? This lake is very much alive. There are fish. I can see them feeding on the insects. See there? I hear birds. I think there are birds very near but they are staying in the canopy. They are not sure if it is safe to leave the protection of the trees yet. And here...see this...possum and raccoon. Both watered here. Think about how much life there might be deeper into the mountains. This is why we are no longer wading in the bodies of insects."

They decided to circle the lake for a while. Even though they both knew that it would take several hours, they could still be back at camp before breakfast ended. He wanted to see if there were other animal trails leading to the water. He pointed out that the mountains were still very much alive, the thick forest canopy had saved many animals, the deer trail to the water also produced sign of a bobcat and several foxes. He told her that he and Dakota had seen coyote tracks on one of their explorations.

He was excited when they reached a marshy area and pointed something out to Gwen. "See those grasses growing in the marsh? Do you know what they are?"

"No, should I know?" she wondered.

"That's wild rice!" he told her. "I can still remember how people used bull boats to harvest wild rice. Maybe we can fashion something to serve. They would bend the grasses over the rounded bull boats and beat the blades to release the rice into their boats. There is enough here to fill many boats!"

"What about those round sleds we saw in the sporting goods store? Would those work?" she wondered, trying to picture what he explained to her.

He grinned. "Gwen, you're a genius! We could just wade in there and use those sleds as bowls to catch the rice."

She was happy to have thought of something so simple and yet so unrelated to the task. They continued their explorations.

When they stopped to rest, Yellow Feather wasted no time and asked softly, "How long do you have?" Her shock must have shown on her face because he reached to take her hand. "Path doesn't see it because he doesn't want to. You remember that feeling, but I think he knows deep down in his heart. Why do you think he began sending others into Denver to do what he once took as his duty? He does not want to waste a moment of time that he could be spending with you. Tell me what you want us to do."

"I want you all to survive and keep these beautiful children safe. There were twenty more who found their way to the Commons last night, and they had no adults with them. The oldest was only fourteen. We put them together in dormitory four, the smaller ones sharing bunks. Imagine being fourteen and brave and strong enough to lead that large of a group." She sighed and turned to him. "I want to know...is this my last, my final incarnation? Will this body, this one so very me, so much my very own...when this body dies, will I die with it?"

"Gwen, why do you think that I will know the answers to your questions? I can tell you what I think. I cannot tell you what I know, because I do not know. I have no greater knowledge than you. I have only the memories of what I have lived, what I have thought, to guide me. I think that our energy will continue to regenerate, as it always has. You may go back in time. We may repeat all of our cycles, and then," he smiled, "we may be walking out there, in another universe, we may walk in the stars...whatever that future may hold, we who are left behind will still have to go on, but it will be so hard for so many. You have touched so many lives. Walk on knowing that you were loved, and with no greater love than his."

"Will you help him? He doesn't do well, he has never done well when I went first...." she said, through a curtain of tears.

"Of course, we will all help him, give him purpose. Gwen, this should be the least of your worries, he is as loved by all as you are, he will never need to face this alone. How much time do you have?"

"I don't know that."

"Of course you do, you have always known, even when you pushed it from your mind," he told her, "there are times you have said to yourself, 'I should have expected,' but you actually did, you just rejected the signs. You timed it almost perfectly when you found out about Tommy's illness, didn't you? You could read the signs, and it allowed him to see his child before he died. You have much more knowledge and power and vision than you think."

"Maybe a month," she sighed. "Not much more than that. I don't know what it is but it's a stronger pain this time. Lacking x-rays and tests, I can only guess." They were silent for a while and he gave her the gift of not having to talk, time to think.

"May I ask you something personal?" She looked into his eyes, "May I ask what your chosen name is? As Path and

I have our chosen names, did you have a name that you most closely related to, your inner identity?" She smiled and squeezed his hand.

"Other than the name my father, Pucksinwah, and my mother, Methotasa, called me? Other than Tecumseh?" he asked. He seemed to think for a long time on this and she realized that he was reliving many of his lives in his mind. Then he looked deep into her eyes and gave her his chosen name. She closed her eyes and smiled, she had already known it, somehow, it was the translation of the word Tecumseh, Panther crossing the sky, or simply, shooting star.

Shooting star.

"Shooting Star, I was cruel in several of my lives," she admitted. "I am so ashamed when I think back on those times."

"Circumstances often make us do things that we regret. I fought in many wars, and shared many skins of many shades, and I exhibited my own share of cruelty, even when it appalled me. Are you thinking that you have to make restitution, Gwen? I don't think that I find that something we need to worry about. Look how many lives you have saved, look at the good you have done."

"Don't worry, I'm not going to go 'religious' on you, my friend," she smiled, "but I do hope that the fact that I am aware of my capacity to be cruel will change that in my next...IF there are lives to come."

"I know that there are beliefs that embrace reincarnation as being a way to work toward a state of grace, or a nirvana. I find that I can be a hero in one life, villainous in the next, so I have a hard time embracing that theory," he told her. Even while they talked, though he gave her words all of his attention, his eyes were seeking life-sign from the forest floor, from the soil around them. "Remember, there are two of us in here for much of those lives," he tapped his head. "Should you take full responsibility for the cruelty that other person would have committed with or without your presence? I have been in the body of someone so warped and twisted that I spent every moment waiting for what you and Pathogent call the Blink, feeling soiled and degraded and evil because the mind I shared the body with had thoughts I could not abide."

She had never considered that possibility and, when he voiced it, it hit her that her own ego did not allow her to consider that the person she occupied might have, at times, been in control of her deeds and that Path, as simply a witness to those deeds, had not known or felt the difference. She smiled, "It almost seems like 'the devil made me do it', like excusing the actions." Then she remembered being pushed out of control by Felix, when he wanted to tend Tommy himself, when he needed to say good-bye in his own way.

"What could you have done? You were not in control at the time. I am sure there was an internal battle, but the stronger wolf won," he stated, simply and clearly, using a tale familiar to many Native American children. "Gwen, those of us who know you realize that there could never have been a time that you were evil; it's just not innate in you. So, if there were deeds done while you occupied an evil person, you were definitely pushed down to achieve them. And I am also certain that it was a difficult battle for the other."

"How is it that I just knew that I would feel better just being able to talk to you again?" she sighed.

"I wish that I had the power to make you feel better, physically, but I'll be content with easing your emotional pain," he told her, smiling. "Now, shall we organize a bath for those little dirty ones? It will be cold, summer is later here in the mountains, but it will feel so refreshing!"

"I'm sure the adult dirty ones will feel better, too!" she laughed. "They will probably be full of gratitude for this discovery."

*

Everyone celebrated the day, the swimming, the bathing, feeling refreshed and rejuvenated, it was a day of smiles and hope. The fact that the mountains might be teeming with wild animals made them all smile. The adults anticipated the campfire for sharing the excitement of their day. It was a happy group that was meeting around the campfire when all the children were finally tucked in and safe in their cabins.

Path led the conversation into talking about religion. He asked if anyone were strong in their faith. He and Gwen were not surprised to find that this group was far more secular than they could have hoped. They talked about reincarnation and most of the group scoffed at the idea and equated the belief to believing in alien landings and Big Foot and chupacabra. It caused a long moment of indecision for both Gwen and Path.

"I knew you were coming here," Gwen told them.

"You sure did seem to," Conner agreed. "I mean, how did just two people and a little group of kids get all that bedding ready, all the food laid up, secure the armory? How did you do it?"

"Determination," she smiled at him. "And I knew that you'd be coming in small groups; but what Path and I didn't realize is," she paused, unsure of her next step, then she plunged forward, "we didn't realize that so many of you would be so closely related to us."

Several of the young people were squinting, thinking hard about what she might mean by this statement. They all seemed very aware of who their relatives were and none of them had ever remembered meeting Gwen or Path before coming to Colorado. Melody was the first to speak, while the others were biding their time, trying to find a comment that might fit. "Gwen, I am really not sure that I understand what you are telling us. I know that you're not a Coen. Are you a Dunning? Was I one of the people you feel related to?"

"This is going to be very hard," Pathogent looked to Gwen and tried to add to her lead, "I know that this is going to be very hard for you all to accept. It will sound crazy. I am sure that it's going to sound as if Gwen and I are trying to blow your minds, but we haven't really thought of a way to tell you."

"We could begin by my telling them that I have known Gwen and Pathogent in many of my lives, in the past, in the recent past, and in the far distant past," Dave stated, offering support. "You see, folks, there really IS such a thing as reincarnation. Many of you probably have reincarnated, you simply don't remember each life, but there are a few of us who do. I am one of them. Some of us call ourselves travelers, movies insist on calling us time travelers. Gwen and Path call the feeling when they flip from one person to another person, and another era as the Blink. I knew them both in the past, and I'm not the only one. Layla is a traveler, too, and she's been a closer figure in many of their lives." He nodded at Gwen and Path. "There you go, my friend, I pushed the ticket for you. Now, let them have the details." He turned to Path and smiled.

"Let me get this straight, if I understand what you were alluding to, Gwen. You think many of us came here because we felt the pull of our relationship to you?" Declan mused. He was staring at Gwen and could see that she was sincerely struggling to make them understand.

"In another life, in my longest and happiest time with Path, I was called Sabd and he was named Nuadu, Declan." She sighed at the look of doubt on his face and struggled, then brightened, "And, much later, I was also Kaitlyn Donnelly. I was a fighter, and a bloody good one, but I carried a wound into my old age. I had been hit by a bullet in the right thigh and limped throughout my life. It never really healed properly and caused me a lot of pain."

Declan's eyes widened dramatically, then he sputtered. For the first time in his life, he found himself unable to talk and sat back to think.

Path looked at Melody. "My parents, Catherine and Saul Coen, lived in Cleveland where he was a doctor and she a professor of women's studies. My mother had a sweet red Alfa Romeo 1900 SS Cabriolet that she drove everywhere. I loved that car! If family pictures survived, there were many taken of us at Lake Erie on vacation. She was a fashionable woman. In the photos she was wearing a huge straw hat to protect her skin from the sun, a bathing suit, and a long silky wrap, tied around her waist; he wore a suit, even on vacation, even at the beach. I was a little squirt in a bathing suit, kneeling in front of them, and I was holding a puppy, a cocker spaniel named Teddy. We were posed in front of the car, squinting into the sun. Uncle Ezra took the photo; he was there with his fiancée, who later became Aunt Rachel."

"I had that picture," said Melody, her voice fading to nothing. And that was all she was able to say.

Gwen smiled at Shawnee and said, "I know that you can imagine our surprise when you told our story. Path and I were Eastern Woodland Shawnee and moved from Tippecanoe to what would become South Dakota in 1819, having given up on being able to find peace with the whites. Our adoptive family were so kind. The father of the family that took us in and helped us to become one with the Teton Sioux, where your cousins migrated from, were Lame Bear and his woman, Shaking Tree. Shaking Tree made a medicine bag to give to me for my future children. Because of her skill with the craft of beading, it would have been a family treasure. It was in the shape of a wolf. She knew my love for them. In the bag was a piece of Ohio flint, a small bit of Catlinite from a trade I made in Tippecanoe, and a lock of hair, my husband's hair, Path's hair, though he was called Siginak. I imagine that you already know that means Raven."

Shawnee put a hand to her chest. Under her shirt, on a leather strap, hung the fetish, handed down from generation to generation of her family, a treasured, almost holy, keepsake. "Oh, Gwen. Grandmother," Shawnee breathed.

"Conner," Path addressed the Englishman and smiled, "your family probably had the most amazing horses for many generations. The stables were behind the summer kitchen and rested in the lee of a hill so that they stayed cool in the summer and were protected from cold in the winter." Path pulled out some paper and a pencil and wrote numbers for a minute, then continued. "Your 19th great-grandfather's favorite horse, back in the late 1400s, the one in the painting that hung in their grand entryway was a sorrel mare, not the prettiest of his horses, but his favorite, nonetheless. He called her Dowager, after King Edward's Queen and widow. That painting hung next to his for many years. It may not still be there."

Gwen added, "It might be near the portrait of Edward's lady...me. The painting was done right after her coming out to society. She wore a green silk gown with high tufted sleeves, a daring, plunging neckline. His grandmother had given her a pearl pendant to wear. It was lovely and simple. Her red hair stood out in the painting, that and her green eyes. That one may not be there, either."

"But it was when I left England," Conner said softly, smiling at Path, smiling at his ancestor. "All three paintings still hung in the entryway."

Gwen smiled and her glance moved to the person seated at Conner's left. "And Gayle," Gwen began.

"Allow me, please," Layla offered, fighting back tears. Gwen realized fully why Layla wanted to deliver this one, and smiled in agreement, nodding. Layla wiped tears and began, "Gayle, my dear. I was once a very privileged person to be able to live safe and loved by two men who also loved one another deeply. My own childhood and young adulthood had been scarred permanently by rape and molestation and I knew that I would never trust anyone enough to fall in love. My name was Hester and I was given a greater gift, during that life, than any of my other lives. You see, I desperately wanted to be a mother. I was chosen to give birth to the man who would become your grandfather. Tommy and Felix were my dearest friends. I could not have loved them more. They gave me a safe place to live. My haven was with them. They gave me two of the most wonderful friendships I could ever have known. When I became their surrogate, they gave me the gift of the most wonderful son a woman could ever have asked for. He would have been so very proud of you. And so are they. You see, Path and Gwen were within Tommy and Felix."

"They were," Gayle tried to reason. She looked from one to the other, incredulous, skeptical, "You were both men?"

"Many times in our lives!" Gwen smiled, "and we've both been women. We only have gender identification of our own invention. Tommy and Felix were real, they were already wonderful people. We just occupied their minds and bodies for a while. That's how it happens with us: we are not always born into a life, we sometimes occupy a life already established. I know this is so very hard to understand. We are not sure we understand it ourselves. And we've both spent lives yearning for one another, not really knowing why we felt so incomplete. The thing we're trying to establish here is that many of you, maybe all of you, are descendants of at least one of the two of us. Well, I mean, we were occupying your ancestors…we shared life and memory with them. It wasn't until we heard your stories that we realized it. I know it's a difficult thing to understand, believe me, we've been struggling with it for many centuries!" She tried to make a joke but knew that it would fall flat. All the eyes that were on her showed confusion and concern.

It was the quietest night in weeks as everyone tried to process the information they had been given. Gwen was exhausted by her early morning explorations and the efforts to get everyone bathed, dried, and clean. She rose to her feet, "Talk to each other, come talk to us, if you need more clarification. I have to go to sleep, I wake so early."

Path stood and she stopped him with a hand against his chest, "You can stay, if you wish, you might want to help them talk it out. We shouldn't both leave them now but I am ready to drop." She walked to their cabin alone, carrying a lantern that Path had lit for her. Waiting outside their door, seated comfortably on the ground, was Yellow Feather. She smiled to see him.

"They will come to believe," he told her, "and, even their doubts should not deter you in any way. You have given them so much, now it is time to think of yourself."

She put a hand on his shoulder and smiled, "Tonight, my young friend, I feel hundreds of years old. I hope that I will feel up to more explorations tomorrow, but I can't be sure."

"Rest, dear Gwen," he said, smiling. "You need to rest and

know that what you have started here will continue to grow, we will be a village. We will thrive."

She looked into his eyes, "And this village will have the greatest leader they could possibly have dreamed to have someday, when you are grown. Now, young man, back to your bed, it is getting late and you wanted us to treat you no differently than the other young ones." She grinned and ran her fingers through his long raven-wing hair and kissed his brow. "Go to sleep, tomorrow promises to be another very busy day."

"Wait! Gwen!" He put a hand to her arm as she opened the door to her cabin and stopped her from going inside. Then she, too, heard it. In the far distance, deep into the mountains came the long, mournful song of a wolf. He smiled at her as the howl was joined by a chorus of other voices, not a solitary wolf but a family, a pack. Though they were many miles away, the sound carried in the mountains in the clear, cool air. Gwen closed her eyes as tears brimmed her lashes and threatened to fall down her cheeks. "They are singing for you, my friend," Yellow Feather said, smiling.

"There are many times in my lives when I have said, 'I can die now', over something so pleasant and perfect that there can be nothing more to wish for, but I have so much more to achieve," Gwen said, her voice tired, her face drawn. "Shooting Star, I am glad I was with you when we heard them," she added. "Serendipity," she mused.

"Me, too, I'm glad I was here. I think there is another word that fits this moment, I will look it up and tell you if I have it wrong. 'Numinous'," he nodded. He turned from her and obediently went to his cabin, careful not to wake the other boys in their bunks.

She smiled and watched him disappear into the darkness. "Numinous, indeed."

*

Conner helped Shawnee follow him up through the rocks, lending her a hand when the ascent required a long-legged stretch to get to the next foothold. When they reached their destination, they stood and took in the vista around them. They had been exploring for hours. The group had worked on scheduling classes and gardening and all the chores to allow each of them to have two days off out of seven. Those who were off were free to go to Denver to explore or anywhere they chose. Several had been to Golden and to Boulder. Others had gone to Colorado Springs. Conner and Shawnee always used their days exploring the wilderness around them. Neither of them had much curiosity about how to replace the fall of one modern society with another. They had carefully mapped out more than a few trails and were delighting in how strong they had remained, not allowing their muscles to go soft from the trip across country. Conner was assigned teaching the children basic grammar. The more advanced students were learning composition. And he was a swimming and relay coach. On her assigned days, Shawnee was leading the children through the forest to identify trees, edible flora, wildlife sign for survival studies, while Mary refined their botany studies more scientifically. Shawnee also had a math classroom so that the kids could learn the basics. Other adults were teaching what their strengths were. Of course, Melody led the music classes and Dave and Clint taught mechanics.

They had found a nice supply of textbooks in their sojourns to nearby cities, loading the truck with other school supplies. They had successfully turned several of the remote cabins into schoolrooms, but many of the classes took place outside, in the forest, in the meadows, in the sunlight. As agreed upon around their nightly campfires, there were no gender roles assigned to any task; all the children were learning to cook, all the children were learning mechanics. The adults knew that, eventually, some of the children would develop and follow their own interests, seeking out knowledge from other sources like the many libraries throughout Denver and science labs scattered throughout the cities. Some of the children had already gone with the adults to raid a library for reading material and had stocked their shelves with favorite reads. One of the young teen-aged girls named Laurel had already put together a decent poetry collection but Shawnee teased Conner that it was more about her crush on her English professor than her love of Rumi.

Yellow Feather, exploring with Coyote and David, had found a cabin that had once been used by the Colorado

Forestry Service, just up Route 70 from the campground. The cabin was set up as an office, but there were skylights in the roof, and the cabin sat in a huge natural clearing so the forest did not encroach on visibility. This was what excited Yellow Feather the most. His excitement was contagious as he explained to several of his teachers what he wanted to do. Clint and Declan helped him find sophisticated telescopes at the universities and they set up a star lab. Books lined the walls for reference and anyone who wished could visit to study the stars. Clint and Janice were as excited about this as the boys, and spent a lot of time in the lab, working with them to make it a great retreat for nighttime star-gazing.

All of the adults and children were becoming accustomed to exploring, even at night. Some occasionally carried a flashlight or lantern but many were developing their night-sense and had lost fear of darkness. They were made aware in their wilderness classes of night predators but nature had not begun to invade their world in any way but to bring them hope and joy. When animals were sighted they received these visitors with respect and awe. They still had seen no remnants of any domestic animals, but then, they were exploring the wilderness, not farmlands or pastures.

Today Conner had asked Shawnee if she wanted to explore with him and she had been happy to oblige. She was getting to like his company more than she allowed herself to admit. He moved at her speed and his observations drew attention to things that she would have sought out herself. She realized that, though worlds apart in their upbringing and lifestyles, they had a great deal in common, not the least of which was the mutual attraction growing between them. When he bent to kiss her, he asked, "Does this feel weird to you, now that we know that we're all…in some strange way, related?"

"Gayle says that, scientifically, the sperm and eggs belonged to the bodies they occupied, so we aren't really 'related', in the scientific, genetic sense; but we all know that emotionally and mentally, we feel strongly connected to Gwen and Path. And, even though this belief in the hoop and the continuance of spirits is strong in my heritage, I am still tripping over it. It's a little much to take in. I noticed that several of those who already established that ancestry connection to them are pairing up." She rubbed her hand over the small of his back. There was something about the strength of the muscles there, the way his back felt strong and taut, that compelled her to touch him there whenever the opportunity arose.

"Really?" he grinned, "I hadn't noticed. I guess I was too busy just trying to get you to myself. Who else is pairing up?"

"Well, we all recognized that Melody was charmed by our Irish friend, Declan, but now it seems that the feeling is mutual and they took a cabin together."

"Heh, is that the new terminology for hooking up?" He laughed, "They 'took a cabin', like 'jumping the broom' or 'hand-fasting'." He grinned. "Yeah, I knew it the first night. I was awake when he came back to the cabin for a few of his things and we talked a bit. Hey, Path and Gwen aren't the only ones who deserve a little comfort and happiness, no?" He ran his fingers along her jawline, tracing the shape of her face. From that first moment, back in Missouri, he had wanted to touch her beautiful, strong face, the high cheekbones, the natural beauty of her, the wisdom in those eyes, the something almost feral yet smooth, and sure about her movements.

"And Brittin is so crazy for Gayle, she doesn't know what to do with herself. But, naturally, Ms. Gayle-I'm-So-Serious-About-Everything doesn't even notice. So Brittin follows her every move and just hopes for an opening. I could just shake Gayle. You can tell she envies those of us who are finding comfort and happiness. By the way, is that how you define it? Comfort and happiness?"

"And so much more, my love," he told her. "I'm never at a loss for words, you know that, shall I wax poetic for you?"

"A little Yeats?" she teased. He recited,

"Never give all the heart, for love

Will hardly seem worth thinking of

To passionate women if it seem

Certain, and they never dream

That it fades out from kiss to kiss;..."

He kissed her lips, "To kiss. Want me to continue?"

She grinned, "I've never known anyone who could just quote Yeats off the cuff like that. Continue the kissing or the poem?"

He smiled and drew her closer, "The kissing, I hope."

*

A special reason to celebrate happened about a week after Path and Gwen had talked to the young adults about their heritage. A group of two adults and four children, two of them teens, came into Denver on motorcycles. Attached to all of the bikes were trailers filled with supplies, but one of the trailers held something all the children delighted in, a large crate with a bitch beagle hound and two puppies.

"How on...where on... EARTH did you find her?" Randy asked. "It has been a while since I have seen a dog that wasn't in a pack and a little dangerous."

"See that little man over there, the red-headed guy?" The newcomer, Brian, pointed to one of the teens. "We were the only human beings in that part of Nashville and he refused to come with us without his dog. We found the first three bikes in Nashville, attached the trailers and got a crate for her. The pups were born two days later, in St Louis. The momma dog is Bella. Travis named the boy pup Archie in honor of crossing the archway. The bitch pup is Lulu, a female form of Louis, I guess, he told the kids."

Brian introduced his wife as Dani. Brian, who was only in his earliest twenties, if that, told them that he had been a farmer in the Tennessee hill country and Dani, who could not be more than nineteen, twenty at the most, was a sous chef at one of Nashville's finest restaurants before, "All Hell broke loose!" They were the first couple that had actually known each other for several years before taking to the road and coming west. None of the children were theirs, or related in any way, but three of the six of them came from Nashville and the others were added along the route, Brian said.

"We found another cycle after we found Lonnie in St. Lou. That helped with the younger kids who doubled up with us, me and Dani. Not too many even heading east anymore. Lots of bodies," he whispered to Randy out of ear-shot of the children. "It's like nature woke up every sleeping virus ever found; people are sick and dying everywhere you look. People passing through Nashville on the way east looked like ghosts, or zombies, so sick, almost too sick to walk."

"It's amazing to have a dog in camp. Bella has the distinction of being the first," Lily told Dani, changing the subject.

"And she may be the last. The big dogs are running in packs. I think all the little dogs have been killed off. Bella and her pups may be the last of her size. The big ones are dying off, too, not many prepared to fend for themselves."

They seemed the bearer of bad tidings and Lily and Randy both hoped that Brian and Dani would be more positive after they saw the progress made in the camp.

"Not sure we want to begin to husbandry animals here; we'll just let the dogs be dogs for now, if we find any more," Randy said. "We talked about that around the campfire. We don't want to repeat the mistakes made in society of breeding dogs into designer packages, something we all agreed was a big mistake. Can't go too wrong with a beagle, though, huh?"

"If they don't get eaten by their cousins out there," the boy called Coyote told them, half joking. "No, Miss Lily, don't worry, there is plenty of game growing up there. The 'coydog' cousins won't need to poke around our camp for a very long time. Me and Dakota and Yellow Feather, and Fawn when she's not hanging on Miss Melody, go all over the woods. We have seen a lot of animals."

There had been debate around the campfire about letting the children run the forest unescorted. It was pretty evenly divided until Shawnee told them that there was no way they would be able to prevent children who had grown up on the reservation from wandering wherever they might want to go. To restrict them would be equal to clipping their wings and she would not stand for it. The argument continued until Gwen and Path finally told dissenters that the children could wander freely and safe from harm for a twenty mile radius and even beyond that, because of the magic "shield" that prevented humans from finding them.

Path told them that the minute they entered camp, the magic shielded them and they took it with them even when they left the perimeter.

"We would be invisible to others? If we went to Boulder or even further, people would not be able to see us?" Darren asked.

"Only when we want them to. You became part of the magic when we brought you here," Path nodded.

"So, if someone is driving by on Route 70…" Lily began.

"They would have no idea that anyone was here, even if they turned off and drove here, they would find an empty camp, like the way it was when we found it."

"The children are safe to roam," Gwen assured them. "It was the first thing that Path and I did on arrival. The magic shield. So many of these children have been traumatized, we want to make certain they feel safe."

"But they could be killed by bears, wolves," Lisa, one of women from Declan's group, argued, still debating in her mind the issue of the children and their explorations.

"True, and the same danger was there for you when you were a child," Conner said. "Did that stop you from exploring? Did you enter woods thinking you would be eaten by a predator? Did you dip your foot into the ocean terrified that sharks were going to dine? Shall we prepare these children for an uncertain future, or are we going to put them in a glass case and call them 'Exhibit A, the

Survivors'? I'm not trying to hurt your feelings, Lisa, I know that you care passionately, but these are kids and we've got to get them to stop having to look over their shoulders like they are the bottom rung on the food chain. More than a dozen children died just coming to this place. These kids have a greater chance of survival here than anywhere else in this country."

Shawnee started to say something more, then held back. To what Conner had just said nothing needed to be added.

*

Three days later, another group came into Denver and followed Dave and Randy to the camp with yet another dog, this one a big, sweet, goofy Staffordshire Terrier named Pompeii who had walked with them from the time their car broke down at the Colorado border. She was only too happy to be smothered in the children's attentions and got along famously with Bella. This group came from southern California, through Phoenix and into Colorado from New Mexico to the south. The leader of the group, Julio, told them that Phoenix was a completely dead city, no one found alive there in the desert at all, even though his group explored for two weeks and found a great supply of food, even water. Julio also told Gayle that what she had seen was the worst red tide ever to hit the coast. "But the ocean is coming back, believe me. I met a guy before I left Cali who had come in off a boat and said that the coasts are ugly but the ocean is healthy farther out to sea. There are still whales, dolphin, all sea life is still there.

The ocean is just reacting to all the volcanic activity and the poisons. What you saw along the north coast is probably gone by now. It's never going to be the same, but there's still life out there."

Gayle had a difficult time being optimistic enough to believe he was right but she did allow a smile of hope. She turned to find Brittin standing beside her. Brittin took her hand and squeezed it, saying, "Gayle, I think Julio's right, the ocean is deeper than mountains are high; there will be regeneration, perhaps even new species will evolve, but it will regenerate. Look at how fast nature is coming back here!" Gayle recognized something deep in Brittin's eyes that she could identify with, a yearning, a need to be touched. She squeezed back and smiled.

It was true. More and more, there was life around them. They were beginning to endure the age-old problem of having to discourage deer, rabbits, and crows from eating their crops. Shawnee told them about Native children standing sentinel on the fields, their job to chase away the freeloading animals. Brian helped even further by showing the children how to make several scarecrows with materials that made noise in the wind. They dispersed them through the fields and called them the sentinels.

They had hauled tons of bird seed from Denver to feed the birds, since there would be few crops this year for those that depended on plant life. The birds had already begun visiting the camp and they had cleaned the area of any insect infestation that might have existed. Not that there weren't still insects, but they were no longer out of control the way they were in other parts of the country. Much to Shawnee's delight, crows had survived, ravens were seen, and owls. She had heard a barred owl the night before last. She recognized that familiar call, paraphrased by naturalists to say, "Who cooks for you? Who cooks for y'all?"

That night, around the campfire, there was celebration and joy. The crops were growing, the children were responding well to the structure of teaching that was less like school and more like play, and the population had grown into a sizeable village. Yellow Feather and Gwen had told them about the lake and their idea of using sleds to harvest rice. That had resulted in a barrel of some of the best wild rice they had ever tasted. Dave was experiencing great success with clearing the streets in the western part of Denver. They had yet to encounter what might be considered hostile humans coming into Denver at all.

There were seldom complaints about the primitive life they were living. A few of them had already commented on the fact that they preferred their new life, their life without civilization and capitalism. They thought about the future, planned what to do in case of attack from another village, if there were another village. Declan asked Path the hardest question, knowing that it was on everyone's mind, "If you and Gwen are gone, will the magic remain?"

"No, I don't think it will," Path admitted. "I think it may weaken considerably if only one of us is here."

Gwen looked away at his words and sighed. Today had been a hard one. She felt weary. For the first time since she and Path had arrived in this time and space, she felt physically drained. There were so many things that she was accustomed to doing on a daily basis now, tasks that she had adopted to remain organized and aware, but today had been a special challenge. Forty more people had come in over the past few days and she helped to direct the preparations for their accommodations. The thought struck her that the magic might be weakening because she was weakening. Perhaps the magic was directly related to her energy source. She was grateful that Path's was still strong. He was as energetic as any of the young men, sometimes seeming to be in many places at once.

Brian was sitting across the fire from her and said, "Gwen, are you tired, should we turn in so you can rest?"

"No, no, I'm fine. Well, just a little tired. It was wonderful watching your gardening crew work today!"

"Watching? I saw you working right along with us. Don't you think you do too much, working with the kitchen, the sleeping arrangements, keeping everything in order? You really did too much today. I was afraid the sun might have been getting to you."

Path turned toward her and the concern was evident on his face. She put a hand on his arm to reassure him and smiled, "No, I think I might have pushed a little too hard, but it's just so wonderful seeing the progress we're making now that we have someone who really knows how to farm directing our efforts."

"The other night we were talking about the fact that we are almost glad that we haven't found livestock to raise. It was a contingency that we don't begin to exploit animals as had our predecessors." Brian grinned, "I can live with that. I've been almost two years without meat and I feel pretty damned good! Had anyone told me this ten years ago, I would have called them radical idiots, but I guess all those people putting out films about vegetarian eating might have been right. I guess the World Health Organization might have been very forward thinking after all, when they advised people to work toward a plant-based lifestyle. I read their reports...over my steak and potatoes," he laughed, jokingly. "But I'm no longer so skeptical."

"I don't think that many of the domesticated animals survived," Gayle, her hand firmly linked in Brittin's, offered. "The poor things probably died standing in fields waiting to be fed, milked, or worse. Any that did survive were probably killed by the same people who were hunting humans."

"I think you might be wrong," Path said. "There might be horses. They might have gone wild. But I do think that most of the people have died off. The last two groups that came in, one from the north and the other from the southeast, said that they stopped encountering anyone at all after a few days of the eastward migration. It seems that a lot of the people who reached the coast turned back but disease was spreading like wildfire and caught many of those who had survived the first wave of viruses. Isn't that what you told us, Lincoln?"

The newcomer nodded and sighed, "I don't know why none of our group ever got sick, we had no choice but to be maneuvering through the bodies. I had my precious black bag with me, my grandfather's black bag, but we seldom needed it beyond a few nicks and scratches. Maybe those of us who were coming here were immune, or..." he let the thought trail off for a moment, then added, "or maybe it's the magic." Tonight he had told them about his family life and about his ancestors who he had traced back to Sauri, Kenya, where she, the grandmother, served as teacher to the village, while her husband healed the people of that village, and for miles around, as their trusted physician. "She had been born in the United States and was sent to Kenya in the Peace Corps, while he was born in the village and was educated in France to later return to the Sauri to help his people. They were both greatly revered by the villagers. My grandfather was their only son and was the first to be sent to the United States to become a doctor. We lived in Atlanta for many years but I moved my wife and kids to New Orleans to open my own practice. This was long before the troubles began." The sadness never left him as he told his story, even when they told him theirs. It was obvious that the loss of his family was a heavy burden for him to bear and he sat quietly listening, seldom joining the high spirits at the campfire. Layla moved to comfort him, speaking quietly and soothingly.

Not that they made anything like race or creed an issue at any time, but Melody couldn't help but notice that the new population had no minorities, and, better yet, no prevailing 'majority'. There were people of all walks of life and all cultures. If there were any culture represented more strongly than the others, it was the Native Americans, and that seemed all right with everyone since they were the strong survivors of the group. Almost every incoming group had encountered and picked up Native American children from the Southwest, Oklahoma, Minnesota, and South Dakota. Shawnee was able to give them history lessons that included the history before white incursion as well as the lessons in the textbooks they had found. A trip to a big Denver bookstore gave her a treasure trove of the books she had grown up reading, the books that might have been considered pre-history to many grade school teachers. All of the children were fascinated by the history she gave them, especially when she could teach them first-hand the physical lessons that went along with it.

Dave and Randy organized burial details among the adults. They wanted no children involved for the bad memories it might implant. They had already buried many of the remains of the people of Denver, respectfully, in the nearby quarry, where they had been able to find earth-moving equipment ready and waiting for the chore. No one discussed it around the fire, it was just accomplished, one day at a time. Dave did say that the one thing that felt very strange to him was all the money and jewelry they found and each realized that these items, though so very important to the people who had stored them, meant very little to the survivors. Jewelry stores were everywhere and had been looted very little during the exodus out of the city.

On one of his turns at burial detail, Conner did enter a jewelry store to find a specific item. When he found it, he tucked it away with a smile, leaving precious diamonds and other stones behind. He stood in front of the store and took in the downtown area, completely cleared of vehicles, empty and desolate, like a movie set with no actors. He thought about how crowded with people these streets had no doubt been at one time. The thought, surprisingly enough, did not sadden him. It was simply a reflection of how far they had come in accepting their plight. Little good did all the glitter and accoutrements of the age do the people of Denver, of the entire continent, for that matter, when Death came calling. He had learned to live in the present, giving most of his energy and thought to the future, none to the past.

Eventually, as the group at the hidden camp grew, they might actually come down to the city and reclaim it, but that was for future generations to decide. Right now, he and his friends were happy to be where they were. Although Clint was quick to remind them that they might feel different after a hard Rocky Mountain winter. With enough food stored away for several winters, few actually worried. Each cabin had a fireplace and the chimneys had been cleaned. All needed repairs had been done and enough wood was split and stacked to get them well into a long winter. Their summer had been spent teaching and preparing; there seldom seemed to be idle time, which was why Pathogent was insistent that their days off were spent doing anything but. He was seldom seen to leave camp and neither he nor Gwen ever seemed to rest.

Early one morning, as they were drinking their morning tea, Path and Gwen were surprised by a light knock at the door of their cabin. They were both accustomed to be the first to awaken in the camp. They were happy to greet Yellow Feather, known to them as Tecumseh, and welcomed him in to join them. Though in the body of a child, he was their wise and trusted friend and advisor. He thanked Gwen for the tea and smiled, hardly able to contain himself. He seemed excited yet apologized for invading their privacy, seating himself in a chair opposite theirs.

"I am so sorry to bother you so early," he said, smiling as Path waved it away. "But I want to share this discovery with you. I want you to know how important it is that your descendants are here to protect and guide the children. I want you to know that what you have accomplished here will, indeed, save humanity. It is far more special and far-reaching that any of us had thought or dared to dream."

He made himself slow his speech down and relax, but the smile on his face revealed his excitement.

"My friend, please share, we can use the good news," Gwen urged.

"Your descendants have played a very important role in gathering and bringing children to this safe haven, and they are continuing to take responsibility by teaching, mentoring, and guiding the children, not to mention all the hard work they are putting forth to make life better, to make life happier for the young survivors in their care. Now, I have something to share with you that will make you even happier that you were part of this plan, this reincarnation of purpose. Your descendants are not travelers, but you and Path are not the only travelers, nor Layla, nor Dave, nor I." He paused, his bright eyes shining as he looked deeply into Gwen's eyes.

She finished the sentence, "The children are all reincarnations, travelers much like us, travelers with full memory of their former lives, skills and knowledge." She let the thought trail off as she and Pathogent stared at one another. Path's smile grew as he realized what they were discovering, what Tecumseh had discovered.

"Nearly every child is an energy being who lived many lives, who created, invented, made life better, worked diligently toward the betterment of the planet. I have been talking to so many of them. Among the native people, Crazy Horse, Chief Seattle, Geronimo, Chief Joseph, and

Wilma Mankiller are here. I cannot believe how fortunate this opportunity has been for us all."

He listed them serenely, pronouncing each name like a prayer:

"Nikolai Tesla, Alan Turing, John Muir, Jane Goodall, Dian Fossey, Marie Curie, Sojourner Truth." The young Yellow Feather closed his eyes and smiled, trying to remember names that Gwen and Path might be familiar with. "If there is a scientist or an inventor or thinker whose life's purpose was to improve life on this planet in some way, they are here embodied in those children. Many of them attend the classes that they could be teaching! But they, too, want to be allowed to be children for a while. They want to be allowed to grow, play, enjoy life. Many of them have had terrible trauma from this life but the past is strong in them and they will eventually take their place to help to put things right, to help rebuild humanity. I am telling you this, but insist that only the two of you, and I, will know this truth, will be able to process what it means to our future."

"There are over sixty children here now," Gwen breathed, this discovery almost too much to take in.

"No, more, nearly eighty," Path told her. "We did a count last night. Just think, eighty of the brightest and best throughout history. I wonder if some of them were geniuses more than once through time."

Tecumseh laughed and looked at Path. "But I don't think you'll find a politician or capitalist among them, nor a land developer or investor. I think those types of people cannot be travelers because they are too much 'in the world' to have far-reaching minds capable of reincarnating and gathering knowledge useful to the survival of all. The good news is that we will not have to 'reinvent the wheel,' so to speak. We will turn them loose when the time is right and they will make just enough improvements to make life better as the population grows."

He caught himself and looked at Gwen. "How are you feeling?" Then he looked trapped, worrying that he had revealed too much.

"Path knows," she assured him, "I told him the same day that you and I discovered the lake."

"Yes, I know," Path grimaced, "and that's another thing I want to talk about. I've discussed it with Gayle and Lincoln, Maria, and Stephanie. We want to talk to you about the possibility of operating."

Gwen gasped, "Path, it's my BRAIN; you're talking about brain surgery."

"I know. Lincoln has performed more than I have and Gayle knows more than both of us put together. Given what you know and how you could actually pinpoint the growth, we would stand a very good chance."

"Pathogent," Tecumseh said softly, "you're talking about a complex surgery with nineteenth century equipment and technology."

"No, not according to Clint and Julio and Randy. They believe that we could use generators to make one of the hospitals fully functional. The generators are already there, they were there for emergency back-up when the hospitals were operating fully. They would install more, giving the back-ups' back-ups. They would tend them constantly, leave nothing to chance. We would have access to all the machinery and Gayle would be able to run lab tests, view scans. We could do this, Gwen, let us do this." His look was haunted, pleading.

"Path, you can't operate on me. It's too risky. We are too close," Gwen said, softly.

"Lincoln would be lead surgeon. I would be there as his assist. Gwennie, these are your grandchildren, they are not ready to let you go. They want a chance to try to save you."

"Path, you know how strong the Fade is. We don't know if there is any way to reverse its 'pull'," she argued.

"We don't really know any such thing. We have never been in bodies of our own before. We must be pure energy, Gwen. We didn't occupy these bodies. They are ours. We have no precedence to know if or when the Fade or the Blink can affect us. Who would have dreamed that you would or could have a growth, a tumor, in your brain?

How could that have happened to you? It wasn't hereditary nor caused by food or environment. Let us try, Gwen. Don't just give up."

Gwen looked from Path to Tecumseh and back. She didn't know what to say or think. If there were a possibility to live another few years, to watch these amazing children grow, given what Tecumseh had revealed about them... She turned her face away and stared out the window and the vista revealed a beautiful view of the hillside and the other cabins around them. The lush grasses had returned, the forest was a mix of hardwood and pine and was dark, mysterious. And that thick canopy had saved the lives of countless creatures deserving of a chance to go on. She had found that she was capable of falling in love with the children and adults who had come here as quickly as they were introduced. The feeling of having purpose and promise helped her to realize that every single person on this hillside had come to be important to her, had given her reason to live. She realized that she did, indeed, want to add time to her life. "I want that, too, Path. I want to try. Promise me this, though. If things go wrong, and you know that they might go wrong, you will realize that I went into this fully on my own, that you did nothing to convince me. I WANT to undergo the surgery, I WANT to assume the risk."

Tecumseh sat back from the edge of his seat and his eyes sought out Pathogent's. He smiled and nodded, "You do understand what she's telling you. She wants to make certain that you allow no one to take blame if this life she is living now cannot be saved. She wants them to understand fully about the Fade, about how little we know about the strength of it. How we cannot possibly predict whether the surgery can or cannot have effect."

Path nodded in agreement. "Gwen and I have lost one another in too many lives for me not to be prepared for that eventuality. I am a realist. That said, I also know that we truly do have some of the brightest and best at hand. They love you, Gwen, they are not willing to just give you up without a fight."

Gwen smiled, "We don't even truly know what we travelers actually are made of. What if they find that the structure of my brain is entirely different from the normal human brain? What if they find that there isn't anything but energy inside my head?" She laughed, for the first time in a long time.

"We are like them, Gwen, in many ways," Tecumseh said. "We, too, are stardust."

*

Nearly two weeks later, they were finally prepared for the surgery. Gwen had worked closely with Lincoln and Gayle, reading the tests, pinpointing the exact location of the tumor. Her experience with brain surgery shocked and surprised her two young descendants, until she explained what she had done in 2028, who she had been, and the surgeries she had performed, even on newborns with brain trauma. They had both studied her advances as her former self in the surgical theater and were awestruck having an opportunity to meet a personal hero of theirs. Her work with neurosurgery had been textbooks during their studies.

Lincoln put a hand on her arm. "I grew up reading your papers; those journals were dog-eared and worn. Your advances in the studies of autism alone..." his hand shook as he patted Gwen's arm. "My grandmother, you have lived many amazing lives."

Gayle stared at the results of the MRI they had performed on Gwen and leaned close to show them the path of entry she found to be best. "We will enter here, less invasive from this point." Her hand, too, shook as she addressed Gwen. Gwen smiled and put a hand over Gayle's, and smiled.

"Tell me you're not going to be too nervous to be assisting. I want you, not Path, at Lincoln's elbow. I really don't want Path to be assisting, should things go wrong." Gwen sighed. "Please just know that you are both far more capable and far more advanced than I was thirty, nearly forty, years ago."

"I am still in awe over what you just told us, but I will be ready to scrub tomorrow, I promise," Gayle assured her. "We can't keep Path from joining; you know that we need him. But I will try to make certain that he is only there to advise, to guide us."

"I don't know that a surgery room has ever been more sterile," Lincoln told her, smiling. "Maria, Stephanie, and Layla have been working non-stop on the room and the instruments. Everything has been tested time and again."

"Clint, Dave, Julio and the others have gotten us enough power to light up seven fully operational hospitals!" Gwen laughed. "I hope everyone will finally be able to relax when this is over. We have children to educate and raise!" What Dave had not told her was that they had cleaned the hospital of the hundreds of bodies they had found within. They wanted nothing of the nightmare they had found when entering that facility to haunt the doctors, nurses, and assistants who would be performing this surgery.

"Don't worry about the children. They are doing fine. I have noticed that Yellow Feather is taking it upon himself to make them all very aware of the animals and the symbiotic relationship with nature that they imply. He will make naturalists out of each and every one of them. I honestly think we have somehow found the brightest and most cooperative children on the planet! They are almost unbelievably teachable," Lincoln commented.

At this, Gwen smiled and cherished the insight given her by Tecumseh. Knowing that everything would be all right, with or without her, gave her the opportunity to face this surgery fearlessly.

Blood tests were run. There were no shortages of donors. Maria took this job on and had everything readied and, although she had never served as a surgical nurse, Stephanie had trained as one and was prepared to do the job, going over everything needed with Lincoln and Pathogent. Pathogent showed no distress over being replaced as attending by Gayle. He seemed almost relieved. And Courteney, a new arrival, was an experienced and skilled anesthesiologist. It was if something were orchestrating this entire thing to be a success.

The surgery was planned for eight to ten hours of grueling, precise, painstaking work but took only four. Recovery was quicker than any could have imagined and all involved were pleased that the tumor, once removed, seemed to be contained and benign. Had it been left in place, it would no doubt have killed Gwen, but now it seemed possible for her to have a full, if not speedy, recovery.

She was not happy about having to stay in the hospital during recovery, one single patient in a hospital designed to house hundreds. Of course, Pathogent stayed with her and she was besieged by visitors daily but her mind was in the camp and she could not help but worry if everything was being taken care of.

"Gwen, my dear," Layla scolded, as she fussed over the pillows and sheets, making certain that Gwen was comfortable, "give us some credit, Lisa has taken over the kitchen and could cook for an army if necessary but there are several of the children already helping who seem quite capable in the culinary arts themselves. She has no shortage of assistance. Dani, Nikki, Blake, and Dave have organized laundry brigades and keep the cabins neat and clean but we have all noticed how helpful even the smallest of the children can be. Classes are going swimmingly and we've even had a few added. Several of the children are teaching archery and it seems that they enjoy competitions. Just last night, little Haylie shut the older boys down by running away with the archery competition; she's a natural. She even bested Yellow Feather, much to his obvious delight," she chattered on, bringing Gwen much wanted news from the camp, detailed reports on how everyone was doing. "Little Constance has cut a tooth and is beginning to crawl everywhere." As she talked, her voice and news soothing to Gwen, Pathogent listened, too, having been away from camp almost as constantly as Gwen had.

Gwen sighed, teasing, "So what you're saying is that I'm no longer necessary."

Layla looked up, surprised and shocked, then relaxed when she saw the smile on Gwen's face. "As if, Gwennie, you know how everyone adores you. You are the undisputed matriarch of 'the clan'." Her voice changed, concerned, "How are you feeling? Are you getting memory back?"

Gwen had slowly begun to remember as her brain healed from the trauma. It helped that Path was there to talk to her constantly of their travels, their lives, the things they had done together. Many things were still a little out of her reach but she knew that they would come back. This touch of amnesia was normal considering the trauma her brain had undergone. She marveled at how skillfully Gayle and Lincoln had been able to accomplish what they had done with a very small entry point and very little invasiveness. They both were happy to have been able to use the lasers, overjoyed by the advanced equipment provided by a first-rate facility, and gave much credit to the mechanics, who stayed with the generators, keeping the power at a level enabling them to fully use everything needed.

Clint and Dave had talked to Pathogent about having several hiding places around the city where they would store gasoline. Everyone agreed that they would eventually run out as the gasoline was already evaporated from many of the deserted vehicles, but they were able to use generators to operate pumps to pull gas up from underground at many of the gas stations closest to their location. They were carefully storing cans filled with gasoline at several locations far apart from one another, so that if one somehow caught fire, through natural causes or otherwise, the explosions would not spread. Should they face another need for surgery, they would be prepared. Eventually, they knew that they would have to think about getting the grid up and running again, but they all wanted to put that off for a year or two.

First they wanted to clear the city of bodies, then prioritize their needs a little at a time. Right now, the pressing jobs were survival and preparing for the winter. They didn't want to think too far in advance of their current capabilities. Everyone agreed that their first obligation was to the children, ensuring that they were healing from the emotional traumas they had faced and learning so that they could influence their own futures.

The meeting place at the Commons was renamed "New Hope" and had been decorated by the children to calm any who might find their way there. The meeting place was checked several times a week in hopes that more children and adults might find their way to Denver. Path took her there on the way back to camp to show her how the archway was decorated with drawing and notes, welcoming newcomers to join them.

Gwen's homecoming was a cause for celebration that lasted the entire day. She waved off those fearful that they were tiring her out by having each of the children get a chance to greet and talk to her. Tears of joy filled her eyes as she greeted those dear little faces, and met newcomers who had arrived during her recovery period and absence from the camp.

"Every cabin is now in use," Conner told her. "And we've built new bunks and rearranged to accommodate everyone. However, we are going to have to build a couple more cabins for the adults. We've got tents set up now, but they won't do for the winter." He and Shawnee had given Gwen a wonderful gift that afternoon, announcing their commitment to one another. Now he raised their linked hands to his lips and kissed the ring he had put on Shawnee's finger.

"Oh, my dear, none of you ever stops working," Gwen said. "I hope you're going to be able to get enough rest!"

"This isn't work. This is survival," Sean grinned as he looked around the camp. "We come up with a project and there are always enough hands to make quick work of it. A little like Amish barn raising: many hands make the task easy. The garden is flourishing, canning food is underway, the larder is filled. Julio even showed us how to make some of the most delicious salsa I've ever tasted. We have shelves of it canned and stored. Lily makes the best jams and jellies you'll ever want. And, young Tess has whipped up some of the best vegan stews in existence! Who knew?"

Her first campfire in many days was another joy-filled celebration as she listened to the survival stories of the newcomers and the discoveries of those she'd known the longest. Several of the older teens were now present at the nightly campfire, joining in with the laughter and tales.

"Do you suppose we're now the only survivors on earth?" Melody put forth. Stories coming in from the newcomers were filled with grim tales of a nation filled with bodies and fewer and fewer survivors to gather.

"I don't think so," Brian said, quietly. "While we may be the only ones on this continent, I think someone told me that you," he nodded towards Gwen, "had said that Africa may be teeming with life. I agree. After all, they were at war with no one at the time all the troubles started. They may still even have the capabilities to fly here, may still have infrastructure intact. We may see them someday."

"I do remember something about some trouble in South Africa," Declan nodded. "But they might have sorted it out."

"It doesn't matter," Yellow Feather said, quietly, "whatever the future may hold, we will have no choice but to face it. Today, however, we need to celebrate being alive, having one another, and knowing that survival just might be possible."

"Not only possible," Gwen said, smiling, "I think we've got the possibility for a bright and shining future. We have been given the gift of one another. That seems to be the purpose for each of us. Funny word, 'purpose', but I truly think that I understand clearly what Path told me a long, long time ago." He slipped his hand in hers and nodded. "There truly was a purpose behind everything that happened to us before now, and a purpose for each of you to work your way toward us. I used to look at the future as grim and hopeless. That vision has been completely reversed."

Around the fire, all those who had once thought that very same thought nodded. The future no longer looked grim, nor hopeless. The survival spirit within each of them was strong.

Several days later, Path and Gwen stood with Declan in front of the Norlin Library on the campus of the University of Colorado in Boulder. Declan had been soaking up knowledge and doing as much research as his downtime would allow. He brought them here with him today telling them he had something that he wanted them to see. They both looked at him and smiled.

"Is it inside?" Gwen asked as they poised on the sidewalk, where she had expected him to lead them to the entrance.

"No," Declan said smiling, "just face the building and look up."

Path saw it and smiled, his arm around Gwen to support her. They looked at one another and smiled, then beamed at Declan.

"I know it was crazy to bring you all the way here for this, but I couldn't help it. I had to have you see it. It's like," he paused, "it's like we were meant to be here, like everything is telling us that we were right to gather here. I can't even tell you how glad I am to know that I am descended from the two of you. I have never met more inspiring and good people than my forefather Pathogent and my foremother Gwen."

"It's a quote from Cicero," Path said, turning to his memory and pulling the words from a former life. "More precisely, *'Nescire autem quid ante quam natus sis acciderit, id est semper esse puerum. Quid enim est aetas hominis, nisi ea memoria rerum veterum cum superiorum aetate contexitur?'* " he recited, in Latin.

"Or, in translation, 'To be ignorant of what occurred before you were born is to remain always a child. For what is the worth of human life, unless it be woven into the life of our ancestors by the records of history?'

"I think that's pretty close. Thank you, Declan, our hope lies in you, my son, in all our sons and daughters."

The words above the entry to the library read:

"Who knows only his own generation remains always a child."

FINI

Author's Note:

When Elizabeth (editor extraordinaire) and Matt (the visionary cover designer) were working on finalizing the book, I was beginning to finally see a dream coming true. Needless to say, everything made me so happy, I was really looking forward to the reality of seeing a book I had written in my hands. I was driving to Oakland, California, with friends to see an Athletics game and one of them discovered an old CD in my giant case of music and asked me to put it in the CD player. It was the **Moody Blues** and we listened to it for a while, singing along with the lyrics. I had completely forgotten I had that CD. On our way home, I dropped one of my friends off at her car and drove alone, turning the music up louder, then the, *"I Know You're Out There Somewhere"* track came up and I started singing along and then it hit me that it was like that song was written for Gwen and Path. If you liked the book, find the track on Youtube and play it and thank Justin Hayward for writing "their" song. I know he had a different relationship in mind, but you'll see how well it fits!

About the Author

Jeanette ("Jenny") Appel Cave lives in Sacramento, CA, by way of Ohio. She has three children (whose open minds and courage inspire her), five of the best-looking grandchildren on the planet, and three great-grandchildren (who make her hope for a better future). She shares her home with her youngest daughter and two Terriers who rescued Jenny from a dull fate. She may be reached at: jennycave49@gmail.com.

This is her first novel. She is working on more Science Fiction, more passionate stories of survival, the environment, tolerance and inclusion, and humanity's moral duty to protect the earth. Look for *"Survival Instinct"* soon.

Made in the USA
Middletown, DE
21 May 2023